CAFE
PURGATORIUM

CAFE PURGATORIUM

Dana M Anderson

Charles de Lint

Ray Garton

Tom Doherty Associates

New York

CAFE PURGATORIUM

A TOR Book
Published by Tom Doherty Associates, Inc.
49 West 24th Street
New York, N.Y. 10010

Library of Congress Cataloging-in-Publication Data

Anderson, Dana
     Cafe Purgatorium : [three original novels of horror and the fantastic] / Dana Anderson, Ray Garton, Charles de Lint.
          p.   cm.
     "A Tom Doherty Associates book."
     ISBN 0-312-85180-4
     1. Horror tales, American.   I. Garton, Ray.   II. De Lint, Charles, 1951–   .   III. Title.
PS648.H6A53   1991
813'.0873808—dc20   90-29260
                                                                    CIP

First edition: July 1991

Printed in the United States of America

0 9 8 7 6 5 4 3 2 1

For Linda, Matt and Jordan

CONTENTS

CAFE PURGATORIUM

by Dana M Anderson

1

A single drop of blood.

Jack Bellows considered the red spot for a moment, then used a tissue to wipe it off the heavy paper of the stock certificate on his desk. It was an inane waste of time to be sitting staring out the window and poking a pin at the tip of his thumb, but that is what he had been doing for the past ten minutes. He realized that he probably would have continued all afternoon if his idle activity hadn't drawn blood.

The precious fluid oozed slowing out of his upraised thumb, trickling down the path of the last drip. Jack licked it away, then squeezed his thumb and watched more blood gather. Then he pressed the tissue against the wound and sat back to resume looking out his window at the traffic-clogged street ten stories below him.

The weather matched his mood, or, perhaps, had created it. It had been well below zero since the new year, two weeks already, and the forecast held no relief. Minneapolis was locked in the humorless grip of winter, with temperatures so low that even the wind lacked the ambition to blow. Below him, the exhaust of the slowly moving automobiles hung in an icy fog over the street. Seemingly immobile, solid, the vapor looked as though it had been painted on the air, giving the scene a surreal foreboding.

Jack imagined the fog of steam and monoxide building up till it reached his windows and began seeping in around him, encasing him solidly in its cold tendrils. He could already feel it holding him to his chair.

No, he couldn't take another day of this routine. Jack was an investment broker, a position he'd been born into and accepted without thought. He was good at it, taking over the family firm with his brother when their father retired, but making rich men richer wasn't ultimately satisfying. Every day was the same, monotonous and meaningless, and the money could no longer explain why he stayed at it. He had slowly come to the conclusion that he should find work he could take pride in, perhaps serve the public in some way.

He wasn't entirely insane, however, and wasn't looking to throw his suits away and beg on street corners. No, he'd chosen a route that should prove profitable, and had already decided to open a restaurant.

His desire to run a restaurant had developed from a slight dissatisfaction with the places where he normally dined into the stubborn conviction that he could certainly do better. But should he try it? Why not?

Not being used to failing, he did his homework: he studied the business and scouted locations in reference to projected city growth, and he even researched shifting trends in popular dining. Starting in the suburbs and moving toward the city proper, he'd felt drawn to the older sections of downtown Minneapolis. There was a coziness to the renewed areas that suited his temperament. What he'd eventually decided, with the help of a more than chipper young woman in a gaudy yellow jacket, was to go all the way and buy a building housing an old Art Deco joint with a history running back past Prohibition.

His realtor had put the place so far down on her list of possibilities that he'd almost given up on her services before they came to it. Once he saw it, however, he'd known it was what he wanted. A strange sense of belonging nuzzled around him in the dusty room, and images of what it was

4

and what it could be filled his head as he stood amid the dust and clutter with his hands stuffed apathetically in the pockets of his heavy coat.

He played it cool, telling her he'd think about it, but the title was already transferred in his mind.

That was yesterday, and now Jack was impatient to get on with the move. He wanted to just walk away, leaving the work in his lavish jail-cell office unfinished. Run away. To hell with the price, call the agent and get it over with now. He didn't feel he could wait another two hours till he met her at the old building.

Outside his window the world was locked into its pattern, frozen into a reality that nobody controlled or deserved, but Jack was going to break away from his groove. He knew it was a safe escape, he was making the break with enough money in the bank to cushion any fall, yet the thought of getting out of his office and into the world excited him with a feeling of recklessness. It was as though no one had ever actually opened a restaurant before this bold experiment, and Jack couldn't help laughing at the image of himself as some kind of pioneer restaurateur.

The laughter broke the spell of his mood, and he went back to the papers he'd been avoiding most of the day. The faster he got his work wrapped up, the sooner he could get on with his life.

"It's only been used for storage since seventy-two, but it's structurally sound. Big enough for dancing, too. I really believe this is the place you've been looking for. Don't you?"

Kelly Dawson ended the question with a smile, turning to look at Jack. He smiled back, somewhat wanly, wondering how the woman managed to get her teeth so white. The woman would be a natural on a Sunday morning church show if she ever got out of the housing racket. But if she would only stop smiling for a minute or two she'd be perfect, and, shameful as it may be to admit, he had chosen

5

her to show him the available properties primarily because of her looks.

Jack glanced around the dimly lit bar. The Cafe Society had remained in remarkably good condition, considering the neighborhood and the years of neglect. The interior design was pure Art Deco, stylized yet functional, and, even empty and shrouded with dust, there was a friendliness, a welcoming feeling to the room. And, the price was right.

"I guess I'm still nervous about taking the plunge," he answered. "You were right about it, though. It's in great shape, and I've always liked Art Deco."

"I think you'll find it to be a wonderful location for a supper club, Mr. Bellows. Urban renewal has brought the neighborhood around again, and with the renovation of the downtown residential areas you won't have any problem attracting diners."

The neighborhood had suffered a long decline since the original grand opening, but it was on its way up again following the rebirth of the inner city. Young families were moving into the sedate Victorian houses nearby, new shops had sprung up along the old streets, and a new movie theater was going in on the block. All the area needed was a good eating place within walking distance, and it would be complete.

Yes, this was his destiny.

"All right, I'm sold. Let's get the paperwork started before I chicken out."

And that was all there was to it; a quick trip to the bank, and he'd become a restaurateur with one scrawled signature.

He drove home to his apartment with the radio tuned loudly to a rock station, singing along as best he could. His whole outlook had been completely reversed. Mere days ago he'd thought of himself as nearly middle-aged at thirty-eight years, but today he felt rejuvenated, ready to take on the world. And if the restaurant business didn't pan out, he was quite willing to move on to something else. Anything was possible.

"You really went through with it, didn't you?" Marion Peters stood solidly before him, arms akimbo, visage fierce. "I suppose you're going to blow your entire savings on that dump, inheritance and all. How could you?"

Jack took his key out of the lock and came into his apartment, closing the door quietly behind him. "Good afternoon, dear," he said, smiling. "Good news travels fast."

"Tommy called," she told him. "He's worried about you."

Jack sighed. Marion, his fiancée, had joined with his brother in a conspiracy to keep him with the firm from the first mention of finding another occupation. It had been a sore topic for months, and their opposition had only strengthened his resolve. Now, feeling as good as he did, he regarded the slim blonde before him with less than his usual affection.

"He's just worried I'll go broke and start asking him for money," Jack said callously.

"You needn't be nasty. It's just that this restaurant thing is so hit or miss. You could lose your shirt."

"Yes, and we'd hate to have you marrying a man without a shirt, wouldn't we? Don't worry, I've got plenty of money and my social status won't dip more than a point or two." He threw his winter coat over a chair and walked toward the liquor cabinet, loosening his tie. "Besides," he said, laughing, "if times get tough, I can always play harmonica on the street for spare change."

"You're being heartless, Jack." Hurt replaced the anger in her soft brown eyes, and Jack regretted his words and the thoughts that produced them. He took the woman in his arms, kissing her cheek softly.

"I'm sorry, it's just that the two of you have been butting

7

your heads against a stone wall on this issue. The whole argument wears thin after a while."

"Yes, I suppose we have been." Marion allowed a smile to assert itself on her full lips. "Maybe I'm just not used to change."

"Nobody is used to change, honey. It's human nature."

"But Jack, if you aren't successful at it, will you be willing to admit defeat and get out?" She snuggled against his chest in an almost feline motion.

"I'm not a fool, Marion. And I'm sure I can rent out the space in the building easily enough."

"You bought the whole building?" She pushed herself away, shocked. "Couldn't you just lease like normal people?"

"It's better business to own the building than to pour money into someone else's pocket, dear. I get the deductions myself this way, and I can rent out office space on the top floor. Besides, it's a great place. It used to be a speakeasy in the twenties, a real hot spot with the local gangs. It's beautiful!"

"Dammit, Jack! The least you could have done was discuss it with me."

"I tried discussing it with you, and you know how far I got."

And so it went, never reaching the point of actually shouting at each other, but coming closer than either liked to admit. Their relationship, based on a childhood friendship that had continued through Marion's first marriage and divorce, had never been forced to stand the test of anger, was never tempered by any need for forgiveness. Even when he'd made his last spontaneous decision and joined the fringes of the peace movement in college, she'd only rolled her eyes and smiled, as if to say that he'd come to his senses soon enough. He had, of course; he'd thought of his career and social status, and he cut his hair and returned his attention to his financial studies. And his life progressed on an even keel.

Now he found that he couldn't explain turning his back

on the external symbols of his life. His work and lifestyle, even their coming marriage, were things that he'd just assumed he wanted, or, at least, would learn to want. He had acquiesced to his existence rather than actively seeking it, and the growing dissatisfaction he felt was always ignored. He'd lived with his sour feelings for so long that they'd become part of the natural order of things, and to have finally acted on them was almost as much of a shock to him as it was to her.

Eventually, Marion went home unsatisfied and he returned to his thoughts of menus and stage shows. Even what appeared to be a serious rift between them couldn't ruin his excitement for long.

2

The world was white, encased in slowly shifting clouds that billowed up around Jack's bed. Into the nothingness, the void, there came a soft sound of laughter, and then footsteps. A man materialized, his face obscured by the mist. He stood patiently smoking a cigarette, and his eyes, dimly seen on his shrouded face, were focused on Jack. He seemed to be waiting for Jack to do something. What did he want? Jack could feel that the man was smiling, sensed his amusement, his inner glee. Then the man was gone, and Jack was sitting in his bed with moonlight spilling cold and blue through his bedroom window. He shuddered involuntarily and lay back in his bed with the covers pulled tightly up to his chin.

3

Late the next afternoon, Jack Bellows used his own key to unlock the door to his future restaurant and entered with an almost giddy feeling of pride pushing at his chest. He surveyed his new domain: touching tables and chairs, blowing dust from the fluted lighting fixtures on the columns, assessing the damage time had done to the kitchen, and fondly running his hand along the chrome railing that skirted the balcony dining area.

It was going to be beautiful.

Heedless of the dust, he put down a chair and sat imagining the finished product. The room was a rectangle about a hundred and fifty feet from the front door to the edge of the stage and one hundred feet wide, with an upper level of seating over the front third. The bar was in the center, a long oval of once-polished oak beginning beneath the balcony and extending about twenty feet into the main-floor dining area. A two-sided mirror and liquor shelves stood within it, connected to the ceiling where the balcony covered the bar and supported on the other end by a fat, round pillar of wood.

It was a versatile room, and he would remain true to the original design, of course, with chrome gleaming bright and live music from nine to one. Forest-green walls, dark and cozy; soft booth seating; indirect lighting. And the stage was even large enough for dinner theater if he decided to take that route.

As he sat, the sun retreated in the sky, sending long shadows reaching in through the dingy front window and deepening the gloom. Stray beams of strawberry-orange light filtered in, catching the motes of dust like a fairy ballet performed lazily in the air, a sparkling movement flashing silver and gold in a hypnotizing, kaleidoscopic array of colors. Jack was tired. It was time to go home.

He stood and descended the stairs to the main floor, stopping at the bar. It was an incongruity, a holdover of Victorian styling in the modern room, but it was beautiful—a tribute to solid craftsmanship that no one had been able to destroy. He slid his hand lovingly across the dusty oak.

It was all his.

And a drop of red liquid fell to spatter on the dusty wood before him.

Jack stared at the irregular spot of moisture on the dusty bar top for a moment, then bent down to examine it more closely. Blood. He smelled musty iron when he got closer. Slowly, he reached out to touch the spot.

A single drop of blood fell, splattering on the back of his hand.

He pulled his hand back as though stung, staring at it, then wiped the drop away with the tip of one finger. The liquid felt slick between his fingertips and wore down to a tacky residue as he moved them together. But where had it come from?

A single drop of blood fell before him and hit the old wood with a quiet tap. Slowly, he lifted his gaze.

And the creature jumped from the balcony rail above him.

Spidery, with glistening, maggot-white flesh; its eyes were bulging and webbed with swollen veins; its translucent lips were pulled back over razor teeth gleaming steel-white and drooling blood; the claws were extended at the ends of seven gnarled fingers—it jumped screaming, its voice a blackboard squeal.

The talons grasped Jack's upraised forearm, puncturing his flesh with hot needles, and blood spurted from the wounds, hissing against the claws. He fell back, swinging his arm around to dash the leathery thing against the edge of a table. The thing's flat, serpentlike head pulped on impact, splattering gray slime over the table, and the claws released their hold.

Jack moved away quickly, clutching his damaged arm and watching the deformed creature twitch on the tabletop, its claws closing on air, teeth snapping frantically, severing its own tongue in its frenzy. With one final spasm, the abomination lay still.

"What the hell—" Jack moved quickly toward the door,

staying clear of the table. Whatever that thing was, he was in no hurry to go after a closer look.

A second creature scuttled in as he ran toward the doorway. Moving apelike on its long, twin-jointed appendages, the thing approached quickly, grinning and flicking its long tongue between bloody lips. With a short grunt, it leapt at Jack's throat.

Jack stumbled over a chair, falling to his back on the dirty floor as the creature landed like a cat on his chest. It bent over, the hand reaching for Jack's face, its mouth working silently.

And Jack was screaming when the last rays of the sun deserted the sky and the lights in the old bar flared on in an explosion of brilliance. He shut his eyes against the light and the all-too-clear picture of the demon's face leering down at him as the cold hand covered his mouth, squeezing his lips shut, pressing his cheeks in against his teeth hard enough to draw blood.

"Vanish!" A voice—booming, echoing. "Be gone! Scoot, you ugly bastard!"

The hand released his face as the pressure left his chest, and he forced his eyes open. The specter was gone. Jack rolled to his knees and spat out blood, staring incredulously at the bright red rivulets that ran down his right forearm.

"This can't be happening," he whispered.

"It is, Jackson. But they're gone now." The voice again, but soft, melodic. Footsteps. "Get up. We're all friends here."

Jack stared at the toes of a pair of brightly polished black shoes, then lifted his head. Wide-legged tuxedo pants, creased to kill, and a red cummerbund beneath the jacket were all he could see. He pushed himself up and back from the stranger, looking hesitantly at the man's face.

The man was anemically pale, but there was a glow to his cheeks and his thin lips were spread in a smile. Inquisitive blue eyes looked out from beneath pencil-thin eyebrows and his hair was slicked straight back, black and glossy, and parted in the middle. He laughed.

"It's all true," the stranger said. "But the worst is over now. Relax."

"What is going on?" Jack's voice was like a rusty spring expanding in his throat.

"We've come to welcome you to your club," the man told him. "You are the proud owner of the late, great Cafe Purgatorium."

Those enigmatic words were the last thing Jack heard before the darkness overcame him.

4

In a red-lit room—a glowing, pulsing room—he watched a small, dark man smoke a cigarette. The man was seated in a hard chair by the window with his back to Jack, who was lying on the bed in what was apparently a hotel room. The man had removed his shirt in deference to the heat and was wearing dark trousers held up with suspenders strapped over his sleeveless underwear shirt. He wore a rumpled fedora at the back of his head. The little man appeared to be waiting for something.

Jack felt himself moving on the bed, and the man snapped his cigarette at the throbbing neon sign outside the window and turned. His hairline dropped to a pronounced widow's peak over his deep-set eyes, and his long, narrow nose carried the downward line of his hair to his thin lips. He wore a goatee trimmed to a neat point, which, combined with the line of his hair and nose, gave his face the appearance of a descending arrow.

The man smiled, teeth glistening in the red light, and winked at Jack. Then he turned back to the window and lit another cigarette.

And there was sudden darkness, as if a black wall had dropped before the smiling man, replacing him with a void

13

holding only a voice that spoke slowly, patiently. Jack vaguely remembered the voice as belonging to the man who'd called off the strange animal in the bar. This is a history lesson, the voice said, a crash course in history of immediate interest to Jack.

Established in 1891, Maxie's did good business as a tavern and burlesque house. The new century was celebrated there by men in derby hats sporting handlebar moustaches, and, later, parties were held for our doughboys heading overseas. Business was destroyed by Prohibition, and the tavern was closed down from 1921 to 1923, when it reopened under the name of the Cafe Society.

In 1923 the Cafe Society was, for all appearances, a successful family restaurant. It was owned by a man named Louis Trent, a transplanted Bostonian with a clipped moustache and a dapper manner, and it did well enough for him to open a second restaurant, the Cafe Philharmonic, which was larger, and catered to a more upscale crowd. That both of his restaurants offered more than coffee for refreshment in those Prohibition days went without saying, and Trent was guaranteed to prosper as long as the Eighteenth Amendment remained in effect.

He did so well, in fact, that in 1926 the cafe became the object in a buy-out attempt by another Minneapolis businessman, Johnny "Spider" Fitzsimmons, looking to expand his holdings in Minnesota's illegal liquor trade. Louis Trent rejected his less-than-generous offer, so Johnny was forced to make arrangements to buy the two eateries from the late restaurateur's estate. The new management expanded the floor show and added a gaming room in back, more than tripling the profits.

In 1927 the cafe again changed hands when Spider Fitzsimmons and three of his "accountants" were killed on the street out front by gunfire from a passing car. The new owner, a lawyer named Donald Petersburg, remodeled the interior of the Cafe Society in 1929, giving it a sleek, Art Deco look and adding the balcony dining in an area that had previously held offices over the front half of the restaurant.

On December 5, 1933, both establishments went legit—Prohibition had been repealed. As joyous as the occasion was, it marked the beginning of the end. Both fell victim to popular tastes, losing most of their nongambling business in the years before the war. Petersburg sold the Cafe Society to Minneapolis banker James Wilson, falsifying the books to cover up the restaurant's sinking profitability. He took the gambling equipment with him to his remaining club, ensuring that profits would drop even further.

World War Two caused a small boom in business as Americans went out in search of diversions from the war. The Cafe Society became famous for its music, introducing the Midwest to some of the finest jazz bands in the country. Those were its glory days. After the war, the city began to grow away from it, relegating the neighborhood to the less fortunate citizens who couldn't afford the move to the suburbs.

In the sixties it enjoyed a short period of popularity when it was purchased by a young entrepreneur named Kaminski who was hoping to establish a rock music club to fill the void left open by the more conservative dining spots in town. He did well for a couple years, again giving the old room the reputation as a haven for good music, but the patrons didn't have the buying power needed to keep it afloat. A series of drug raids in 1969 spelled the end of that enterprise, and the club was sold by the court to pay off its debts.

It ended its long run as a strip joint, coming more or less full circle, and closing in 1972 due to lack of interest and finding some use as a warehouse.

The Cafe Society was left to gather dust and memories. And it remembered . . .

In November of 1926 Joe Waterson, Wesley Timm, and Milton Andrews, members of the Dave Cornish Dance Band, were mistakenly shot to death in the dressing rooms beneath the stage by one of Spider's boys acting on a tip that they had been sent in by a rival liquor dealer with weapons in their music cases. A search of their equipment revealed only a clarinet and two saxophones. The mix-up was covered over by paying off the band and giving the bodies a quick burial after dark in the broad Mississippi River.

On April 1, 1927, Spider Fitzsimmons personally knifed to death a woman named Elaine Denver in the ladies' room. She'd been in the chorus when he took a liking to her and set her up in an apartment downtown. He carried on their romance until he found out she was using her penthouse to dispense her favors to other men who also knew how to express their gratitude. Spider confronted her after closing on the morning of the first, striking her several times with his fists before she escaped to the false safety of the ladies' room. She too joined the muddy Mississippi on its way south.

In 1941, Clara Montgomery, a business executive's wife, choked to death on a piece of filet mignon while laughing at a third-rate comic named Charlie Brell.

A wino named Dickie Billings passed out and froze to death in the alley behind the Cafe Society in January 1952. The wizened old creature remained frozen up against the wall for three days before a policeman found him.

In May 1965, Robert Anderson and Christine Parker overdosed on smack that had been cut a little too pure for their tastes. They died in Robert's blue Mustang parked in the same alley where Dickie Billings had drained his last bottle thirteen years earlier.

And, on July 4, 1971, a stripper and part-time hooker named Fay Browning hanged herself in the shower stall of her dressing room. She was twenty-two.

There were other deaths in or around the Cafe Society over the years, various muggings, rapes, car accidents, and heart attacks, but they were of little importance in the scheme of things. They passed through the veil like smoke and were gone, leaving only their families to remember their passing. It was the other ones—Joe, Wesley, Milton,

16

Elaine, Clara, Dickie, Robert, Christine, and Fay—who mattered. They stayed.

Something inside them had been unwilling to die. Even Fay, who'd give up on everything, found that she wasn't ready to give up what little life she had. As she kicked away the wobbly old chair and the noose fashioned of pantyhose tightened around her slender neck, she found a part of herself that still had courage. She refused to die, and went on to join the others.

They found themselves adrift in the world. Disembodied by day, they had to content themselves with watching the activities of the living world, but at night they could do as they pleased, with bodies as substantial and essentially the same as the ones they left behind. And, they were free to make the choice denied most mortals—the choice between Heaven or Hell.

They had gained this freedom by slipping through a crack, or, more appropriately, making use of a loophole in the natural order of things. It was simple, really. It hadn't been their time to die, and, though their bodies were claimed by natural laws, their souls didn't have to be. All it took was a little willpower to escape absolute cessation.

And, over the years of decline, when the Cafe Society was fading along with the generation that built it, it gained a reputation in dark circles that far outshone any of the meager fame it had once known. It became a gathering place, a bar held in high esteem among those in the know. The liquor was always free, the music excellent, and the company jolly in the Cafe Purgatorium.

Others came from across the country to join in the fun, people who, like the local group, found themselves at liberty between the seams of things, came to dance and drink till dawn. If anything, the closing in 1972 increased the club's popularity. Now they didn't have to wait until after hours to move in each night. Now they needed only wait till dark.

5

Jack felt himself floating up from darkness into bright light and the shadow of someone leaning over him. He felt an urgent need to ask about the man in the red hotel room, but, as consciousness rushed back, the pain in his right arm obliterated all memory of the dream and the questions he wanted to ask.

Shaking his head groggily, he strained to focus his eyes on his forearm. It was bruised darkly where something had gripped him, clearly showing the imprint of six long fingers and a thumb, but the skin wasn't broken. How could that be? Jack clearly remembered the blood spitting out around the claws.

"It cut me," Jack said quietly. "What happened to the wounds?" He looked up at the stranger in the tuxedo crouching beside him on the floor.

"Illusion," the man replied. "They're not that strong yet. Not strong enough to draw real blood, anyway, though they've become quite solid."

"What are they?" Jack forced himself to sit up, realizing that there were others there behind the man. "Who are you?"

The man smiled slightly, seemingly relieved to allow the second question to preempt the first. "Milton Andrews," he said, holding out his hand. "Call me Doc. I'm one of your new tenants. Come, I'll introduce you to the regulars."

Jack took the offered hand and allowed himself to be pulled to his feet. The room wobbled slightly around him as he took a tentative step toward the people who stood behind Doc.

"Joe Waterson," he said, indicating a man with a thin moustache who smiled and shook Jack's hand. "Wesley Timm." A sallow man with flaming red hair stepped forward with a nervous nod. Both Joe and Wesley were wearing tuxedos identical to Doc's.

"This is Elaine Denver." Doc escorted a slender, dark-haired woman forward with a hand on her shoulder. She was wearing a long red evening gown with spaghetti straps and a large silk flower at the left hip. Her hair was bobbed short and she wore dark red, almost black lipstick that echoed the color of her long fingernails.

"Dickie."

An old man in ragged clothing stepped up with a sly grin. "Pleased to meet ya," he said in a high, laughing voice. "You'll like it here, boy. Have the time of your life."

"And our lovebirds, Bob and Christine." He motioned toward a couple of kids in jeans who stood slightly back from the rest and smiled shyly. Both were clean-cut, of the boy and girl next door variety, and Jack was struck by the thought that neither one looked like a heroin addict.

Why would he think they were junkies? He missed the next introduction in his confusion, but he already knew that the plump woman wearing a brown suit with heavily padded shoulders was Clara Montgomery. But how did he know?

And the dream came back slowly, seeping up into his mind like a cold spring spilling forth the realization that the dream was real; it was the truth. And he looked around him, noticing for the first time that the white shirt beneath Doc's tux was stained with blood, and the other two were marred by similar stains; that Elaine's form-fitting gown was slashed and stained nearly as black as her fingernails above the flower that rode her hip; that Dickie's unshaven face was unnaturally white and marred by rough grooves that could have been gotten by falling asleep against the bricks of an alley wall.

It was true, but couldn't be true. Doc's left hand couldn't be shattered by what appeared to be a bullet wound that sent splintered bone up through the top of his hand and twisted it into a claw, and that tidy-looking boy didn't have dark

19

bruises hidden in the crook of his elbow just below the short-sleeved shirt. None of it was real. Was it?

Jack reached out and touched Doc Andrews lightly on the shoulder, then gripped him hard.

"I'm real," the man told him. "Real enough, anyway."

"Oh, God." The lights seemed to dim slightly, and he began to tremble.

"You need a drink, buddy," Dickie chirped.

"Good plan," said Elaine, moving up to take his arm.

As he turned he saw the air begin to shimmer at the front of the restaurant. The door and front wall wavered in his vision as though someone had dropped a pebble into the pool of his perception, causing it to ripple and distort what he saw. The watery movement continued, moving in a definite line of distortion along the walls and floor toward where they stood by the long bar. Behind the flowing ribbon of unreality the furnishings had changed. The dirty door shone with careful polishing and the headwaiter's desk changed from dirty white paint to sleek gray enamel trimmed with chrome and a large fern grew luxuriously in a pot beside it. The walls bled into gentle pastel shades of blue and green as the dust evaporated, and the ragged, faded coverings on the booths exploded with geometric patterns. The distortion passed, and the floor beneath them melted into a shining pattern of black and white tiles.

Jack spun around in time to see a circle of shimmering light shrinking in the center of the curtains over the stage where it popped out of existence. He turned back to the others, who had moved on to the bar.

The bar itself was shinning, reflecting the soft lighting back from its highly polished surface, and rows of bottles were stacked—full, waiting—before the mirror on the long cabinet that sat like a castle within the moat of wood.

Milton "Doc" Andrews walked through the solid oak of the bar to take up position within it as bartender. Jack staggered toward him, staring openmouthed.

"Scotch, neat. Right?" he asked, taking the stopper out

of a tall, green bottle. The mirror behind him reflected the entire scene, though he and his friends seemed slightly hazy. Jack could see that he was the only one whose reflection was entirely clear.

"Yes, neat. Is the booze real?" he asked, then heard himself laughing at the absurdity of the question.

"It'll do the trick," was Doc's reply as he poured.

"Yeah, we specialize in spirits here," Dickie said, chuckling.

"Poor Richard," Elaine mumbled in a bored tone. "That joke was old in thirty-two."

Jack moved like a puppet on tangled strings, tripping over his own feet and stumbling to the empty stool between Elaine and Joe and hoisting himself onto it awkwardly. He took the short glass in both hands and swallowed the amber fluid quickly, slamming it down for a refill. Yes, the booze seemed real enough, and it burned a path down to curl up in his stomach with a satisfying fire.

The booze was real, and that was the only important thing at the moment.

"How do you like the place?" Doc leaned on the bar, his face close to Jack's, smiling. "It'll be one hell of a party tonight. You'll get a kick out of some of the people who show up here."

Jack said nothing, but held out his glass.

"There's a boy after my own heart," Dickie chirped, pouring himself a water glass full of Jack Daniels. "Eat, drink, and be merry!"

"For tomorrow ye shall die," Elaine finished quietly. He could feel her watching him in an unmistakably carnal matter, radiating desire like an open oven and concentrating her sex in the solid probing of her eyes.

"Feel better?" Joe grinned. "A shock, ain't it?"

"Our boy is a tough cookie," Doc said, his eyes very serious above his smile. "He'll be all right."

"As long as I make the assumption that I'm not insane,

I'll be fine," Jack said, staring back into the other man's eyes. "I'm not a great believer in the occult, though."

"What, you mean Ouija boards? Hocus-pocus? Sophomoric parlor games?" Doc's eyes consented to a humorous twinkle. "Forget about that, Jackson. This is the real thing."

"Life after death?"

"Between death. I suppose you could call this limbo. But it isn't that, either. We're nowhere, out beyond the reach of belief. They can't touch us here."

"Who can't?"

"Those mud puppies you met earlier, for one example," Joe explained at his elbow. "And others."

"Shhh!" Dickie shook his head frantically behind Elaine. "Don't worry, Mr. Bellows, there ain't nothing here to hurt you."

"Come on, Dick," Joe said. "The man's got to have the lowdown. He's got to protect himself."

"Against what?" Prickles of ice crawled across Jack's neck.

"Nothing." Dickie was adamant.

"Joe's right." Doc silenced the old man with his gaze, then looked back at Jack. "Everything here can hurt you if you let it."

"But why? If I understand this correctly, you don't mean me any harm. Do you? How can I be hurt?"

"Because you ain't dead yet, Jackson."

6

Mamma went to Heaven
Papa went to Hell
I moved into Limbo
And I'm doing very well.

The band used an eclectic combination of instruments ranging from electric guitars to a harp, and put out enough sound to wake the few dead who weren't already in attendance. Jack was surprised to find that this odd collection could even agree on a key to play in, but they were quite good, with a repertoire covering nearly a hundred years of popular music. Jack relaxed in the hard pulse of their song, a little rock and roll ditty the leader, a blind, bearded giant named Max, called "The Ballad of the Not Quite Dead." The irony of their situation was not lost on anyone. In fact, they reveled in it.

They wore smiles and makeshift bandages. They wore the signs of their deaths, the crushed limbs and cyanotic faces, the gaping, bloodless wounds. In deference to Jack, they covered their pustules and the ragged ends of bones as best they could. The dead became his friends; they were very friendly people.

Jack felt narcotized by the dream, the history lesson Doc had fed to him, lulled into accepting the evening as it came at him. Though the more rational part of his mind rebelled at the scene, he found it made a certain mad sense. Human history contained too many references to ghosts and hauntings for all of it to be garbage. After a while, with enough liquor in him, it became an enjoyable party.

He sat with Doc at a table near the bar. They drank Chivas and ate beer nuts. They eyed each other warily, then grew garrulous with drink.

"I am satisfied with things as they are," Doc insisted over his glass. "I like my death. Sure, I'd like to be up there with them, playing some of the old licks, being in the center of things, but you've got to play the cards you're dealt. Hell, I held my hand out like maybe it would stop the slug. Can you imagine that?" He laughed, and sipped his drink. "You could say I dealt myself a bum hand," he said, holding up the ruined appendage with a crooked grin.

"You people are very well adjusted to things," Jack admitted. "It must have been hard at first."

"Hard? Hard to believe my good fortune, you mean. I can go anywhere and do anything I damn well please. I even went to France once. Imagine that, Milton Andrews from

Jersey going to Paris. It's a pip. The cat's meow, we would have said back in my life, though it's hard to remember why."

"Don't you want to move on?"

"To where?" He raised one eyebrow.

"Heaven, I guess. I don't suppose you'd choose Hell."

"They're all the same, man. You pays your money and takes your chances, and either way it's all over. They put you into your little niche and that's it for eternity. No, thanks."

"No, there's more than that, isn't there?"

"Sure there is. Gabriel will blow his horn, and the world will explode, or some such malarkey. Then the dead will all rise from the grave with their teeth pearly-white and their halos held in place with bobby pins. It'll be one big picnic from then on, buster. You betcha."

Mamma plays her harp now
Papa stokes the fire
You can tell me that they're happy
But you're just a dirty liar.

"Can you imagine what it'll smell like when all those corpses come bobbing up out of the ground?" Doc giggled.

"He'll get you for talking like that." Jack laughed.

"Who? The great muckety-muck in the sky? Mister, if God wanted our smiling faces up there, we'd be tuning our harp strings right now. Free choice, chum. That's the key. Predestination is just a lie the sin-and-salvation boys use to excuse all the big shots who get away with murder. The will of God, sinner, and you're stuck with it. Hell, Joe Pulpit knows what side his bread is buttered on. But God, or whatever, doesn't make any such demands on a person's time. Everyone has a thinking organ so they can come to their own conclusions. Our own choice, pal. That's why we're here, and that's why God can't do anything about my backtalk. It's those Holy Joes who have everything wrong."

"But you all prefer this existence? You like walking around looking like a bunch of broken toys?" Jack looked around the crowd, finding a woman sitting several tables away. "Does she like spending eternity with half her face torn off? The woman is a walking scab. It's horrible."

"Horrible? Man, you don't know horror at all. She's the Mona Lisa. She's Clara Bow. Helen of Troy. You haven't seen horror yet."

The Devil sends his gargoyles
Jehovah sends his saints
They all say come and join us
But we'll just stay here by the gate.

Jack danced with Elaine, losing himself in the feeling of her cool body against his and the faint scent of jasmine that clung to her hair. She held him close, whispering, seducing, and Jack was hard-pressed to find a polite reason for refusing her. He broke away mumbling a lame excuse, thinking of Marion and wondering if being faithful was worth it in the end.

This woman is dead, you idiot, he reminded himself. It was so easy to forget. Unless he came up against someone who'd died in an exceedingly violent manner, he couldn't see any difference between these people and the crowd at any other bar in town.

"Having fun?" Doc was at his elbow, grinning, slopping his drink on the floor.

"I wanted to talk to you, Doc," he shouted in the man's ear.

"So, we're talking. Say your piece."

"When are you going to explain about my being hurt here? What about those things that jumped me?"

"Gargoyles is what we call the little monkeys." Doc smiled. "Everybody wants us to come play at their house, and those things are just Old Nick's little helpers. He's planning a snatch."

"But why would they hurt me? And, for that matter, how could they?" Jack had a hard time trusting the man, no matter how friendly he was, and hoped to pin him down on an answer.

"They want to scare you away." Doc put an arm around Jack's shoulder and leaned in close. "They can take us down with them if they catch us alone, so our safety is in numbers, see? Lately, this last year or so, they've been getting stronger. Pulled a frail right off the dance floor one night. Business has been slow since then, not like tonight."

"What does that have to do with me?"

"You're our protection, buddy. You own this joint. That's the ticket right there—ownership. See, they can't do anything to us unless you invite them in. This place was abandoned before, though I suppose somebody owned it, and we were left as caretakers by default."

"So you had to invite them then."

"Wise up, buddy. Dead people can't give permission for anything. The Devil doesn't need to ask us squat. His agents just weren't strong enough to overpower us, is all. Get it? Now that you have taken ownership, he has to have your permission."

"I didn't ask them to attack me."

"He can scare you, I guess. I'm not sure, but I have an idea." He peered into Jack's eyes, breathing booze in his face. "I think that we've been hanging around here so long that we've kind of worn a groove in the place. The barriers have gotten weaker, and that's why he's stronger."

"So go somewhere else." Jack shrugged his arm away. "Take your show on the road."

"But Jackie, we like it here! It's comfortable." Doc laughed and finished the rest of his liquor. "You got a swell joint." Doc made a small salute with his glass and staggered off in the direction of the bar.

"Great." Jack stuffed his hands into his pockets and watched him walk away. A bunch of drunken ghosts were going to get him in trouble with the devil.

A one-armed man and a woman whose face and left arm were burned to tatters of blackened flesh danced between him and Doc's retreating form. Jack shuddered slightly and looked away. Couples were dancing happily around him: a kid in bloody marine fatigues waltzed with an overly made-up flapper; a tall black man whose zoot suit still looked sharp even though it was marred by the bloody evidence of a shotgun blast twirled a hippie girl whose arms were flaming with needle tracks; an elegant gentleman, whose wing collar almost covered the ragged gap in his throat, carried a legless girl, no more than fifteen, around the floor in broad circles. They were all so happy, so satisfied, and their happiness began to seem a bit cloying to Jack. He was their meal ticket now, their promise that the party would continue, and it was a role he didn't want to play. He felt himself being manipulated again, forced to live someone else's idea of his life, and it was a realization that spoiled the good time he'd been having.

Jack checked his watch impatiently. Four A.M. already. What the hell was he doing? He had to be at the office in five hours. Somewhat angrily, he began searching for his coat.

He bumped into a woman carrying three full glasses to her table. "Excuse me," he said absently. She glowered at him with her good eye and moved on. People moved around him, laughing, kissing. A pretty girl with shimmering black hair smiled at him briefly before she was obscured by dancing bodies.

Jack suddenly felt an urge to cry.

Who was that? Jack changed his course abruptly, maneuvering through the crowd toward where she had been sitting. Her place was empty when he got there, and he scanned the room for a glimpse of her. Something about the girl had captured his imagination even while his mind protested against taking special interest in a corpse.

He couldn't see her anywhere.

She had seemed so alone, so empty. He'd felt her

27

loneliness like a tear within him, as though that one glance had made an empathic connection between them. He couldn't leave until he'd found her.

You made me love you
I didn't want to do it
Didn't want to do it
You made me want you
And all the time you knew it.

The band had switched eras, and a skinny crooner, one arm hanging limp at his side, slid through the song as though his heart would break. His maudlin interpretation saddened Jack after the feeling he'd absorbed from the elusive young woman.

Five o'clock. Jack sat at the bar staring into his whisky. She had disappeared, if she'd ever been there at all.

He felt a sense of loss in the pit of his stomach.

Six o'clock. He had searched every available space in the building, forcing entry into the dusty offices upstairs and the dressing rooms below the stage as well as searching though the kitchen and restrooms. Nothing.

"Doc." He called out, walking quickly to grab his arm. "I'm looking for a dark-haired girl. Pretty."

"Lots of dark-haired janes here, Jackie boy." Doc's eyes were bloodshot and unfocused, and he had to keep shuffling his feet to remain standing in one place. "What style of hair?"

"Long, about shoulder length, and straight. Well, almost straight. She had an oval face. Shy-looking."

"So how was this chippie dressed?"

"I don't remember. Short skirt, I think, but modern, not a flapper. And bright colors."

"Straight hair and bright colors sounds like the sixties, doesn't it? You people showed such godawful taste back then." He hiccuped and laughed.

"Yeah, could be then."

"Probably Fay. She's damn shy, Jack. You should look up Elaine." Again, he threw an arm around Jack's shoulder, but this time it was more for support than comradery. "Elaine ain't the least bit shy, no sir. She's a fast one. And she likes you, Jackson. You two could make a swell couple."

"Where can I find Fay?" Jack was angered to find out that a drunk was still a drunk no matter what corporal state he was in. "Come on, Doc."

"Can't find her if she don't want to be found. Us disembodied spirits can make ourselves invisible, don't you know? Could be standing beside you listening to us talk. Forget her. Failed suicides are all screwy."

Jack pushed him off and walked away angrily. He'd find her on his own.

It was six forty-five when he came upon her sitting on the floor of the coat checkroom. She was huddled in the corner holding her legs up against her chest and pressing her face hard against the patterned nylon stretched over her knees.

"Fay?" he said, leaning on the Dutch door. "Hello there."

She looked up quickly, blinking. Tears pooled in her dark eyes and streaked her cheeks, and a strand of hair clung damply to the side of her face. Again, Jack felt a twinge inside him.

"Hey, don't be sad," he whispered, opening the door and entering the small room. "What's wrong?"

Kneeling beside her, he could smell strawberry perfume and something herbal in her hair. He touched her, smoothing his hand down her arm. Merely making contact with her sent his heart thumping hollowly in his chest.

"Please don't cry." He felt pathetically useless trying to comfort her.

"I didn't mean for you to follow me." Her voice was small and caught in her throat. "Don't bother with me."

"It's no bother." He took her chin in his fingers and lifted her face, dipping his head slightly to meet her eyes. A livid

29

purple bruise circled her throat, the only outward sign of her despair. "I felt—well, I felt lonely for you. I wanted to meet you."

"You're very nice." She smiled. "I could see that."

Jack's stomach clamped on his happiness when she smiled. It was a feeling he'd forgotten, the feeling of hopeless love.

"I'd like to get to know you," he said.

She looked down demurely, seeming to shimmer in the dim light. Then her face grew indistinct, and his fingers slipped up through her chin and past her lips.

"It's dawn," she said as her image dissolved before him.

"Wait!" But he was alone, kneeling on the dusty, litter-strewn floor and staring at the cobwebs on the wall.

The restaurant was empty, returned to dirt and decay. It was as if none of it had happened, and only the light-headed feeling from the whisky in his stomach kept him from losing his belief. He got his coat and walked out into the cold air and feeble sunlight, and even the effect of the booze began to fade.

But it had happened. She had happened. And Jack walked to his car feeling happier than he could remember ever feeling before.

7

"Where were you all night!" Marion's voice was a strident yelp on the telephone. "I tried calling you."

"Tom's been asking me the same thing all morning." Jack lowered his head to his free hand and worked his fingers back into his hair. "The two of you should put that to music."

"Listen, buster, your snide comments don't answer the question. I was worried about you." Her voice settled into a cold, hard tone as dangerous as the growl of a mountain cat.

"I was at the cafe most of the time, then I went out for something to eat."

"All night? I called well after three A.M."

"It's good to hear your clock works, Marion. I told you where I was, but I doubt I can come up with any witnesses." None you'd want to meet, anyway, he thought.

"Yes, I doubt it, too." She hung up.

Jack frowned at the telephone for a moment, thinking about love and the world of Marion Peters. Hearing her like that, her voice harsh with barely controlled rage, made him think of all the times she's used the threat of her anger to sway his actions. She played him like a concertina, squeezing him this way and that, until he wasn't sure who had been the author of their plans. Their marriage was something that got planned along the way. The fact that he'd remained single through her first marriage and divorce seemed to say that he was waiting for her, silently implying his intentions. He'd gone this far in life without really knowing what he wanted.

This morning he knew what he wanted. Unfortunately, it was something he couldn't have.

The liquor had worn off rapidly in the sunlight, evaporating as quickly as the woman in the coat checkroom, leaving him feeling tired, worn down to his lowest reserve of energy. He hadn't stopped for breakfast, but hurried home to shower and change clothes, arriving at the office right on time. Now he was paying for it as he yawned over his eighth cup of coffee and struggled, cross-eyed with fatigue, to study the papers on his desk. By noon, he realized that it was useless—no work was going to get done today.

"I'm out of here, Tommy," he called out as he twisted into his coat and started down the hall.

"Wait!" His brother, a balding man in his shirtsleeves with an ample spread of belly pushing at his belt, emerged from an office and hurried after Jack. "Have you got those accounts straightened out yet?" He was puffing slightly when he caught up with Jack.

"Pretty close, Tom. I'm dog-tired, though." He continued past the receptionist and to the double mahogany doors.

"Jack, you've got to handle your end of things before you desert us. I can't put up with the extra work now." He stopped the younger man with a hand on his arm.

"The way I feel today, I couldn't advise my garbage collector on where to invest the trash. I don't want to do a second-rate job, okay?"

"That's fine, just fine. Why didn't you think of that when you were out all night, Jack? You still owe the firm a little loyalty."

"Tom." He looked seriously at his brother. "You're absolutely right, and I'm sorry, but I just can't handle it right now. It wouldn't be fair to our clients or the firm. Why don't you give some of my accounts to Dave Martin? He's been with us long enough, and certainly knows his stuff. You could take on a couple yourself, couldn't you?"

"But we're swamped, Jack. Why the hell couldn't you wait till middle age to have your middle-age crisis?" Tom said sourly. "Why now?"

"Because I have to get out before it kills me." Jack leaned against the door and smiled sadly. "It's been squeezing me for years but I didn't feel it till now. It may sound strange, but I didn't know how much I dislike my life. I've been letting life happen to me, never taking charge, never deciding anything. I have to change things, before it's too late. Do you understand?"

"Maybe I do," Tom admitted. "Oh, hell, I guess I can shift your accounts and move Dave up to your slot. I may be selfish, but it's hard to lose my wonder boy without a fight."

"Things will work out, bro." He gave Tom a playful slap on one cheek. "And anytime you want a free meal, you'll know where to find one."

"Sure, as if I need more food." He laughed, patting his

stomach. "Just don't expect any commission off work we do."

"Boy, you sure bounce back fast, don't you? See you around." He opened the door and stepped out into the hall.

"Yeah," Tom called at his back. "Say, get your tail back here on Friday and we'll have a going-away party."

Jack waved his assent as he turned the corner and was gone.

On his way home, Jack made a stop at the office of the *Star Tribune*, where he spent an hour using a microfiche reader in the newspaper's morgue.

As expected, there were no obituaries for the three musicians, but Fay Browning was listed. The short paragraph stated that Fay Marie Browning, twenty-two, was found dead in the dressing room of the Cafe Society, where she was a dancer. She had hanged herself in the shower stall. Fay was an orphan, and was buried by the city.

It wasn't much of a summation for a lifetime, even one as brief as hers. It said nothing about her dark eyes and the full pout of her lips, made no mention of her soft, innocent voice. The obituary wasn't about the woman he'd met at all.

He drove home in a sober mood, allowing his thoughts to turn inward to feelings he'd never examined. There had been a time when he knew what he wanted, when his goals were as clearly visible as a beacon on a clear, still night. He'd wanted his own business from the start, beginning with a boyhood dream of owning a riding stable. Always, he'd imagined himself as the architect of his own destiny, never following anybody's orders. He'd imagined himself a free man, and never saw the lie that was his life. While taking over the family brokerage house with his brother might be interpreted as being his own boss, it didn't give him control. That had been given over to his father, a stern businessman who always knew what was best for his sons. He introduced them to reality and showed them their places in it. He had determined the course of Jack's life, choosing his college and profession, his clothing, his hairstyle, and locking him into his predetermined future while giving him a wall to serve as his horizon. Now Jack could see it, and admit it. And, five years after the man's death, he could see the love and concern in his father's decisions just as clearly as he knew it was time to break away from them.

Marion was the cause for his most painful emotions. Jack felt a leaden clot of guilt in his throat when he thought of her, guilt over promising his love when it was more an obligation that he felt. It was so clear now. They were accustomed to each other, and he'd never found anyone else, so it was logical that they marry. Logic, not emotion. But logic had been his substitute for love, and his guilt had bent him to her will as she guided them to all the right social events and the introductions to the right people. It made her happy; it was good for business. It was garbage, mere posturing and thoughtless actions, and there were times when he felt the pain of living would drive him to kill her one day. And that thought bred guilt that grew into more posturing and more stifled rebellion.

But he had suppressed those feelings just as he suppressed his own desires. Keeping everyone happy became his goal, and the beacon light went out.

At home, lying in his big bed, he allowed himself to think the truly unthinkable and contemplate the rekindling of the beacon. Twenty years after a torrid relationship with Mary Swanson during his senior year of high school, Jack Bellows was in love.

He was in love with a woman who died in 1971.

Love is a painful emotion. It tears at the fabric of life, rearranging priorities and challenging every cherished belief. But the pain is gloriously beautiful. It reminds the soul that it is alive, and that anything is possible.

Jack had gone beyond questioning his new love. He didn't want to examine it, just revel in it and hope it would last. It was enough that she was solid and alive after dark; the metaphysics of the situation didn't matter. And, as he drifted off to sleep, the scent of her strawberry perfume floating through his mind, he knew with cold certainty that he was willing to die if that's what it took to join her.

8

The sign outside the window flashed like a heartbeat, pumping red light like hot blood into the dingy room. And the light took on a liquid quality, seeming to lap at the edge of the bed. The walls dissolved, leaving the sign hanging for a moment flashing CAFE SOCIETY before it too disappeared, and Jack felt the bed bobbing, awash in an ocean of blood that stretched unbroken to the horizon under a jet-black sky.

The small man rose up from the vile ocean to stand beside the bobbing bed. He smiled, then placed a cigarette in his lips and lit it with the tip of one finger. Dark things played in the liquid at his feet.

"You want the bitch?" he said, in a voice like steel ringing at the blows of a hammer. "She's yours, sinner. I can bring her."

And the bloody ocean hissed, evaporating in an odorous cloud until a blasted landscape rose up around them. Two of the demon things were running across the rocky plain dragging something behind them. They laughed as they ran and stopped at the man's feet. The object behind them appeared to be a tarpaulin rolled up like a rug, which they lifted and laid parallel to Jack's bed. At a nodded command from their master, they hunched their backs and tugged at the ends of the tarp, sending it unrolling toward the bed.

Fay was in it—dismembered, eviscerated. Her limbless torso flopped once, releasing the viscera across the tarp with a wet, slapping sound; severed hands clutched at the air; bone gleamed white at the hacked joints; and her long hair was bloody and matted against the head that rolled to stare at him with eyeless sockets, her lips parted, the thick, blackened tongue pressed against her blood-encrusted teeth.

Jack heard a scream like gulls crying, a wailing cry that tore at the bowels of a living pain.

"I can put her together for you, dear boy," the man taunted.

But Jack wasn't listening to anything but the desperate sound of his own anguished cry as the flies began to gather on the savaged body of his love.

His own cry, like a child whimpering in the dark, seemed to echo in the empty bedroom as Jack sat up in bed blinking in the glare of the sunset that filled the window. A sunset like blood spraying over the frozen wastes of the city.

9

"Flowers, Jackson?" Doc met him at the door, cocking one eye at the bouquet in Jack's hand. "For me?"

"No, sorry." Jack flushed under the man's unwavering gaze. "I, uh, I see the joint is hopping."

"Certainly is. But you're changing the subject. Who're the posies for?"

"Maybe they're for Elaine," he said, looking through the crowd as they walked in.

"Maybe you lie." Doc's laugh sounded oily, conspiratorial. "Besides, you don't need to waste flowers on Elaine. She was born on her back."

"Where's Fay?" Jack felt light-headed, and couldn't keep the words back against the hammer blows of his heartbeat. He had to find her and not waste a minute of the hours till dawn.

"You probably don't need flowers for that one, either," Doc said coldly.

Jack swung his fist around, putting his full weight into a punch that sailed right through the other man's face. Jack stumbled through his target, thrown off balance by his momentum, then turned to face him angrily.

"Sorry, fella." Doc cut off Jack's words with an upraised hand. "Rather callous of me, wasn't it?"

"Damn right it was." Jack had swung reflexively, surprising himself as much as the startled spirit. He felt like a lovesick schoolboy fighting over every slur, real or imagined, to the reputation of his love.

"You're in for heartache, buddy. The worst move a man can make is to fall for some broad he can't have." Doc's voice was compassionate, quite contrary to his normally cynical attitude. "You do know how stupid it is."

"What I know doesn't matter, Doc. You understand that, don't you?"

"Absolutely." He waved one hand toward the crowded tables. "She's in a booth up by the stage. I'll have drinks sent over."

They spoke without words, reaching out intuitively with heart and soul to touch and hold each other in the cradle of their understanding. A marriage of true minds, conceived in the shadows between worlds, between day and night, Heaven and Hell. Each shared the other's grasping need and filled the other's empty spaces, becoming their own quiet universe within the cacophonous revels of the dead.

Jack Bellows and Fay Browning had found what they'd been searching for.

"I haven't been a good girl," she admitted, the blush in her cheeks enhancing the dark pools of her eyes.

"I don't care," he replied, watching her, letting his eyes drink in every nuance of movement that enlivened her face.

"I was lost, I guess," she continued, speaking in the abstract tone of someone who is trying to comprehend the complexities of their own emotions. "I guess I reacted against the good, Catholic upbringing I got at St. Matthew's orphanage when the going got tough, rather than drawing strength from it. They were so strict, so righteous in their morality, that I could hardly breathe. So, when I ran out of money, and the only dancing jobs I could find all involved taking off my clothes, I said to hell with it and gave in. I thought I was strong enough, but I wasn't. Life got to be too much of a bummer. I couldn't hack it, and every day was just more of the same, so I copped out. Blew it, though, didn't I?"

"I'm glad you did," he told her. "It's as though God, or fate, or something kept you on earth so we could meet. If anyone had tried to tell me this was possible a week ago, I would have laughed in his face. But now that I've seen and touched all of this, I know it's true. And now that you're here, I know why it's true."

"I was never in love before," she told him.

"I've told myself I was a time or two, but I wasn't. I know that now."

"But why now? Why do we find love when it's too late?" She bit her lip against a halting sigh. "What did we do that deserved this punishment?"

"Enjoying the party, kids?" Doc slid into the booth behind Fay, leaning over the bench beside her and stroking her cheek with his ruined hand. "You guys ought to mix a little."

"We're happy where we are, Doc." Jack felt a possessive anger wash through him at the sight of the man's hand on her face.

"I can see that." He smiled slyly. "Well, maybe you should tell her about your daylight lover, old boy. It should make for sparkling conversation." He slipped away before anyone could say a word.

"Who does he mean?" she asked him softly, as though afraid of his reply.

"Marion," Jack said, his mood soured by the thought. "My fiancée, more or less."

"I knew this was too good to be true." She held her smile in place, but her eyes had dimmed slightly, and Jack felt sickened by her sadness.

"Oh, yes, it's a marriage made in Heaven—the union of

38

two wealthy families. We're sure to produce retarded children."

"Don't talk like that," she scolded. "I understand."

"No you don't. She's one reason I'm here. It's, well, I guess I bought this place partly because she didn't want me to. Like a three-year-old who has to have his way, you might say. Do you see what I mean? We're a mistake, she and I, a serious misunderstanding."

"Come on, man, I've been led on by better liars than you." She laughed as she said it, but it was a protective laugh, an attempt to soften the eventual defeat. "If you wanted to get laid, I probably could have been persuaded."

"No. I'm not lying. It's over, and I finally have the guts to admit it."

"Sure, but I'll bet you haven't told her yet."

He could see every lie she'd ever believed, every come-on and proposition that led her to a nylon noose in a shower stall, written on her face as she spoke.

"No, I haven't," he admitted.

The band had been playing swing tunes, but now they stopped abruptly, as though someone had pulled their plug. A tense feeling of listening pervaded the room, and the sound of someone knocking at the street door drifted through the frozen dancers.

"Run and hide! Run and hide!" Doc shouted, laughing and throwing his hands into the air like a chorus member in a minstrel show.

"I'll be right back," Jack told her as he stood. The knocking was louder now. "Wait here."

"I'll wait," she answered, as he hurried to the door.

"Are you deaf, Jack?" Marion stood bundled in fur and shivering outside the door. "I came to see your new club." But the look in her eyes was colder than the January weather; she'd come to disapprove of the club.

"Kind of late, isn't it?" he asked, standing instinctively in her way. "Looks better in daylight."

"Come on, Jack, aren't you going to let me in?" Disbelief passed over her face. "It's cold out here!"

"Yes, uh, sorry." Jack shook himself into movement, standing aside to let her in. "Just didn't expect you, is all."

"I should say not," she said, sweeping past him.

"I'd like to explain about the bar," he was saying as he hurried to lock the door. "Don't be shocked. These people are great once you get to know them."

But when Jack caught up to her, standing in the center of the large room near the old bar, there were no people, no band, no rows of bottles behind the bar, only dust and memories. He stood, openmouthed, staring at the sudden emptiness.

"People, Jack?" Her voice held laughter and a hint of pity. "There's nobody here."

"But there was . . ." He let the sentence trail off with a wry grin. Of course they'd disappear when she came in. She had no part in the festivities, didn't belong there. "The dead, of course," he stated lamely. "The long-gone spirits, all the sorry souls who passed through this place in the past."

"My God, Jack, are you crazy?" The question was rhetorical, and she went on to answer it herself. "You'd have to be, in order to buy this dump. You could burn it down for the insurance, I suppose, but it's outlived any other use."

"No, it hasn't," he said, with an unexpected emotion. "I'm at home here, and I'll make other people feel at home, too. Just wait till I get it fixed up. You'll see."

"I don't know about you, Jack." She softened her tone then, reaching to grasp his forearm as she spoke patiently. "Maybe you really are insane." Then she laughed, sliding her hand down to take his. "I didn't mean insane, actually, but what happened? Did the pressures get to be too much? Couldn't take life in the grown-up world?"

"Marion, don't start anything," he warned her.

"I don't want to start anything. But you're not acting like

40

yourself lately. It's as if you suddenly can't stand being a responsible adult anymore, and you want me to follow you down the garden path. Just because you've decided to become some kind of entrepreneur, you think everyone should understand."

"I can't fully explain it, Marion. I just want more fulfillment in my life. Let's just leave it at that." Jack struggled against the sour ball of emotion in his stomach. What he had to tell her would be harder than any of their arguments.

"And this is how you find fulfillment? Should we all go out and open bars so we can find the meaning of life conversing with drunks and hookers? Is that how it's done?"

"No, probably not," he admitted. "Come and sit down, Marion, I have to talk to you." He led her over to the bar, indicating a stool for her to sit on.

"I can't sit there." She spoke disdainfully, looking at the dusty stool. "It isn't exactly hospitable here yet, after all."

"No, but I don't think our conversation is going to be the kind to have standing up."

"Oh." Marion paled, staring at him blankly. "Then it's true?"

"What?"

"You. It's more than this restaurant, isn't it?" She bit her lower lip thoughtfully, her eyes soft and loving. "You've found someone else, haven't you?"

He looked at her for a moment, finding it far harder to admit to her supposition than he'd have thought. And at that moment, he realized that he had loved her all these years. He'd loved her quiet understanding and sharp humor, loved the small smile that moved onto her lips when she looked at him. But it had been a complacent love, a love worn because it was easy. Their disagreement about the bar had colored his thinking recently, disguising the love that had been there all along. Still, if it came to a contest, his feelings for Fay overrode all others. So he nodded his head to her question, feeling like every kind of fool.

"Sure, I understand." Marion laughed bitterly, pretending to study the top of the bar. "You and some little girl have been playing games, and I'm in the way. It wasn't the bar, it was the chance to exercise your virility with some new conquest that brought you to this. Do you and your girlfriend laugh about me, Jack? Poor, stupid Marion, making her useless wedding plans." She blinked rapidly, tightening her lips into silence.

"Please, Marion, it's not like that at all." Jack slipped his hand up to her cheek, feeling his own emotions billowing within him. "I've only known her a couple days. After I bought the bar, actually. I just didn't think it would be fair to keep it secret."

"Yes, I'm sorry." She looked at him then, the sadness in her eyes tempered by affection. "I don't want to be bitter, but it's hard."

"It's hard for me, too. I didn't know how hard it would be until now."

"I'm going to go home, Jack." She backed away, fighting a smile to her lips. "I do wish you well, you know. And I want you to be happy."

"But I want you to be happy too, Marion." He followed her.

"You're far too thoughtful sometimes," she told him, moving slowly toward the door. "You've got every right to think of your own happiness. But, please, if it doesn't work out, give some thought to us, won't you? I mean, I still love you, no matter what."

"And I love you, Marion."

"I know. Good night, Jack." She hurried to the door and was gone on the breath of the icy wind, leaving Jack standing alone in the decrepit old bar with his farewell unsaid.

He stood looking at the door, standing unaware as the noise and laughter returned and the band began playing again. Then he turned at the touch of Fay's hand on his shoulder.

"I love you, Jack." She spoke softly, smiling past tears running freely down her cheeks. "I'm afraid you're too good for me."

"Dance with me, Fay," he whispered, slipping his arms around her. "Dance with me till dawn so I can keep my arms around you."

And so they danced through all the eras of music provided by the band, danced until the others had collapsed at their tables, danced until the band tired of playing, danced until the hour before dawn. The dance was everything, the movement of two as one, the movement of their impossible love.

10

Sunlight made an oven of the small hotel room and broiled his skin to a dry, prickly texture as he lay, once again, on the bed. He blinked himself awake, moving experimentally, then stood. The old floorboards squirmed beneath his feet like starched snakes, but he kept his footing and took a tentative step.

The room was scantily furnished, with only the bed and an old bureau with a mirror hanging over it on the gray wall, and there were three doors. Presumably, the single door on the wall opposite the window opened onto the hall, so the other two should be for a bathroom and closet. He wasn't certain, but it didn't seem correct for a hotel of this era to have separate bathrooms, so the extra room would only be there for the purposes of the dream. The little man who had been there the other times obviously wanted Jack to open the bathroom door.

Feeling strangely confident, knowing even within the dream that a dream couldn't harm him, he walked to the bathroom door and opened it.

A dirty sink and mirror, a toilet with an overhead tank, and a crusted tub and shower combination were crowded into the room. A broken pipe beneath the sink dribbled brownish water, slicking the floor. The small room was alive with the stench of stagnant water. As he stepped into the room, the air in the tub enclosure darkened and congealed, as though the drifting dust had gathered to form a shape beneath the shower arm.

Her head was twisted away from the moldering gray length of nylon tied to the shower head, and her hair hung back lank and dull, sticking slightly against her bare back and limp arms. The skin on her back and buttocks was gray and shrunken in against the bone, mummifying as she hung like a side of beef in the shower. And, as he stood looking at her, the rotten nylon shuddered and parted above the thick knot, letting the stiff body drop the few inches to the floor of the tub, bouncing slightly on its heels.

He stepped forward, reaching out, as it twisted slightly, turning toward him even as it toppled like a rotten tree falling in a storm. "Fay!" he called, catching the corpse by the shoulders. The skin crumbled in his grasp, shredding away from the bone as she slipped toward him through his arms. "I love you," he whispered, and her lipless mouth grazed his cheek as he circled her with his arms, the parchment skin dusting up into the air and floating around them like swarming flies. Then the body crumbled in his grasp, bone leaving bone to clatter to the wet floor, and he was left alone again.

"Nobody can hurt us now," he whispered.

The bathroom dissolved to pale gray, re-forming as the old hotel room again, and he awoke on a filthy mattress shoved into a corner of the room. Outside the window the neon sign hung dark and soiled with pigeon droppings. And this was not a dream.

"I just can't get to you, can I?"

Jack sat up quickly, searching for the source of the voice. The small man walked in from the air and stood by the mattress. He smiled, hitched his creased trousers up slightly, and lowered himself to sit beside Jack. He was wearing a cool white Italian suit and a pale gray fedora. He smelled of English Leather.

"I meant that as a most sincere compliment, Jack." He spoke softly, leaning toward Jack in a confidential manner. "You have developed a very strong sense of—how should I put it?—of reality, I think. A strong sense of reality. I can't seem to make you sweat anymore."

"Why are you here in daylight?" Jack spoke in a low monotone, fighting to quell his fluttering stomach. "What do you want?"

"Daylight?" His visitor laughed, and placed his arm on Jack's shoulder. "I have no restrictions on me. No fear of the sun. I am not like those semishades, your friends. Though I am your friend, in a way."

"You haven't answered me."

"What do I want?"

"Yes." The man's arm was hot, and Jack felt sweat greasing his neck beneath his collar.

"Nice room, eh?" The man smiled. "It was when you brought your little girlfriend in here, anyway. Strange how things look different in the strong light of day. You really tied one on last night, didn't you? If the liquor here was a bit more substantial, you'd have a nasty hangover."

"I'm not interested in that right now. I want to know what your game is, and what part you expect me to play in it."

"Still a bottom-line type of guy, eh? Okay, I'll get to the point." He floated up and lowered his feet to the floor. "I want them. All of them. And if I can't scare you off, I'll cut a deal. That's fair, isn't it?"

Jack scrubbed his fingers back through his hair, blinking away the sleep in his eyes. That the confident little man standing before him was real, he had no doubt, but the idea of making a deal with him was rather hard to grasp. Does anyone routinely strike bargains like that?

"I don't think I'm up to dealing with the Devil," he

admitted, smiling up at the man. "You better just try something else."

"Your candor is absolutely wonderful!" The man clapped his hands together and shook his head in wonder. "No braggadocio, no macho posturing. I'd not have thought a human could be so honest in a situation like this. I do have you at a disadvantage, though. I am not Lucifer. I don't pretend to such greatness."

"That explains why you've been unsuccessful so far."

"Honesty and humor. You are a find." The man's eyes hardened into black pebbles. "Is it this *love* of yours that gives you such courage, do you suppose? You didn't possess it a week ago. No, you weren't nearly so self-sufficient."

"Listen." Jack was annoyed with the whole thing: tired and stiff from sleeping on the thin mattress, sick of nasty nightmares and taunting little men. "I don't want to talk about my private life with you any more than I want to sign any contracts. Understand me? Now, if you don't have anything else, I'd like to go home and get some decent sleep." He stood tiredly and started toward the door.

"Yes, to sleep, perchance to dream," the man mused behind him in a stage whisper, then he called out, stopping Jack at the door. "But you haven't heard my proposition."

"Fine, say your piece and get it over with."

"It's very simple, really. You get the hooker, Browning, and I get all the others."

"What?"

"You heard me. That's what you want, isn't it? The bitch?"

"Don't talk about her like that, you fuzzy little twerp!" Jack ordered in unthinking anger.

"Yes." The man grinned, coming closer. "It *is* love that gives you that foolish courage. It's amazing, when you think of how badly I could hurt you." His voice held absolute, cold certainty. "That is my deal, though. She'll be alive again."

"You can't hurt me any more than you can deliver on your bargain. You're just a lying little bastard doing scut work for a lazy master. Go away."

"Oh, I can deliver. In fact, they could do it for themselves." He placed one hand on Jack's shoulder, massaging his fingers slowly against the ridge of bone. "They enjoy a special position here and don't even know it. Just as they avoided death with the strength of will they once possessed, they could bring themselves back to life if they had the energy or the desire to try. This is the only realm of reality where they have that power. But they are complacent, weak, too used to their liquor and parties to remember what it was like to be truly alive. In short—too human. Strange, isn't it, that only at the moment of death do you humans realize the full joy of living. Only then is the desire to live strong enough to do you any good."

Jack licked his lips, thinking about what he'd said. If it was true . . .

"I see you're thinking about trying it. Now that you know it's possible, you believe your little slut can perform the miracle for herself. Don't you?" His smile brightened, and he slapped his hot fingers lightly against Jack's cheek. "No chance, buddy. She's the weakest one of the lot. Never had any self-esteem—not in life, not now. Your friend Doc, he might be able to do it. His desire is still fresh, no matter how hard he masks it. He is the force who kept us away this long. Yes, he could do it, but young Fay would never survive the trip. Not without my help."

"Why do you want these people? What good are they?"

"Ever heard of Armageddon, Jack?" The man raised one eyebrow mockingly. "The book of Revelation is, of course, just so much horse manure, but that's the closest analogy I can think of. The battle won't be on Earth, won't have anything to do with Earth, but it's coming. The final battle. I'm just a recruiter—a collector, if you will. Everybody is busy building up their armies."

"And you're doing your bit for Uncle Satan." Jack smiled, rubbing his eyes.

"You make us sound so bad. It was just our misfortune that the other side got their propaganda mill rolling first. That's all. He painted us into a corner with his horror stories. But we've learned that there are plenty of people who are attracted by those lies, so we play the part. Do you honestly think your nocturnal friends would still be here if they truly believed that Heaven is the better destination? No. They can't choose between Heaven, Hell, and that stinking, breathing world of yours. And they don't believe they have any other choices."

He held Jack's eyes for a long moment, then shrugged his shoulders and sighed. "Well, I'm not specifically here for you, though I feel you could be taken. What about my offer?"

"Even if you're not lying, I'm not making any deals."

"Just think about it, Jackie." The man stepped back, seeming to liquefy as he did. "But make your choice soon, dear, or I'll suck you down with the rest. It might be fun to have a live one."

The little man's face melted away from the lattice of muscles beneath the skin, and his eyes burst in their sockets as the muscles withered and dried against the bone. Fat black spiders crawled from the eyeless sockets and danced across the ruined face. The hideous jaw flopped open. "Boo!" it said, and disappeared in a gale of laughter.

11

"You can do it."

Talking quietly, away from the others, he told her about the little man's information. She didn't believe it, didn't have faith in her abilities. He had no proof, had nothing but faith, and he held her close to him, whispering his assurances, and trying to imbue her with his impassioned belief.

It wasn't easy; she had a lifetime of failure working against his words.

"I've never done anything right before, Jack," she said, smiling. "Why can't we just enjoy what we have?"

"Because we won't have it for long." Urgency and frustration pressed at his words as he sensed the end of the party approaching. It was a feeling he'd been unable to escape through the long day, the feeling of fate sweeping over them. "He said they'd be coming for everyone."

"But how can they?"

"I don't know." But Jack was beginning to think he did know. He'd been unable to sleep for thinking about the proposition, and had spent the long hours till dusk arguing within himself—thinking that he should have made the deal. Even now, with the sound of music and laughter swirling around them and his lovely Fay nestled in the security of his arms, he found himself contemplating the odious exchange. If it were only true; if he could trust the little demon; if he could reconcile trading everyone here for the life of one woman, he would certainly consent to it. Only his uncertainty, mixed with fear, had kept him from agreeing in the dirty room that morning. And he'd begun to feel that his warring thoughts may have already extended the invitation. Perhaps he'd already agreed in his mind.

And so he fought his thoughts while mouthing assurances to Fay. Their only hope was for her to believe in herself and learn to control her own destiny. He didn't know any other way to make this dream come true.

"Please, Fay, I know you can do it." Whispered softly as a dancing couple passed their booth.

"How? I don't understand how it would work. I don't even know how I ended up here. Tell me how to do it," she pleaded, her eyes moist. "I want it so badly."

"That's a start. I don't know what else to tell you."

"Before I met you, the last thing I wanted was to live. The very last thing. And I felt so safe here. Now that you're

49

here, I don't feel safe anymore. I feel trapped. God, Jack, I want to be alive with you. I love you."

"I think it's the wanting that makes it happen." He sighed against the sweet scent of her hair. "But I'm so afraid that it's too late already."

The band finished a set of Gershwin numbers, and a frail woman in a low-cut gown was helped to the stage by two bearded fellows wearing Hell's Angels colors. She was missing her legs at some point above the hem of the long gown, and the two men balanced her in a canvas director's chair that had one arm removed to accommodate the guitar a third man handed to her. She smiled and began to slowly pluck her instrument, building to a crescendo of intricate sound.

Jack and Fay were silent as the sound descended into a melodious drawl.

"It's culture time, kiddies," Doc announced, standing by their booth. "That's Janet Delveccio."

"How did she arrive here?" Jack asked softly as he motioned for the man to sit across from them.

"Slipped under a departing train in Penn Station back in nineteen forty-two. I hear she was bidding her fella good-bye, but the dame won't talk about it." He smiled. "You have something to tell me." He pointed one finger at Jack.

"I guess I do," he admitted, watching the other man closely.

"No need, friend. I met the little guy years ago."

"Did he offer you a new life? A human life?"

"Of course. What else could he have to offer? Doc laughed, shaking his head slowly. "My life for the souls of all these fine fools."

"But you didn't believe him," Fay said.

"Of course I believed him. Just didn't think it was much of a deal at the time." Doc waved one hand at the bar, and they all waited while a bottle and three glasses were brought over. "It wasn't as easy as simply consenting to the deal. He needed me to separate them, get them alone and away from the safety of the crowd. I couldn't do that."

"Don't you want to live?" Jack spoke low, leaning in slightly. "He said you could take yourself back to life if you really wanted to."

"I suppose I could." Doc sipped his drink and smiled down at the table. "I'd sure like to play my saxophone again."

"So, why don't you do it?"

"They need me," he stated, a hollow look in his eyes. "Look around you, buddy. Some of them have been on a continuous binge for forty, fifty years. That's all they want to do. They don't want to live or die, just drink and dance. This is heaven for them."

The people around them sat at the tables and booths talking loudly, laughing, making broad gestures with glasses in their hands, totally oblivious to pain and worry. The woman on the stage played "Jesu, Joy of Man's Desiring" flawlessly, each note expressing the depth of her feeling and talent, and each note falling on deaf ears.

"They wouldn't stand a chance," Doc said. "The little man is right. They're too damn human."

"So what happens now?"

"It's over, pal. You did something, I guess, gave the bastard a handle on us."

"But I didn't agree."

"I don't know all the rules, Jack, but I can feel him coming. Tonight, the bill comes due." He drained his glass and refilled it unsteadily. "Can't you feel it?"

"I feel nervous, like someone was watching over my shoulder."

"See? They don't even feel it. What a bunch of dopes."

"You should have left them long ago, Doc."

"No. I left home when I was sixteen. Bummed around, saw the world. Even got married for a while. I left her, too. I left everything." Doc quietly sipped his whiskey, staring at the laughing crowd, and his silence was more eloquent than any words.

"You sure brought little Fay around," he said at last. "She was the biggest—what's that word you use, Fay? Downer? Yeah, she was the biggest downer in the place. Always moping about how everything was all bitched up. Couldn't even die right. Now look at her. I've never seen you smile before, Fay. Maybe it was worth sticking around just for that."

The guitarist struck a discordant note, a single twang like a champagne glass breaking, and Jack looked around as the woman disappeared, her guitar thudding to the stage. One of her escorts ran onto the stage, stopping by the empty chair, then spun quickly, clutching at his face. He stumbled back, stepping on the fallen guitar and snapping the neck off, then he was gone.

For a second there was total silence in the club, then the sound of wind, like someone breathing slowly. The celebrants began to run.

"I love you, Jack."

He turned as she vaporized beside him and the arm that had circled her shoulder fell limp against his side.

"Fay!" He rose quickly in the booth, but they grabbed him even as he shouted her name and pushed him down on the padded bench, laughing and drooling over him as they pinned him down. One gargoyle sat on his throat thrusting its elongated, bulbous head forward on its scrawny neck to stare into Jack's eyes while the others held his legs and arms. The creature grinned, breathing a sewage stench in Jack's face as it held up one hand and slowly waggled the seven long, straight claws.

"You can't hurt me," Jack panted. "The pain is an illusion."

"No," the creature croaked in a guttural facsimile of speech, slurring the words around its ragged teeth and lolling tongue. "Real." It laughed, selecting one claw to point into Jack's left nostril.

"No!" he screamed.

With a gleeful squeal, the demon forced in the four-inch claw.

A white-hot amphetamine burn traced the nasal passage and up, arrow-straight through flesh and bone, popped through the dura, and sliced into the left frontal lobe, exploding in ice-blue starshells that ricocheted off skull through cerebral tissue while he screamed, "No! No! No!" making no sound after the nerve connections were destroyed, but still holding the thoughts, the feelings, the pain, impossibly thinking, "This isn't real!"

And he was sitting in the booth staring at Doc's ironic smile while the pain still sizzled in his mind.

"That's it, Jackie." Doc spoke over his whiskey as though nothing had happened. "The party is over."

"But I didn't invite them," Jack insisted.

A pallid creature pulled itself up over the edge of the table and paused, cocking its head toward Jack. Then it grabbed the whiskey bottle by the neck and swung it against the tabletop, shattering the base off the bottle as though it were made of blown crystal. He lunged, pushing the jagged edge like a spear into Jack's eyes.

A slash of green glass, looming, expanding, pressed hot and wet, slashed through skin and muscle, against tough corneal fiber, eye bulging against penetration as the twisting shard split the eyelids and the red haze flowed to match the haze of pain.

And Doc complained, "You spilled my booze, Jack." And he melted, changed, rotted away.

Eyeless, the skin drawn tight and dry over the skull, Doc sat in a rotted mourning coat holding his empty glass. Wisps of dark hair clung to the parchment scalp as though waxed into place, and his lipless mouth showed two rows of yellow teeth grinding together. He raised one hand, a fat black spider clinging tenaciously to the bones of the index finger.

"Stop it!"

Standing, Jack screamed down at the man and flailed his

53

arms as though movement would send the vision away. But the man stood, hands held out questioningly.

"This is not real! This cannot hurt me! Cannot hurt me!"

And Doc returned to normal, his cynical smile in place.

"He's keeping you busy, Jackson. Keeping you down while he sucks all those lovely souls away." Doc raised his empty glass in a salute. "I'd better get a fresh bottle."

"No. Wait!" Staggering around the table, Jack grabbed at his shoulder. "Why didn't they take you?"

"Every bar needs its regular clientele, Mr. Bellows." Behind him, the little man spoke happily. "Wouldn't you like that, Doc? To be the only one left?"

They turned toward the stage, where the collector sat on the director's chair like the emperor of the world giving an audience in the now empty tavern. He was dressed completely in black now, with a diamond pin holding the shimmering silk of his tie in place.

"No one invited you here." Jack's voice was hoarse, defeated.

"Yes you did, and I thank you." The man smiled. "All we needed was the thought, the belief. Now they're all gone, and you and your friend can discuss the good old days over your whiskey sodas every night for the rest of your meager existence. Sounds like fun, doesn't it?"

"I've got no beef," Doc said, walking to the stage.

"I told you long ago that I dealt harshly with people who stood in my way."

"Won't there be any new ones?" Doc used a chair to step up onto the stage beside the man.

"Certainly, but they won't come here." He laughed, holding up one finger toward Doc. "And they won't stay long once you come calling. You're marked now."

"Well, I can't say you didn't warn me," Doc said, stooping to lift the neck of the guitar by the strings that curled up like strands of silver hair. "I can get used to it."

"Where are they?" Jack walked up to the stage, standing helplessly at the man's feet. "Where did they go?"

"They're safe for now."

"Where? Where is she?" Jack ran at him as the room expanded, the stage rushing away like a departing train. "Where is she?"

The floor dissolved beneath him, and he sank to his hips in a molten substance that hissed around him, igniting his trousers with small puffs of flame. He froze, fighting the illusion, and it stopped.

"You're getting good at this." The collector smiled. "Sorry, no time to chat now. Got to run."

As the little man stood to go, Doc stepped back slightly, twining the E string around his good hand and smiling at Jack past the demon's shoulder. In one, sure movement Doc lifted the neck of the ruined instrument up and brought the looped strand of steel down around the collector's throat, pulling it tight.

The room shook to a heartbeat throbbing, and Jack fell to his back as tables and chairs jumped and skittered on the floor. He rolled to his knees, watching the little man jerk and flail against the constriction of steel, seeming to stretch as Doc pulled him back over the chair and lifted his feet from the floor. The demon's face blackened, snarling; his hands clawed back, reaching for Doc's face, tearing shreds of skin away below his eye. Jack watched, mesmerized, unable to move to help his friend.

The strand of steel sliced through skin, blood spurting out around it, and the demon smiled. The blood hissed and bubbled around the string with a crackling sound like dry twigs popping in a campfire, and the guitar string snapped with a loud *ping,* sending Doc staggering back, the string dissolving in his hands.

"Damn you!" Doc screamed, and threw the neck of the guitar at the little man.

"Too late for that." The collector held out his hand to Doc as though demanding payment. "I think I will take you after all," he said. "Now."

Doc's eyes strained open, as though they were trying to

fly out of the sockets, and his body tensed against the pull of the man's demand. His face reddened, darkening almost to black as he took one unwilling step forward, then stopped.

"Come," the demon demanded. "I command it!"

But Doc only smiled, relaxing slightly.

"Now!" the little man said more urgently.

"Kiss my ass!" Doc stepped forward and slapped the demon with the back of his hand. "Hit the road, you little twerp."

"You—" The little man started, staring incredulously at Doc. "You did it."

"Damn right." Doc smiled, moving in almost chest to chest with him. "And you can't hurt me until I die again. Probably not even then."

"Bravo." The little man clapped his hands together and laughed, stepping back to glance at Jack. "You may get up now, Mr. Bellows."

Jack stood, still watching the stage.

"It seems that I have two stubborn humans to deal with now," the collector said, laughing. "But I also have the white queen. And in this game, that seems to mean checkmate."

"No." Jack ran to the stage. "I thought we had a deal."

"We made no deal."

"You told me that it was my invitation that got you in here tonight. My invitation!" Having done the deed, unwillingly or not, he wasn't about to get screwed out of the reward. "I invited you!"

"Certainly. But we made no deal." Smiling, condescending, the little man dismissed Jack's demands with a small tilt of his head. "No deal at all," he said.

Jack grabbed at his ankle, and his hand was thrown away by an electrical shock. "You lying bastard," he shouted.

"It's part of the job." The little man smiled.

"Come on," Doc said, smiling lazily and standing with his hands in his pockets. "Live up to your little bargain.

You don't want to keep her anyway. All she does is whine and complain, and she's no damn fun at parties."

"Please." Jack's anger evaporated in the heat of his need for the missing woman.

The collector smiled slightly, tilting his head back, then turned to look at Jack. "You want her? Okay, lover. Come and get her."

And the air clotted around Jack, drawing in tight against his face, heavy with the smell of wet leather. A pulse, like the movement of time as a physical sensation, the throb of the earth revolving, shook him, vibrating his bones together as he felt himself falling. He was falling into light from the massive darkness, falling into soundlessness from the garbled drone of babbling humanity, falling into death like an old friend, a lover, warm and intoxicatingly beautiful, falling from the mundane cares and responsibilities of life into quietude and peace. Falling into the lie with only the promise of truth to shield him.

12

There was no desolation, no brimstone and fire, but only an endless landscape of slowly rolling prairie knee deep with summer-brown grasses. Overhead, the sun burned hot and gold.

Jack stood at the crest of a low hill, his clothing damp with sweat and uncomfortably hot and tight under the glaring sun. He shielded his eyes with one hand and looked around him, searching for some sign, a direction to go in the directionless landscape. Below him on the hill were a series of what appeared to be marble pillars standing in the field. They were of various sizes, seeming to have been worn away by time, and were placed randomly throughout the expanse of grass. He shrugged off his jacket and walked down toward them.

But they weren't marble worn away by the elements; they

were his friends, claimed by their new owner and standing frozen like statuary on display in a vast museum. The dead stood naked and rigidly straight, their hands at their sides and heads held up proudly. Their skin was white as salt and hard as bone, gleaming in the sunlight; their wounds were heeled, bodies made new again.

He hurried among the waiting dead, looking for Fay among them, but she wasn't there.

"Stay with me, Jack."

He spun at the feminine purr behind him. Elaine moved slowly among the others, her body, released from the spell, seeming to glow with health in the summer sun. She held out one hand as she walked, her breasts quivering slightly with each step, and her smile seemed to draw in all the radiance of the sky and reflect it as her own. He felt his desires straining toward her, wanting this once cold body as though she were the only woman ever created.

"No," he whispered. "You're dead and gone."

"Please, Jack." She placed her hand softly on his cheek, stroking down to the line of his jaw as she smoothed her other hand over her own belly. "I'm not dead here. I'm alive, Jack. I need you."

"He owns you." Jack stepped back, turning his face away from her hand. "You're just a feeble trick, a delaying tactic." He backed away slowly, wanting, yet dreading, and cursing his unthinking lust as a betrayal of his love.

"I need you," she cried, loneliness twisting her features. "Don't leave me!"

"Go away." Jack turned and ran before she could say anything else and hurried through the field of the dead to the crest of the next hill without looking back.

And the sky darkened as he descended the hill, blackening overhead as the air became cold against his damp shirt. The terrain was rocky, dropping off to a winding road far below him. He could see the gargoyles dragging something white along the rutted path, pulling it with ropes and running as best they could against its weight.

58

He scrambled down the broken hillside, reaching the path as they rounded an outcropping of rock a hundred yards ahead. The wind roared against him as he followed, blowing stinging particles of dust and ice into his face like buckshot, and when he made the turn they had gained another two hundred yards on him.

"Stop!" He squinted against the blowing dust and trudged on, not knowing where they were going or how he could rescue her once they got there. All he knew was that he had to get her back or he might as well stay with the others on the field of the dead.

And at the next turn of the road, he saw that the landscape flattened out again, changing into a plain as regular and featureless as a tabletop that stretched unbroken across the horizon, a land seemingly made of polished steel. The demons skated across the surface, pushing their burden ahead of them.

The path ended abruptly at the metal surface, and he skidded onto it, falling to his knees. It did, indeed, feel like steel, though it was warm to the touch. Tentatively, he stood and shuffled after the creatures who moved so surefootedly on the slick surface. The effort to keep his balance was torturous, bringing cramps to his groin and thigh muscles, yet he continued walking for what seemed like hours until the horizon became barren around him, an endless gleam of steel.

He was gaining on them now. In fact, he could see that they had stopped and were busy standing their burden up on end. He did his best to run, forcing himself past the pain in his legs and the stinging of cold air in his tired lungs.

"Yes, run." The collector moved beside him, floating in tandem with Jack's shuffling trot. "Run to her, Jackie-boy. She's waiting. Faster, boy. Here, let me give you a hand."

He clutched Jack's hair and flung him ahead, sending him through the air to land sliding on his belly toward the jibbering creatures.

He rolled, trying to stop the slide, but continued on till he

DANA M ANDERSON

slammed against her ankles; it was like hitting an iron post. He forced himself to stand painfully as the man approached smiling, stooping to pet one of the gargoyles.

"You have no right," Jack said panting. "I made no deal with you."

"But I've got them now, don't I?" the demon taunted.

"Not for long."

"Really? Okay, then. Be a hero." The collector moved one arm behind his back, then brought it around holding a glimmering sword. The blade hummed through the air as he swung it in a flat arc at Jack's legs, slicing through them above the knees.

Jack fell to the ground, flopping helplessly as the creatures carried his legs away and the little man stood over him, laughing.

"This isn't real," Jack said, his breath coming hard against the pain. "I don't believe it."

"That's right, Jack, keep a good thought." The collector lifted one foot, pointing the toe down at Jack's slack, panting mouth. "What you don't believe can't hurt you, can it?"

He thrust the toe of his shoe between Jack's lips, breaking teeth as he forced it back against his throat. "Is she worth it, Jackie?" he asked. He kicked the foot forward and Jack felt a sudden snap as his head was separated from his neck and lower jaw.

The steel horizon spun, flipping over and over as Jack's head bounced across the plain until it was stopped by the collector's pets. They carried him by his hair, running back to his sprawled body.

"Is this real, Jack?" The collector took him from them, lowering him to look down at the legless, decapitated body lying in a pool of blood. The gargoyles were busy tearing its clothing off while he watched.

"What's wrong, buddy? Cat got your tongue? No, I guess the lower half of your mortal remains has your tongue, hasn't it?" He laughed, turning Jack's head around to look

60

into his eyes. "Let's try another test of your grasp of reality, Jack. Shall we?"

This isn't real, Jack thought, as he was dropped to the ground to lie watching the demons gutting his discarded body. *It isn't happening.*

"Look, boy, up here!" A toe turned him up as the man raised the sledgehammer into the air slowly, his black coat spreading like wings.

No! No! No! No! The hammer came down in the middle of his forehead with a flash of pain like fire and ice united into one sensation. *No! No! No! No!*

"She is worth it." A baritone voice, soft and reassuring, whispered beside him, and he opened his eyes. "Any human being is worth every bit of pain that loving them causes."

Jack was lying on his back staring into a mist, a warm cloud that seemed to be physically caressing him, soothing the pain from his limbs and calming his frightened mind. He felt soft cushions beneath him, a pillow supporting his head. He moved his hands wonderingly over his body as he pulled his concentration around to the voice that murmured beside him.

"Should I let you have her?"

Jack turned his head toward the voice, finding a man dressed in flowing robes of silken red and yellow sitting on a low chair that appeared to float in the mist beside Jack's divan.

The man was nearly perfect, an example of everything the male of the species should be. He glowed, exuding an aura of masculine beauty so pure and strong that no one could avoid being touched by it. His features were regal but understanding, chiseled into decisive lines, strong and proud, yet playfully boyish around the lips. His eyes were the color of a stormy sea, his hair dark and sweeping down across his shoulders in gentle waves. Jack couldn't take his eyes away from the man.

"My first thought is to let her go." He smiled, and Jack felt a wave of reassurance flood over him. "Suicides are of little use to me," he continued. "They have no will, no spark. But I don't feel I'd be doing you a service by giving her to you."

"Please," Jack heard himself say. "I've come so far." He sat up slowly, seeing that he was wearing only his torn and dirtied pants, which had been sliced off at the knees.

"We salvaged your trousers, but the rest was beyond repair. Those little monsters tend to get carried away when not held in check, and my collector is not so much in control of them as he thinks he is."

"But my legs. All of me, for that matter. They cut me up."

"Believing makes it so, but it doesn't necessarily make it permanent," the man said. "I put you back together—this time. You'll have to be stronger if you plan on any more such activities."

"Are you—" Jack cut the question off. It was foolish.

"Satan? I am what you say I am," the man answered simply. "For myself, I say that I am the master in this dimension. No more, no less."

"I thought you would be different."

"Horns? Blood-red skin and a pointed tail?" The man laughed, filling the shrouded space with the rolling echo of his mirth. "If you haven't read the Bible, you should at least try Mr. Milton's work. Christian mythology would say that I am Lucifer, reported to be the most beautiful, most intelligent and cunning of your God's angels. I am the best of the lot. That script was written by the being you call God, of course, but that's of little matter. Let's just say that the historical facts are somewhat different from your myths, but they've got the physiognomy right enough."

He clasped his hands before him, relaxing into his chair to lecture his captive audience.

"You have a saying, 'Ugly as sin.' Have you ever considered that if sin were truly ugly there would be far fewer sinners in the world? But no, sin often seems to be the most wonderful course to follow, doesn't it? It's a case · where perceptions are more compelling than facts."

"Then your beauty is a lie," Jack stated.

"I was told of your honesty, and I do find it refreshing." He laughed. "Is it a lie? I'm not telling you what to see when you look at me. It's up to you. Understand? It's all your choice." And the lie of his smile was so compelling that Jack felt his resolve slipping, found himself wanting to stay and talk longer with this charming man.

"So, what do you want?" Satan asked.

Jack fought against the steady gaze of those steel-gray eyes. "I want Fay Browning," he said, struggling to get the words out. "I want all of them, for that matter."

"That is the one thing I envy about mortals," the man confessed, leaning forward slightly. "This love of yours is such a hopeful emotion. Look where it brought you. This may truly be the place that you call Hell, boy, and yet, even if it is, you seem to expect to be able to leave again. You become so foolishly optimistic, so strong, because of love. It's beautiful."

"What do you care about love?" Jack stood, flexing his legs.

"Don't believe everything you read. I love, too. But I can't achieve anything with love, can't be loved in return. I am not the same as you, not even the same as any of the others here with me. They respect and fear me, lust after me, but none of them love me. Do you understand?"

"This is too much to understand." The smell of wood smoke, sweet and comfortable, wafted through the air.

"Your God also lacks love." The being smiled—sadly, it seemed. "They fear him, obey him, even follow him into death, but that is not love. Their love is reserved for the Christ, the martyred part of him. His human lackey. We are alike in our need."

"I don't believe you."

"The belief of one man makes little difference. In this

game, only the masses count." He stood up and motioned for Jack to follow him over to the fire that had materialized in the mist behind his chair.

"No, you needn't believe me. But the fact is, the being you call God chose to be Lord of a pack of comely monkeys because he saw their awakening intelligence and thought they might come to love him. All he ended up with was you. A rather ironic twist of events, isn't it?"

He put his hand on Jack's shoulder and smiled, and Jack felt a tremble of fear at the power this being held over him in this place.

"We're not here to argue my reputation as a liar. If I am who you say I am, then I am a liar when it suits my purpose. The Prince of Darkness, Lord of the Flies. Unsavory titles, but I will wear them gladly. They gave me a name, a *raison d'être*. I am all that you chose to believe about me and not one bit more. But I am actually rather insignificant. Only human beings have value," he said seriously, looking into Jack's eyes. "No God or Devil is worth a damn, for we are nothing without you. And when we finally screw up the courage to enter the battle we've been threatening for so long, it will be humans who fight it for us. That's why we court you fools like anxious suitors after the banker's plain daughter. We can only use those of you who willingly and completely choose to follow our banner and those, like your friends, who manage to fall somewhere short of dying. The rest, naturally dead, if you will, slip beyond our control to a far better place than either God or I can promise."

"That makes no sense." Jack stared into the fire, his thoughts racing through the new, though questionable, information. "Where do they go? Heaven?"

"Another plane of existence. Another life. Another chance. But, of course, I'd prefer that they stay with me."

"But if you want us on your side, why choose such dark methods? Why attack us?"

"I sow confusion, discord, and let nature take its course. That's all. Contrary to popular belief, I have never possessed a living soul in my life. That is the work of those before me. No, I tweak Jehovah's nose with the reputation he created for me. He got here first, so he wrote the script."

"You play games while building your army."

"Exactly. I do what I can to piss off the pompous old goat and collect the souls who come to me."

"That's hardly fitting behavior for a man of your stature," Jack said. "I'm disappointed."

"As I said, I am the master here, in this place. My power extends only far enough to whisper in the proper ears and claim those souls who wander too close to my seat of command. But within this place, my power is something to be reckoned with.

"Humans are a perplexing bunch," he said slowly, as though attempting to come to grips with the mystery of the human mind. "You breed monsters, your Hitler and Jim Jones, yet also Picasso and Beethoven. You laugh and dance and murder and maim. You sing of your freedom while enslaving others. Then, when things get out of hand, you blame it all on me. Your guilt is short-lived, but your love is eternal. You seek love in everything, accepting sex or power temporarily, but always moving toward love. And when you die, you even love death. I admire you, but on the whole, I don't envy you. Only humans could find the spirit to continue living amid the pain they create.

"And that is why I think this woman-child would be best left with me. Or, perhaps, sent on to the next realm. The girl has no spirit save what you can give her, and she knows too much of suffering to ever be happy."

"No," Jack told him. "She had a rough ride the first time around. This time it'll work."

"No it won't. You live in an angst-ridden world, Jack, with the unfulfilled dreams of billions of souls resounding through time and space. Some of you, such as Fay, are more attuned to the sound of it. She hears the sadness around her, feels it pressing against her shallow self, and that intimate knowledge of humanity's pain drags her down. It killed her once, and it will again."

"You're wrong," Jack said defiantly. "We love each other. We can be strong for each other."

"Maybe. I've been wrong before, but I think not this time. When she lives again, she'll know, she'll feel it again. And someday you'll come home to find your love lying with the empty pill bottle clutched in her cold hand. Then you'll know, too."

"You won't talk me out of trying." Jack drew himself up tall, presenting the most noble façade he could to the demon. "I love her."

"I know, but love is brutal. It has killed more of your kind than warfare." Then he smiled, drawing his robes in to him. "All right then, you may have the woman, Jack. Take her and go."

"Just like that?"

"Why not, she'd be a useless soldier."

"And the others?" Jack faced the imperious man, maintaining a posture of determination. "They didn't consent to come here, and I didn't consent to have them taken."

"Do you love them, Jack?"

"No, not like Fay if that's what you mean."

"Then you can't have them. They are here and will stay here until I'm ready to use them."

"That's not fair! Even your collector said that I had to agree to let them go. I did not agree! I made no bargain!"

"I think that for a moment you did. There are no take-backs here." He smiled thoughtfully, his patient eyes holding Jack's gaze.

"I won't leave without them." Jack spoke with sudden and unexpected resolve, wondering why he should bother even as he did.

"Is this your sense of honor speaking now? Or is it guilt? Is that what causes you to push the issue?"

"Maybe, but it doesn't matter as long as I'm willing to push it. I won't go without them—I can't. And I don't think

66

you can force me to leave." And he knew he was right once he said it. As the man himself had said, everything that happened was Jack's choice. "I have my free will, don't I? I'm alive here, and I can choose my destiny."

"Alive, and perceptive." The man laughed. "You're right, of course. You are all too much alive. You aren't supposed to be here at all, and my collector made a big mistake in bringing a living soul through. You are the only human here with free will, and I cannot force you to leave. I can, however, allow my creatures to kill you."

"But you won't do that, will you?"

"Won't I?" The eyes that had just held such friendly understanding seemed to ice over as he spoke now, and Jack felt a chill jump through him. "I don't know what would happen to a human who dies in this place. It might be interesting to find out."

"I want all of them," Jack repeated.

The man frowned for a moment, but then let a smile grow until the dark look passed from his eyes. "I cannot send them back to where they were. The laws of physics won't allow it, and though my power is great, it isn't absolute. This love of yours is enough to carry Fay, but you have no love for the others. And, in simple truth, my collector is the true possessor of their souls at this time, for he has not yet given them to me. The only way to free them is to defeat him."

"Defeat him?"

"Yes. He brought you through, so if you try to leave past him, he'll have the power to stop you. Even to kill you. But if you can beat him and escape, you'll be breaking his hold over the others as well as yourself. You'll all be free to leave."

"But if you send me away with Fay, won't that achieve the same goal?"

"No. He can't possess you in the same way he does them. I don't need his permission to send you out, so that would not be a defeat of his will."

"You're lying."

"Maybe, but those are the rules I've chosen for this situation. But I am, in my own way, a fair man. I'm a wagering man, as well, and I'm willing to make a wager with you."

"What's the bet?"

"I'll bet their souls against yours that you can't get out of here past my collector. If you do, I'll not claim your friends once he loses his hold. Is your determination to have them free strong enough to survive a fight to the death?"

"I think so."

"You'd better know so, Jack, or you'll lose. Belief is what counts here, remember."

"Yes, I understand that. But what if I win? You said that you can't send them back."

"No, I can't, but I can allow them to pass on to the next plane of existence. I can give them their so-called life after death."

"And Fay comes with me?"

"Of course."

"How do I know you'll keep your word?"

"You don't, do you?" He smiled as the firelight began to brighten, shimmering on his hair and creating cruel hollows of his eyes. "But mine is the only game in town."

Jack turned his face toward the fire, watching the flames rise hot and yellow before him. "All right, you've got a bet. Do we shake on it?"

"No, your word is your bond here. There she is, Jack." He waved one hand negligently toward the fire. "Any man who gets this far deserves to have what he wants. Take her. And take the others if you are able."

She appeared in the fire, an ivory statue tinted rose by the dancing flames. Jack hurried to her, determined to show the strength of his belief and determination by walking directly into the fire without hesitation, even while fighting to convince himself that it was an illusion. He stood in the flames stroking one hand over her cold shoulder and smiling back at his host. There was no heat there now and the flames were only shadows flickering on the man's smiling face.

"You do understand now, don't you?" Satan laughed. "Reality is something to be molded here, but it's your enemy if you let it get the upper hand." He shook his head, smiling benignly. "Of course, you still have to get out of here. My man has the home-court advantage, I'm afraid, but you're strong. You may succeed in getting past him. And think of the story you could tell if you do. You'll be the only man who's come to Hell and gone back alive. It's just too bad you'd never dare share the tale."

"Yes, it is." Jack couldn't help smiling at the thought. "So, what do I do to get out of this joint?"

"I'll send you back to the field, and you're on your own from there. I won't put you together a second time if you lose."

"I won't lose." Jack picked Fay up in his arms. She was stiff, but light as a balsa sculpture.

"Perhaps. Remember, reality belongs to the one strong enough to control it. Go now."

And the fire roared up around them, its heat suddenly seeming all too real, searing his flesh. Jack took a deep breath and thought of the field where he'd first entered the infernal realm. The heat lessened again, and he stepped forward, walking through the wall of flame into the field of grass and sunlight.

Fay softened, her legs bending, arms flopping down loosely as her head lolled back and she became heavy and warm against him. She breathed in with a slight gasp, like a swimmer coming up for air, then settled down to sleep peacefully in his arms.

Jack's heart raced from the nearness, the warmth of the woman in his arms, even as the collector began to laugh.

13

"Hello sucker." The collector was seated on a rock up the hill from Jack and dressed incongruously in a conservative gray suit with a vest and a red carnation on the lapel. "Have you come to say good-bye?"

"Yes." Jack shifted Fay's body slightly and began to walk around him toward the crest of the hill where he'd first come through. "It's time for me to leave," Jack said, nodding toward the white forms of his friends below them on the hill. "Time for them to go, too."

"But they aren't ready to leave yet, Jack." The collector smiled, his face seeming translucent in the watery light of the foreign sun as he dipped his head to smell the flower that adorned his jacket. "Stick around. Don't be a party pooper."

"No, I'm leaving. You can't keep me here."

"Of course I can, Jack. Or didn't he explain that?"

"He explained everything quite well."

"No doubt he offered to send you and your suicidal squeeze away himself. You should have accepted his offer rather than come to me."

"He said that I can gain more than Fay this way."

"All or nothing, perhaps?" The demon's smile broadened, and he stood to remove his jacket and laid it carefully aside on the rock. "Was that his deal?"

"You know it was." Jack wasn't sure how to face this man. Armed only with his frail belief, he felt naked before the demon's knowing smile.

"What if I ruined your grand plan by giving you my permission to leave?" The demon smiled wickedly. "What if I decided not to risk my booty on your little challenge?"

"You won't do that." Jack spoke confidently on this point. "You want me most of all. Both of you want to collect a live soul, don't you? I think that's why he offered me this choice."

"How sly of him. Yet you still came? Foolish boy."

Without warning, the grassy hill was gone, replaced by a Technicolor blue void in which they were falling but not falling while the collector laughed and lunged at Jack and his slumbering burden. His touch sent a jolt of electricity through Jack that blasted him away, dropping Fay as he fell back on nothing and bounced into a blue fog that sucked at his limbs like tar.

Not real. Not happening. It took a concerted effort for Jack to overcome the illusion, believing in the solid feeling of the ground beneath his back rather than the swirling sense of infinity that confronted his eyes. "It isn't real," he called, pushing himself to his feet. "And you can't stop me from setting them free."

"My, my, you once refused to accept responsibility for their destiny. Now you seem to think you are their master." The demon spoke calmly as he appeared to stab a bayonet into Jack's stomach and lift him from the ground on the end of his M-16. "Prideful little bastard, aren't you?" He fired a burst directly into Jack's belly.

It didn't hurt, Jack thought, finding a key to victory in the fact that the bayonet hadn't hurt when it slid into him and that the bullets had passed through like nothing more than a blast of hot air. "No," Jack said, twisting himself off the man's weapon. "I'm just their friend." He wouldn't be fooled by the blood that flowed from his abdomen, not now. The collector hadn't given him time to believe in the reality of the gun before attacking with it, and that was a bad mistake.

"Friendship," the collector mused as he swung the butt of the rifle around inches from Jack's head. "I haven't seen a friend yet who wouldn't stab his dearest friend in the back for a buck or a rung on the social ladder. How did you get to be so noble?"

The demon clipped Jack's shoulder on the backswing,

71

knocking him down. Then he threw the gun aside to produce the sword that had been so real before, had cut him down to be handled by the gargoyles. The hillside re-formed as he stepped forward to swing it in a short arc.

"Send them back." Jack ducked and rolled toward where Fay lay sprawled on the brown grass. "Put them back where they were. Let them make their own choices."

"They have no choice." He sent home the tip of the sword in the meat of Jack's thigh with a very real slash of pain. "They are dead. Refuse." Pulling it out and stabbing again in the other thigh. "They became worm food long ago, and all they can do is mark time until I get them. Why not save them the work and worry of fighting me?"

"They can be alive again. He told me." Jack's wounds burned, blood like fire flowing to paint his legs beneath his torn pants, and the blade was coming down again. Fighting the pain, Jack twisted and grabbed the sword in both hands and pulled it away heedless of the blade cutting into his fingers. "They can live again."

"In a better place, no doubt. How can you stand to be so gullible?" The collector released the sword suddenly, and Jack fell back dropping the weapon. He wasn't even breathing hard.

"It's the truth," Jack insisted, panting with fatigue and pain. Two of his fingers on his left hand had been severed by the blade, and now they were crawling away from him like bloody worms. "You had no right to take them away from the bar." Pain radiated from his hands, shuddering up his arms as he tried to quell the nausea twisting his stomach and squeezed the stumps of his fingers to stop the blood flow.

"You gave me the right, Jackie. You opened the door with your indecision." Opening a glass vial, the demon leaned over Jack and poured steaming liquid on the escaping fingers. "Acid," he said.

And then it was acid, and the fingers smoked as the flesh melted away, the bones crumbled. Then he turned toward

Jack with the half-filled vial. "You gave them to me, and I accepted them. Don't be a poor sport."

"A random thought isn't binding." Jack forced a deep breath into his lungs and stared at his wounded hands. *Not real.* The blood stopped flowing, but the gashes remained and the first two fingers were still missing. "I didn't consent," he said, as the liquid was thrown and became water before it reached his face. Now it was Jack's turn to smile. His belief was getting stronger, and he felt certain that he'd get out of here yet.

"It doesn't matter." The man bent to lift Jack by his throat. "You thought that perhaps these fine drunken souls would be better off here than wandering aimlessly, didn't you? You despised their weakness and inaction. You wanted them to go away."

"It was just a thought." Jack brought his knee up into the man's groin and grabbed his throat in return.

The collector released him, slapping his hands away like swatting a fly. "But your thought allowed for a possibility, and that possibility remained in your mind. I had the power and used it. Now they are mine."

The gargoyles were scampering over the grassy slope, and Jack backed up until he was standing beside Fay. "They belong to themselves," he said, watching the pallid creatures approach. He knew they were real and couldn't be thought around. No amount of belief could convince him that they were as powerless in their own home as they had been in his.

"But your friends didn't care," the collector said. "They only cared about getting another drink to blot out their uselessness. Heaven or Hell, it makes no difference to them who captured them. Somebody finally made a decision for them. Now, they have a purpose."

Jack glanced hopefully toward the hilltop. It was shimmering slightly, the air spinning into a faint image of the tavern, as though a hole were beginning to open in the fabric of the air, allowing a peek into another dimension. It was no more than fifty feet to the opening. Could he get there with Fay before the gargoyles got to him?

"But Doc cared."

"Yes, that's why I couldn't take him. I lied when I said that I had allowed him to stay. He was the only one who consciously wanted to stay. It was a mistake to try taking him, for I forced him to make the final decision. Now he's beyond our reach."

"As Fay will be when I bring her back."

"She'll be back. Suicides always come back."

The gargoyles were almost to them, and Jack knelt quickly and scooped Fay back into his arms and ran toward the hilltop. She was unbearably heavy, and his legs ached from the wounds in which he still believed, but he staggered on toward the image of the bar that grew more solid with every step. The tables were bare and covered with dust, just as they had been when he'd first seen the place. He could see Doc sitting alone, staring at his hands clasped on the tabletop. Why doesn't he see them here?

The bar was no more than twenty feet away when Jack felt the tearing grasp of the little monsters on his back and was driven to the ground by the weight of them. Razor-sharp claws slashed against his cheek, piercing through into his mouth as other claws tore at his legs. Releasing Fay, he rolled and grabbed one of the vile creatures, snarling in inarticulate rage as he seized its neck and twisted. The creature kicked and thrashed above him, jabbing Jack's forearms with its claws and Jack broke its neck.

The other creature had torn open the calf of Jack's left leg, pulling gleefully at the muscle fiber as blood spurted from a severed artery. "Not real!" Jack cried, slamming his fist down on the creature's thin skull. "It isn't real!" He pounded again and again, until the gray thing lay limp across his legs.

"But is it real, Jack." The collector stood calmly below him on the hill. He was laughing as though the fight were won. "They were no illusion, I assure you. Neither are your

74

wounds. And it seems now that the laws of nature would dictate that you bleed to death. I win."

"I'm not dead yet." Jack pushed himself up, falling to one knee immediately as his leg gave way. "And you're just a goddamn liar." He slipped his bleeding arms beneath Fay's knees and neck and stood supporting himself unsteadily on his good leg.

"Liar, liar, pants on fire," the collector taunted. "Am I a liar?"

The hill tilted, stretching up and away, and Jack lost his footing, falling and sliding on his back holding Fay tightly. His blood had made her slick, hard to hold as he rolled down the hill that was convulsing into a mountain, sliding down toward the demon waiting below. "No," he said. "It's not real. Not really happening."

But he had lost the distance he'd gained and lay beside Fay at the collector's feet before he could convince himself of the truth. He lay there panting, and looked toward the shimmering gateway. Fifty feet to the bar, where Doc was standing now, staring out at them. He shouted something, but Jack couldn't hear him. Then he pointed, and Jack rolled instinctively, ducking away from the descending blade of the collector's scimitar.

"You are a dead man," the little man said.

"Shove it," Jack gasped, struggling to regain his feet as the earth shook beneath him. Staggering blindly for solid footing, Jack kicked the rifle that the collector had discarded. Discarded, but not destroyed. It was real and solid, and the demon had created it himself.

"Lie down and die, Jack," the man called from behind him. "You're only making it worse for yourself."

"No, you die!" And Jack turned, bringing the weapon to bear and firing it at the approaching demon. "You must believe in this, asshole! You're the one who made it."

The bullets struck the little man in the chest and raked up into his face as the recoil knocked Jack back off his feet. Her jerked backward like a tangled marionette, blood exploding from him as the rounds pummeled his body and reduced his smiling face to a bloody mulch of torn tissue and broken bone. Then he fell on his back with a startled cry.

Jack dropped the gun and lifted Fay once more, tripping and staggering toward the bar where Doc stood holding his hand out to him. Behind him, the collector began to scream, the noise finally congealing into words. "What do the dead eat, Jack?" he called. "What can they live on?"

Jack was barely conscious of the words, stumbling to his knees and up again as the loss of blood began to take its toll.

Fay snuggled against him, awakening to kiss his neck. "Let's rest here," she said. "You're tired." Her hand moved sensuously up his cheek as she nuzzled his throat, giving him renewed inspiration to struggle on. "Please stop, just for a moment."

Then, with animal swiftness, Fay bit his throat, her teeth tearing through his flesh and into the artery. Blood spurted over her face, splattering in her hair as she worried his throat like a dog.

What do the dead eat?

"Not real! Not real!" he shouted, almost dropping her in his pain. But he clutched her body, fighting the pain, and staggered toward the bar. "It isn't real!" But he could feel the rough strokes of her tongue as she lapped the blood from his neck, felt the burning pain of fingernails digging into his face. Still, he continued to hold her desperately close to him, struggling to attain the safety of the bar.

One more step.

She was slick with his blood, sliding from his grasp, and his goal was growing indistinct, hazy. He stumbled to his knees, fighting against the desperate need to release her.

Doc stood within the dark tavern, holding his hand out, shouting. Jack threw himself forward, rolling, looking away from the hideous, snarling face of the woman in his arms, straining to reach Doc's hand while the collector howled behind them.

His flailing hand passed through a barrier of some kind, like a cold rain of electricity, and contacted the tips of Doc's fingers, grasping, pulling.

And he felt himself rising into darkness, into the sadness and the useless fury. He was floating up holding the woman he loved in his arms as she slept unaware of the journey completed in her sleep or of the hideous use her image had been put to. They rose through dark clouds and cold mists that swirled around them, through the blood thoughts of suffering and the shouted needs of the constantly dying race of man. And they arrived with a sigh on the dusty floor of a decayed bar with nothing but each other to blot out the sounds of despair.

"Christ, Jackson, what a mess." Doc was there, wiping the blood from his eyes with a towel. "But you made it."

"Oh damn, oh goddamn!" Jack moaned, rolling to his side as his body clenched up into a ball of pain. "Get a doctor. Get somebody. Please."

"You don't need a doctor."

Doc jumped to his feet at the sound of the voice behind them, and Jack was aware of the collector's footsteps crunching on the dirty tavern floor.

"All wounds heal, you know," the little man said. "Blood washes off and pain fades. Don't be a wimp. You're as health as any of your kind can be."

It hurt, but Jack set up and looked at his torn legs. They were brutally scarred beneath the sheen of drying blood, but the scars were old, already healed. The fingers were still gone, though those wounds too were healed.

"You lose, turkey." Jack laughed, looking up at the little man standing by the bar. He no longer bore the mark of the bullets that had beaten him and wore a disconcerting smile on his restored face. "Winner take all, right?"

"I lose," he admitted. "You did yourself proud by using my own weapon against me. That was really the only way out, you know."

"Yes, you had to believe in it if you wanted it to work on me."

"You're a smart man." The collector wasn't smiling. "But then so am I. And I have the advantage of being a vengeful man. I don't like to lose."

"But there isn't much you can do about it now, is there?" Doc began to walk toward him, his fists clenched at his sides. He stopped when the demon held up a restraining hand.

"I've found that one sure way of being certain of not losing a contest is to arrange for there to be no winner." Now he smiled. "A victory that costs more than it gains is no victory, is it, Jack?"

"No!" He stood, stepping between Fay lying uncon- scious on the floor and the grinning man. "I won't let you harm her."

"I wouldn't dirty my hands on your whore," he an- swered. "You three knew what you were getting into from the start. Harming you would only result in a draw. No, I want you to lose. I want you to suffer. I've been thinking about a young woman named Marion. And then there is a human male whom you used to be in business with. A brother, I believe. I wonder what I can do to them? Do you wonder, Jack?"

"You can't harm them. You have no power here." Jack stepped toward him, preparing himself to stop the demon at any cost. "You're lying."

"No I'm not. Love and death, Jackie, are the ties that bind. Love binds Marion to you just as you are bound to me by death. I can touch whomever you touch just as I touched your fine, dead friends here. And I'm going to touch your lovely Marion very, very hard. She won't know what hit her. And then you'll be a loser, too," he added, with a malicious snarl.

"No!"

"Do you doubt me? After everything you've been through, you actually doubt I'd do it? Well, seeing is believing, isn't it? Come with me and see if I'm as good as my word."

Jack threw himself at the demon desperately, clutching his throat even as the air darkened and congealed, pressing like black concrete around them.

And then they were gone, leaving Doc standing uselessly beside Fay as she began to stir and call out for Jack in her sleep.

14

"I'm so glad you decided to come, Jack." The collector's voice was a friendly sigh, a caressing sound in Marion's dark bedroom. "You humans are such a masochistic species, and I knew you wouldn't want to miss a minute of this."

"Stop." The word barely came out, and Jack had to lean against the door frame to steady himself. The crushed feeling of the air solidifying around him still lingered in his mind, and he was in no condition to fight the demon who was sitting on the edge of Marion's bed casually holding a knife. "Please stop."

"I don't want to stop, Jack. And you've offered me no incentive to do so." The collector smiled. The moonlight spilling through the opened curtains on her balcony doors created harsh shadows on his face. "Besides, I'd only be finishing what you've begun."

"What do you mean?" Jack tried a tentative step into the room, and another when the demon didn't move to stop him.

"Judging by the soiled tissues on her nightstand, I'd say you've done a fair journeyman's job of giving her pain. Crude, I'll admit, and probably not permanent, but real pain nonetheless." He looked down at Marion, a dark shape in the bed. "Do you enjoy making her cry? Does it please you to reduce this cosmopolitan woman to the state of a blubbering child? It would please me."

"I'm not like you." Another step, and Jack's breath was coming easier now.

"A bit, I think. Aren't you the least bit eager to exact some punishment for her manipulative expertise over the years? Don't you want to make her pay?"

"No! I don't want her harmed. No one harmed. What do you want me to do?"

"Come on, Jackie, let's cut the bitch." The collector spoke with wide-eyed glee. "I know, let's take one ear off. That'll surprise her in the morning, won't it?"

"Stop it!" Three hurried steps carried Jack to the center of the room, but he froze when the man moved the blade around to align it with the back of the sleeping woman's ear.

"Come on, Jack." He laughed. "You can keep it in a box on your mantelpiece. A little souvenir." With a small flick of his wrist, he nicked the lobe of her ear, bringing a dark drop of blood to the surface. Marion moaned slightly, turning her head toward them.

"Stop!" Jack lunged, catching the point of the knife in his forearm as the collector threw him back against the wall. He lay stunned for a moment, feeling fresh blood flowing from the throbbing wound.

"Death is real, Jack," the collector said, "and I am death. There are rules, of course, I can't take her soul, for instance. But I can kill her. I can kill anything connected to your mind, everyone you love or hate, everyone you have a passing acquaintance with. I can send their souls down to the Cafe Purgatorium to wait. They could be your new customers. How sweet."

The collector ran the knife down along Marion's cheek, drawing blood in a gathering stream. "Or I can disfigure her as she sleeps and allow her to wake in a pool of her own blood wondering how it happened. I can ruin her, Jack. Would you like me to do that?"

"What do you want from me?" Jack stood again, near

tears, afraid to move and push the demon into fulfilling his threats. "I can't change anything. What use is all of this?"

"You've claimed my prizes, Jack, but the master has reopened negotiations on that claim. I can get them back. You must give them back to me. You must release them, all of them, to me or he will let them go free."

"So take them!"

"But you don't want to give them up." He lifted Marion's face around delicately and then cut the sleeping woman's other cheek, her blood soaking into her pillow. "What you say doesn't matter. Only your thoughts count, only your desire."

"But I can't change my desire! I want you to leave Marion alone! I want you to go away!"

"But you want your drunken friends to escape, too."

"I can't stop myself from wanting that."

"You will. Ah, but we need light for the operation." The collector switched on the bedside lamp and stood to draw back the sheets and hold the knife above the shimmering fabric of the nightgown covering Marion's stomach. "Your nobility works against you, Jack. Are you your brother's keeper? Are you their savior?"

"I didn't claim to be." Jack stepped forward again, stopping as the knife moved to touch the gown.

"You're an awfully mediocre hero," the collector said. "Say, have you ever seen open-heart surgery?"

"Stop this! You don't want her, anyway. You want me. You still want a living soul for your army, don't you, and this is just a scam to get me back there. Take me, you maggot. Just stop this sadistic game."

"You're right, son. Let's skip the cocktail banter and get to the fun part. Say good-bye to Maid Marion." And he thrust the knife in just below her rib cage and twisted it up toward her heart.

Jack threw himself at him and they both fell rolling to the floor. Grasping the collector's hair, he slammed the side of his head against the floor, flailing blindly and pounding his fists into his face, until dark blood colored the demon's features.

"Get off me, won't you, dear boy?" With a convulsive thrust, the collector sent Jack flying back and out the open door behind him. Then he stood, still smiling, his face unmarred. "You can't beat me, you know. Can't kill me. Can't control the outcome. I said that you were going to lose, and you shall."

And then the knife was back in his hand and he turned back toward Marion as Jack rushed into the room.

As he jumped at the demon's back, Jack could see Marion lying on the bed. For an instant, it seemed that she was unbloodied and sleeping peacefully, but then the vision of blood returned as Jack threw his arms around the collector's neck and pulled him away from the bed.

The collector spun in his grasp, throwing him over the bed toward the glass doors leading to the balcony. Before Jack could recover, the collector was on him and had buried the knife deep in Jack's ribs. Instinctively, Jack grabbed his arm and held him close, spinning to drive him into the glass.

The force of Jack's falling thrust propelled them through the doors and against the railing ten stories above the avenue.

"Now I'll collect you, too." The demon turned him against the railing, trying to pull his knife free and push him over the edge.

"No, you won't have me!" Jack insisted, his breath spraying blood against the demon's face as he clutched him tightly to him. "You can't hurt me. You didn't hurt Marion at all." As he spoke, the hideous pain of the knife twisting in his lung lessened slightly, the blood stopped spraying. "And I can control the outcome."

"You're dead, Jack!" He pulled the knife free, pushing back to slash it across Jack's throat with a spray of blood.

"You can't hurt me if I don't let you!" There was no pain, and the bleeding stopped as Jack moved toward the collector. "You aren't real here. You don't exist! That's why you want those people, because they are real and you aren't. You only exist in your own narrow dimension, but human beings exist everywhere." Grabbing the lapels of the demon's coat, he shook him against the railing. "You should have gotten to the point right away but you didn't, and that was a mistake. You gave me time to think, time to stop believing you! You damn liar, you haven't harmed Marion at all but only made me think you did. This is my world, asshole. In my world, you only exist in my mind."

The demon cried out in inarticulate rage and stabbed the knife at Jack's face. The blade passed unfelt through flesh and bone, followed by the demon's entire arm.

Jack laughed. "You're nothing if I don't believe you. And not only do you not exist," he said, "we never left the cafe."

The demon was fading.

Kill the lingering doubt; kill the demon. Put faith in your beliefs, prove them.

Jack stepped up on the railing and jumped.

And was standing in the cafe with dust swirling through the air around him like a fairy ballet lit by the morning sun.

15

She gave him three months.

One afternoon, he returned from a conference with the builder in charge of renovating the cafe, and found her in the bathroom. She lay peacefully in a tub full of blood-stained water, the many deep gashes in her wrists giving evidence that, this time, she'd been quite certain about her death. There was no note, because she knew that he'd understand.

He knelt by the still-warm water and cradled her head in his arms, blinking away the tears that dropped on her smiling lips. He did understand, and was not sad for her, but shed tears for the reason all tears are shed, for his own loss. He knew that she'd endured their time together all for him, because she loved him and understood the pain her death would cause. She'd done all she could for their love, giving in to the sorrow after a valiant struggle.

For there was sorrow. Pain blew like a wind through the mind of anyone tuned to hear it, and Fay had always been attuned to its sound. The fear and frustration of a struggling world howled from mind to mind, and Jack understood her final defeat because he could hear it too, if only faintly. And he knew it must have been torture for her to endure it as long as she did.

But she'd also managed to attain happiness for herself in their time together. He'd heard her laughter and had known it was genuine. For fleeting moments, he'd brought her happiness, touching her life as positively as she had touched his. And now she was gone.

"You gave her a beautiful funeral this time around," Doc said, fingering the keys of his saxophone as he sat on the edge of the stage. "She was a good kid."

They sat in the empty bar with the scaffolding and half-finished construction in disarray around them.

"Was I wrong to bring her back?" Jack pushed sawdust idly around on the floor with one toe and stared at the stumps remaining on his two severed fingers, a reminder of his struggle to attain the unattainable. "Was I being selfish?"

"No. She wanted it. Neither one of you understood what it would be like. No more than I did, I guess. We're different now. We feel it, too."

"It was worse for her. She'd always felt it, just didn't understand what she was feeling."

"I know."

Doc put the instrument to his lips and created a long, low wail, ending in a note poised perfectly at the edge of despair. He expanded on it, then sweetened it in the upper register, letting it drop off into silence.

"I was a callous bastard the first time around," he said, smiling ruefully. "But here I am, the new, improved Doc

Andrews, reborn to play the blues. Even got my hand back in one piece. I am immaculate." He laughed.

"You're an idiot." But Jack understood the emotion behind Doc's jest. There was joy too in the sounds of the world—joy in the feat of survival, in the fact that people could create beauty and make happy moments out of the pain and disappointments of life. There was great joy in the knowledge that reality was something to be molded, and it was only an enemy if you let it get the upper hand.

Jack stood.

"Where are you off to?" Doc watched him with concern.

"I don't know. Thought I'd take a walk, do something time-consuming."

"Want company?"

"Not right now. Thanks."

Doc stood, blowing intricate joy through the reed as Jack left the bar.

Jack hadn't seen Marion in several months when they met in front of the Hyatt Regency Hotel downtown one wet May afternoon. She'd sent a card after Fay's death, but hadn't talked to him since that night in the bar.

He hadn't expected her to have retained any feelings for him after what he did to her, and he was somewhat surprised when she smiled and walked over when she saw him. They exchanged greetings and mouthed clichés about the weather.

And Jack felt her pain in their separation, the feeling of loss his absence had created in her. Even as she laughed and carried on about a joke overheard at the theater the night before, he could feel her frustrated need to tell him what she felt. It was the same need that he felt within himself.

So Jack Bellows took her in his arms and held her tightly to him, creating a tiny piece of beauty in the world by choosing to love. The world was warmed slightly by their spark, and by their choice to endure its heat.

It was all up to them.

DR. KRUSADIAN'S METHOD

by Ray Garton

1

They were screaming in the Campbell house again.

The bitter, garbled shouting was something to which the other residents of Galaxy Heights had grown accustomed over the years. The Campbells weren't the only ones; the Graftons two blocks north had their share of window-rattling shouting matches and the Tillys one street over seemed to destroy all the glassware in the house each time they had a disagreement. But none fought with the tireless regularity of the Campbells. And none were as private about their disputes.

When the Graftons fought, Suzie Grafton covered her street like a missionary handing out religious tracts; she went from house to house to have coffee and talk about her husband's latest affair.

The Tillys went one better. For a month or so after one of their domestic battles, they tried to get everyone on their street to take sides. They became politicians canvassing the street for votes until they finally made up again; then they laughed about their differences as if the whole thing had been a joke staged for the amusement of their neighbors.

The Campbells weren't like that. They said nothing of their quarrels, their domestic uprisings. In fact, they said little to their neighbors at all, with the exception of the Royers, who lived four houses down. Dani Campbell and

April Royer were best friends; they often spent mornings together ironing clothes and sometimes took turns sitting one another's sons. Other than that, however, the Campbells kept to themselves and probably would have gone unnoticed entirely if it weren't for the screaming. Even that went largely ignored; it had become as commonplace as the barking of dogs and the chirping of crickets.

So no one knew exactly what went on within the walls of the two-story gray house with white trim at 3575 Milky Way in Galaxy Heights when the screaming started, only that things were not as right as they might be.

But then, when were they ever?

The Campbells kept a neat and tidy yard. The grass was mowed each week; the shrubbery that grew along the front wall of the house was always evenly trimmed. Dani kept a flower garden along the front of the lawn that was visible through the redwood post fence running along the sidewalk the length of their yard. It was an immaculate garden in which a single weed was never allowed to see the light of day.

Their nine-year-old son Jason always put his outdoor toys in the garage when he was through playing with them, unlike so many of the other neighborhood children, who often left their front yards littered with skateboards and Big Wheels and wagons. The neighbors took this to mean that Jason was an orderly, well-behaved boy and, for the most part, he was. But the real reason Jason put his toys away was that he was afraid of what would happen if he didn't.

Dani Campbell did not care much for housework, and when she did it, she did it haphazardly and without conviction. Before Jason was born, she'd kept the house spotless, but in the last six years or so, she'd lost interest in dusting and sweeping and scrubbing. It seemed pointless when she knew that her work would be virtually unnoticeable within twenty-four hours. She still did it, but not with the regularity she once had and she supposed not as well.

In fact, there were a number of things Dani did not do as well as she used to. During the first few years of her marriage, she'd exercised regularly and watched her diet and weight as intensely as a broker watches the rise and fall of the stock market. Back then, her body was picture perfect and she was proud of it; she shopped for clothes that best displayed the results of her devotion to fitness and went to the beach regularly to bask in the sun as well as the admiring stares of both men and women.

Not anymore.

Somewhere along the way, she'd slowed down. Her activity had decreased by minute intervals over the years until the only exercise she got was walking from one end of the shopping mall to the other and climbing the stairs in her house. She began to pay scant attention to what—as well as how *much*—she ate and it wasn't long before she was ignoring the more revealing outfits on the racks at Macy's and Weinstock's and searching, instead, for baggy, more concealing clothing, hoping to hide the porridge-like lumps on her thighs and hips and the roll of flesh that now oozed over her belts. Even her hair, the color of rich honey, had lost its shine and taken on a dull, unwashed look that no amount of shampoo seemed able to erase.

Some days—not often, but once in a while—it would suddenly occur to her, just hit her like a slap in the face, that her lack of enthusiasm toward those things that had once been so important to her had something to do with the fact that she and Richard ended each day by polishing off a couple bottles of wine. Maybe three. Or so. Sometimes she didn't wait for Richard to get home to open a bottle, and on those evenings, she usually just slipped frozen dinners into the microwave or got some take-out from the Colonel or Wong's Cantonese Palace. She didn't care much for cooking anymore, either.

On the evening of what would be the last chorus of hoarse

screaming to come from the Campbell house before Dr. Krusadian arrived, they had eaten Kentucky Fried Chicken and coleslaw on paper plates in front of the television set. The Colonel himself smiled from the side of the red and white striped bucket that sat in the center of the coffee table. Two empty wine bottles stood at attention at the end of the table closest to Richard's recliner where he sat eating, a Coors glass filled with Sutter Home white zinfandel on the lamp table beside him. On the floor next to the chair was a third bottle, half full.

Dani sat on the sofa staring blankly at the television. A pile of unlaundered clothes clogged the other end of the sofa and four days' worth of newspapers were scattered over the floor beneath the coffee table.

Jason knelt on some of the papers, hunched over his untouched dinner on the coffee table. His Daffy Duck glass was filled with grape Kool-Aid, watered down by melting ice cubes. Beside it stood Dani's Tasmanian Devil glass; a few drops of wine were growing stale in the bottom.

They ate in silence, as always.

A rerun of *Family Ties* was just getting over on the television.

Richard browsed through the paper during the commercials.

Jason toyed with his food noncommittally.

Dani ate the last of her chicken breast and muttered, "Jase, pour Mom another glass of wine, will you?"

He took the bottle by the recliner and emptied it into her glass.

Dani chased her meal with a couple gulps of wine. She'd finished off a bottle of Blue Nun by herself earlier that afternoon, so by the time she sat down for dinner, her thoughts were covered with peach fuzz and her vision was only slightly, but pleasantly, unfocused. Now things were beginning to clear up and she planned to nip *that* in the bud.

She looked at the pile of laundry beside her as she drank, deciding she would have to get it done tomorrow. And she could probably stack the papers beside the fireplace, get them out of the way.

They seldom used the fireplace anymore. There was plenty of wood stacked in the backyard, but no one ever brought it in. The nights were getting crisp as October neared November and they'd been using the gas heater to keep warm. Dani decided to bring some wood in tomorrow, too. Might as well if she was going to do laundry. Wouldn't hurt to pick up around the house a little, too.

Staring at the black, lonely fireplace, Dani noticed that two of the pictures on the mantel had fallen forward. Although she couldn't see them, she knew exactly which ones they were. One was a picture of her, Richard, and Jason at Disneyland with Mickey standing behind them, arms raised happily. The other was of the three of them at Richard's parents farm in Colorado. The two other pictures on the mantel—Richard and Jason at the County Fair and herself and Jason on a horse at a friend's ranch—were laced with cobwebs. She would have to dust tomorrow, too.

Funny, she thought, squinting at the pictures through a zinfandel haze, *Jason never smiled*.

Dani had noticed that Jason was smiling in none of the pictures several times before, but, as always, she noticed it again as if for the first time. Wondering if the two pictures lying facedown were any different, she set her plate aside and rose unsteadily, went to the mantel, and righted the fallen pictures.

Jason stared at her from within the chrome frame, standing between her and Richard and in front of Mickey; his chin was tucked in slightly, the corners of his mouth turned downward just a bit, eyes shadowed and deep. He was a Dickensian urchin, a lost little elf far from home.

Does he always look like that? she wondered.

He did in the four pictures on the mantel.

Dani returned to the sofa, splashed some more wine into her glass and took a couple healthy swallows.

The telephone rang.

93

On the third ring, Richard said slowly, "I suppose I should get that?"

"Mm-hm." Dani nodded, suddenly interested in the news break on television, because *she* didn't want to answer the phone.

Richard set his plate aside, stood, and stretched. He was just under six feet, wiry but muscular, hard, with impossibly wavy brown hair that refused to be combed or styled; it just did as it pleased, curling here and sticking out there, defiant. He went to the telephone in the hallway with a put-upon sigh. His voice was muffled by the opening theme of *The Cosby Show*.

They used to have a telephone in the living room, but Richard had broken it a few weeks ago and neither of them had gotten around to switching the hall phone into the living room jack.

Dani watched Jason do everything with his dinner but eat it as he watched television. He was a small boy with his mother's blond hair and light freckles and his father's strong features and deep brown eyes. He prodded his chicken leg with his fork.

Richard laughed in the hall, but it sounded forced.

"C'mon and eat your chicken, Jase," Dani said, reaching over to pat his shoulder.

"Not very hungry." His voice was hoarse, his words garbled by the fork as he slipped it between his lips and bit it.

"Well, you've gotta eat, hon. Wanna grow up, don't you?"

He shrugged, using his fork to stir his coleslaw.

"Do you feel okay?"

He nodded.

"Well, why don't you at least—"

Richard slammed the receiver down so hard, Dani heard the sharp ring of the phone in the living room.

Jason's fork slipped from his small hand and clattered to the plate.

Dani silently braced herself.

"That was George Winter," Richard said as he came back down the hall. His voice was different. The lazy dinnertime drawl was gone; his words were succinct now, crisp.

Dani looked over her shoulder, knowing what she would see; she was correct.

He stood at the hallway entrance the way he always stood when he got started: hands in his back pockets, elbows out at his sides.

"You know George Winter, Jason," he said. "Randy's dad? Any idea why he might call this evening?"

Jason stiffened and his lower lip trembled.

Randy Winter was Jason's best friend. Dani had met the boy's parents at a school picnic; Richard had stayed home.

"Seems there was a little program at the school tonight," Richard went on. "A student art show. All the parents were invited." He crossed the room as he spoke until he reached the coffee table, where he leaned forward, his face tensing, eyes narrowing. "All the parents but *us*."

Jason slumped forward a little, pulling his shoulders up to his ears.

"How come, Jason?" Dani asked softly, puzzled.

"Forgot," he whispered.

Richard repeated the word, spat it from his mouth with contempt as he spun around and got his drink from the floor by the recliner. He finished it off and quickly reached for the bottle, but it was empty.

There was a brittle silence as Richard walked a slow circle around the recliner.

Dani knew what was coming, what always came when Richard paced and circled and, as always, she gave it no thought. Instead, she wondered why Jason hadn't told them about the art show. They always attended his school programs; *she* did, anyway, even if Richard sometimes didn't. Why would Jason deliberately keep this one from them?

"Do you know how this looks?" Richard asked. "Do you

know how this makes *us* look? Like we don't care about our son's progress in school, like we don't—" He stopped abruptly and wiped a palm over his mouth once, twice, a third time. Another sign of what was coming. "Get out of here!" he barked, sweeping a hand through the air in Jason's direction.

Jason was up and running for the stairs before Richard had finished the sentence.

Richard paced again, still holding his empty glass, muttering to himself every few steps. ". . . have everyone thinking we don't give a damn about him . . . don't even show up at his goddamned art show . . . and he won a prize, for Christ's sake." He spun around to face Dani and shouted, "Can you believe he won a goddamned prize and didn't even *tell* us?"

Before she could respond, he went to the kitchen to open another bottle.

Dani listened to him slamming cupboards and throwing things. Glass shattered, he bellowed, "*Shit!*" and broke something else. "Why don't you clean this goddamned place up once in a while? *Huh?* Just once in a while?"

She knew he would come out with a new bottle, sit in his chair, and change television channels rapidly with the remote control as he mumbled and cursed. Halfway through the new bottle, he would decide enough had not been said and would go upstairs to shout at Jason some more.

Why would Jason do that? she wondered. It was such a small thing, but so unlike him. Jason loved arts and crafts, was very creative; it seemed he would be proud of his art project, would want them to see it.

The only explanation Dani could come up with was one she didn't want to think about . . . one that made her want some more wine.

Richard returned to his recliner and strangled the freshly opened bottle of wine between his thighs as he shot at the television with the remote control. ". . . goddamned kid . . . what'm I supposed to say when someone asks why we weren't there at the . . . Jesus . . ." He curled his lip back, shaking his head back and forth as if he were running his teeth over a file.

The room moved just a little when Dani got up, drank the last of her wine, and went to the kitchen for her own bottle.

Two coffee cups were shattered in the sink.

She opened their last bottle of Sutter Home, making a mental note to buy more tomorrow, and poured until the wine rose above the Tasmanian Devil's head. As she drank, she heard Richard slam the bottle onto the coffee table and get out of the recliner.

Dani lowered her glass, closed her eyes a moment, then drained it and poured another, starting on it immediately. She felt calm, a little numb, relaxed. Prepared.

"Unlock this door, goddammit!" Richard screamed in the hall upstairs.

Dani went back to the living room, sat in the recliner, found a movie on television that looked interesting and turned up the sound until Richard's words were undecipherable. She could never shut out his voice completely, not once he got started.

Something crashed against the wall upstairs.

Dani wondered vaguely if it was Jason and turned the sound up a bit more.

Cosby's over, she thought, realizing it was later than it seemed. She looked out the window and saw that it was indeed dark outside. Had been for some time, she knew.

Dani relaxed a bit more. She found it comforting, seeing blackness outside the windows; it meant the day was over.

She changed the channel to an old rerun of *The Brady Bunch*; she'd always liked that show.

Jason's voice rose above the television's volume in a shrill scream: "*No*, Daddy, I'm sorry, *don't*—"

Glass shattered.

Dani finished her wine, released a sweet, quiet belch, and filled her glass again.

"—'cause you're ashamed of us? Huh?"

"—please *don't*—"

"*I'll* give you something to be ashamed of, goddamned little—"

"—*noooo!*"

Dani's knuckles burned; she looked down at her right hand and saw that she was clutching the glass so tightly that her knuckles were the color of skim milk. She gulped the rest of the wine like cold water and put the glass on the coffee table beside the bottle.

There was a clamor at the top of the stairs and Dani turned as Jason tumbled from the hall onto the landing. He shielded his face with his arms as Richard stood over him, fists clenched, teeth bared like an angry dog.

"Don't you *ever* do that again," he growled, towering over the boy, "you understand? Huh? Or by God, I'll . . . I'll . . ." Richard paced three steps forward, spun, stalked back, his face a mottled red, and pulling a foot back abruptly, he kicked Jason in the ribs.

The boy rolled once and stopped a foot from the stairs, eyes clenched, head pulled back with his mouth yawning open as he made a long miserable retching sound.

Richard paced again, cursing under his breath.

Dani saw it coming, saw it clearer than she'd been seeing the television all evening, and she surprised herself by shooting to her feet and calling her husband's name in a voice ripe with warning. Her shin hit the coffee table and the bottle fell over and rolled a few inches. Wine made gulping noises as it spilled to the carpet.

Richard ignored her.

He kicked Jason again.

The floor tilted beneath Dani's feet and her vision blurred as another wine-flavored gas bubble burst in her chest and she watched, rooted to the floor, as her son went down the stairs in a blur of small arms and legs.

It happened so fast, and yet it seemed to take forever for Jason to reach the bottom of the stairs. Dani heard a sound rise above the thump and tumble of Jason's body hitting the carpeted steps; it was an instantaneous sound, there and gone so quickly that she realized she might not have heard that brief wet crunch at all.

When he finally hit the floor, landing flat on his back, Jason released a burst of breath, as if he'd been holding it all the way down. Then he lay still, staring up at the ceiling with those big fudge brown eyes that blinked so rapidly, as if he'd just awakened and was thinking, *Boy, that was some dream!*

Dani couldn't move or speak at first, couldn't even breathe, could only listen to the thick liquid rushing sound in her ears—as if she were moving underwater—and stare at her son.

Jason lifted his head, gave it a little puppy-like shake, and sat up. His left arm lay between his legs and he dragged it over a thigh, started to lift it, then let it drop to the floor as if it were just too heavy for him.

"Mommy?" he croaked, sounding puzzled, confused, as he stared at his arm, his round little face clouding with worry. "Mommy?"

"Yes, Jason, yes, yes, Mommy's here," she slurred, hurrying to him unsteadily, nearly falling when she dodged the lamp table by the recliner. She saw the bone when she was halfway there, dropped to the floor, and scuttled the rest of the way on her knees as he began to scream.

"Mom-*meee!* Mom-*meee!* Mom-*meee!*"

His left arm had broken halfway between the elbow and wrist and a jagged shard of bloodied gray bone jutted from his broken skin like a steak knife trying to slice off a bite of meat.

Dani felt the blood drain slowly from her face until her cheeks felt ice-cold and her mouth worked numbly for several seconds before words actually came out; even as she spoke, she knew it was the wrong thing to say.

"Oh, we'll have to put some ice on that, Jase. That's gonna swell."

In fact, it swelled right before her eyes, like a flesh-colored banana-shaped party balloon with a pretty red and gray design in the middle. It seemed a long time before she realized it wasn't the swelling that really mattered; no, it was that bone . . .

Richard was groaning at the top of the stairs, groaning in black, sticky waves . . .

As Jason continued to scream, distorted thoughts limped, wounded, through Dani's mind: *Listen to Richard groan . . . look at Jason's bone . . .*

The horror of what Richard had done finally sank in and, before it could become the horror of what she'd *allowed* him to do, Dani took in a long deep breath as she slowly lifted her head to scream at him and—

—he was still standing at the top of the stairs groaning, such a deep, sickening groan, and—

—when her eyes finally found him, her voice lodged in her throat like a thorn because—

—Richard was doing something, a horrible thing that made Dani think for a moment, that somehow, her whole life had been a tragic mistake, and—

—it was that thing, that horrible thing that her husband was doing, not the sight of her son's exposed and splintered bone, that made her sick on the carpet.

2

Jason felt better after the shot.

The nurse who'd given it to him was nice. Tiny, like him almost, with bright red hair and freckles, *lots* more than he had. Her voice was very high, like an elf's, and her name was Tina.

Tina had been so afraid of hurting him, acting like maybe he was going to start crying when she brought the syringe to his bedside.

"Okay, Jason," she'd chirped, "you're gonna be a big

boy for me now, aren't you? 'Cause this'll only hurt for a second, and it'll make you feel a whole lot better."

He'd been in too much pain to protest, even if the needle *had* scared him. It hadn't, though. A needle wasn't so much.

Tina stood by his bed after the shot, rubbing the stinging needleprick gently with a rubber-gloved little hand. As the minutes passed, ticked away by the unholy throbbing in his broken arm, Jason began to relax, stopped crying and breathed easier until he began to feel like . . . like . . . yeah, like cotton candy, the kind you get at the fair, real light, fluffy and sticky.

"Fellin' a little better?" Tina asked, lightly patting his behind.

"Mm-hm."

"So how'd this happen, big fella?" she asked, tossing the needle and syringe into a plastic-lined silver trash bucket. "Were you fightin' off the girls?"

"I tripped on a roller skate and fell down the stairs," he replied without a second for thought.

"Mmm." She walked around the bed to face him. "Well, that ice'll make the swelling go down, then Dr. Saunders'll fit you up with a brand-new shiny white cast for all your friends to sign. How's that?"

He tried hard to smile as he nodded, but his lips felt a little numb.

Tina left him alone behind the mint green curtain.

If everyone in the hospital was as nice as Tina and as funny as the chubby man who had taken X-ray pictures of his arm earlier, Jason hoped he'd get to stay for a while.

Otherwise, of course, he would have to go home.

At least he'd done nothing more to upset his dad. When he left the hospital, he could honestly tell his dad he'd answered the doctors' and nurses' questions just as he'd been told to do in the car on the way there.

The curtain squeaked in its plastic track on the ceiling

when Dr. Saunders pulled it aside and stepped through, smiling.

"Jason," he said, "how's that swelling coming? You got it down for us yet?"

Jason just smiled a little; his tongue was much too heavy to speak.

Dr. Saunders had snow white hair that was very short, cut high above his big ears. He wore black-rimmed glasses on his craggy face; the lenses made the little twinkles in his eyes look much bigger. He was tall and skinny and his long arms seemed rubbery within the sleeves of his white coat. His voice was rough, but soft, and his breath smelled of sweet smoke, like burning cherries.

"That shot's a whopper, huh?"

Jason nodded.

"Makes you feel sorta like your head's a balloon and the string's coming loose, huh?" He perched himself on a stool and wheeled it over to the bed, adjusting his glasses on his sharp nose and looking down at Jason through the bifocals.

"That falling down stairs, Jason," he said solemnly, "that's no good. That'll have to stop." He took a good look at the ice bag wrapped around Jason's arm, then looked at his face for a long time. "Tell me, Jason. How did you get this little scar here?" He touched a fingertip to Jason's upper lip.

"Fell on the sidewalk."

"Well, what're we gonna have to do with you, son? Put you in a wheelchair?"

Jason laughed wearily. He wasn't used to adults joking with him; it was a pleasant, refreshing surprise.

"You're all alone in here, Jason. Most kids want their mom or dad in here with them. Keeps them from crying. But not you. You're a brave boy."

Jason closed his eyes for a moment; Dr. Saunders' voice was soothing.

"Don't you want your mom or dad in here? Don't you wonder where they are?"

After a few seconds of warming up his rubbery lips, Jason said, "S'okay if they had to go."

"No, no. They haven't gone anywhere. They're right outside. You don't really think your mom and dad would go off and leave you. Do you, Jason?"

He licked his lips slowly; his mouth had gone dry. "Maybe to clean the carpet. 'Fore it stains. S'okay."

Dr. Saunders frowned and took Jason's right hand from the bed, holding it in his big palm as he looked at the pink, slightly raised scar on the pad of flesh between thumb and forefinger.

"And where did *this* come from?"

"I was . . . playing with . . . matches." Jason was beginning to feel very sleepy and didn't really feel like talking, but the responses came automatically, cutting through his foggy head, just as rehearsed.

"And this one on your finger? A cut?"

A heavy, slight nod. "Mom's . . . sewing . . . scissors."

"Aaahh. Jason, where was your dad when you fell down the stairs?"

"Be . . . side me."

"I see. Too bad he couldn't have stopped you."

"S'o . . . s'okay."

Jason's leaden eyes closed very slowly as Dr. Saunders said, "You just relax, Jason. I'm gonna give you another once-over."

"I want a cigarette," Dani whispered. Her voice sounded harsh in the empty waiting room.

"I thought you quit."

"You *know* I quit. But I want one."

Richard stood and the sofa's green vinyl upholstery crackled its relief. "I'll get you a pack."

"Where are you going?"

"Cafeteria. For coffee. You want some?"

"Yeah. A cup."

Dani realized they were both speaking in flat monotone voices, barely above a whisper, like alien invaders in a bad movie.

Richard left and Dani stared up at the black and white television mounted on the wall. *Cheers* was on, but the sound was too low to hear. It was an old episode, way before Diane Chambers ran off with her ex-fiancé to write a book instead of marrying Sam. That meant it was one of the syndicated episodes, so it had to be somewhere between eleven and twelve o'clock. She tried to remember when they'd arrived, couldn't, and gave up trying.

Her gray shirt was splotched with blood from holding Jason in her arms in the car. The blood was drying to a stiff crust.

The ride to the hospital had been a nightmare. Jason screaming in her arms, quaking in pain . . . Richard trying to keep an eye on the road as he said over and over. "Now, what are you going to tell the doctor, Jason? Remember? About the roller skate? What are you going to tell the doctor?"

Dani was glad Richard was gone, glad she was alone. She didn't want to be near him. She leaned forward, folded her arms over her knees, and rested her vaguely aching head.

"Where's Mr. Campbell?"

She snapped upright. Dr. Saunders stood over her, hands in his coat pockets.

"He . . . went for coffee." She stood clumsily and hugged her purse to her stomach. "How is Jason?"

"Heavily sedated and in a tremendous amount of pain. Will you come with me, please?" He didn't smile or look her in the eye, didn't even wait to see if she was coming, just turned and started out of the room. He stopped at the reception window and said to the graying woman at the desk, "Jessie, when Mr. Campbell comes back, would you send him straight to my office, please?" Then he was gone, out the door and down the corridor.

Dani tried to keep up with him on weak legs, thinking, *It's serious, bad, maybe they'll have to operate or . . . Christ, what if he loses it, what if Jason loses his arm?*

She followed Dr. Saunders into a small cluttered office that smelled of pipe tobacco. He closed the door, cleared some books from a folding chair, and gestured for her to sit. When she did, he leaned his hips on the corner of his desk, folded his long arms over his chest, and said, "Which one of you beats Jason, you or your husband?"

Dani's jaw dropped, she released a gush of breath and stammered, "Wh-what—what're you—I don't under—"

"Or whatever it is you do, beat him, burn him, cut him. You or your husband? Or do you take turns?" His creased face was colder than death and his eyes were steel bearings glistening in their sockets.

"We-we-we *told* you, he slipped—"

"—on a roller skate, yes, you told me. But, unfortunately for your son, I'm neither blind nor stupid, and *I'm* telling *you* that I don't buy it. You have a lot to drink tonight, Mrs. Campbell?"

"I-I-I . . ." She stopped, knowing that any further attempts at speech—let alone an explanation—would be futile.

"Your husband, too, hm? Smells like wine, am I right? And it *does* smell, Mrs. Campbell, don't kid yourself. It's a wonder you weren't all killed on the road."

Dani felt light-headed, trembly, like she might pass out. She let her purse slide down between her feet and clutched the edges of her chair, as if to keep from floating away.

"We . . . just had . . . some wine . . . with dinner."

"Some wine," he said doubtfully. "How many bottles?"

Before she could attempt a reply, there was a knock at the door.

"Come in," the doctor said.

Richard peered in uncertainly, stepped inside, and closed the door. His face was expressionless at first, but when he looked at Dani, he frowned, sensing her discomfort.

105

She took in a deep breath to tell him . . . what? She didn't know and didn't try to speak.

"I'd offer you a chair, but I'm short," Dr. Saunders said. "Which is too bad, because I think you'll need one. I was just explaining to your wife here that it's pretty obvious to me you're unfit parents. Both of you."

Richard stared at him blankly for a moment and when the words registered, his eyes became stormy. "What . . . what the hell're you—"

"Shut up, Mr. Campbell. Give me any trouble and I'll have you canned for DWI. You'd probably set a blood alcohol *record* in the lab." Saunders spun, stepped around his desk, and took a seat.

Dani felt sick.

"By law," Dr. Saunders said, "I'm required to turn you in, no questions asked. But I've been that route before and I'm not too keen on the way the system handles this kind of problem. They seem to think that—"

Richard's face was the color of strawberries when he barked, "Wait a minute, here, just who the hell do you think you are, goddammit, telling us—"

"I think I'm what you've been dreading, Mr. Campbell, and if you don't shut your mouth and listen to what I have to say, I'll make things much worse for you than you've imagined, I promise."

"B-but . . . he *slipped*," Richard said, his voice suddenly drained of anger.

Dr. Saunders gracefully locked his bony fingers together beneath his sharp chin and he spoke softly. "Mr. Campbell, that boy has more nicks and scars than my favorite pair of black leather motorcycle boots, which I've had since seventy-*four*. No one . . . *no* one . . . is that clumsy. Now, if I turned you in, Jason would be taken from you. But that usually does more harm than good. So I'm not going to do that. I know of something better."

Dani looked at Richard; his face had become slack, cheeks sagging, jaw loose. Even his shoulders drooped in a physical display of guilt and defeat. He leaned back heavily against the door looking sick.

Dr. Saunders went on. "I know a doctor. Dr. Krusadian. He works wonders. I don't know what his methods are, but I've seen the results. So here's what we'll do. No trouble, no hassle, we're just going to handle your problem in the quickest, most efficient way I know. If it doesn't work, we'll go from there. I'll call Dr. Krusadian and tomorrow—"

Richard stepped forward suddenly, face white, mouth working. "Listen to me," he breathed, lips trembling. "Listen to me, please, I . . . I don't want any trouble. If we can just . . . just forget about this, maybe I could . . . well—" A desperate, pathetic little chuckle wiggled from his throat and Dani, for a moment, almost pitied him. Almost. "—maybe I could add a little something to . . . to your bill? You know? May . . . maybe?"

Dani suddenly wanted to throw up.

Dr. Saunders stared at Richard for a long time. Smiling. When he finally spoke, he did so softly at first, slowly building to a growl as he rose to his feet and dug his knuckles into his desktop.

"Have you ever seen a ruptured anus, Mr. Campbell? I don't mean one that's just torn a little and bleeding. I mean an asshole you can stick your arm into up to the elbow. I've seen that, Mr. Campbell. I used to be a prison doctor. Ugly. *Ugly.* That's the kind of thing they do to child abusers in prison because they hate them. All those murderers and rapists? They *abhor* people like you, and to tell you the truth, I wouldn't mind running an industrial power drill up your ass *myself*, but because I'm not in a position to do that, I'm trying to help you straighten up and keep your family together, and if you don't shut the fuck up and cooperate, I promise you, I'll recommend they throw you into prison for the rest of your miserable life and you'll be shitting into a cholostomy bag within your first *week*. Do I make myself *clear*, Mr. Campbell?"

He stared at Richard with hateful, deadly eyes, and when he got no response other than a look of impossible horror and dread, he returned to his chair and cleared his throat softly.

"I'm going to have Dr. Krusadian drop by and see you tomorrow evening. He will then proceed with his treatment and, whatever it is, you will cooperate. You will cooperate happily. Otherwise, I will, quite simply, ruin your life." Another smile, big and flashy and filled with satisfaction. "I'm keeping Jason here for the night. You can pick him up tomorrow afternoon. I will see him once a week for the next six months. If he shows up with so much as a mosquito bite that I don't like, I'll crucify you. Clear?"

They both stared at him silently. Dani knew she would vomit soon.

"I said . . . *clear?*"

Richard nodded silently.

"Now, Dr. Saunders said, "if you don't mind, I'd rather not look at you anymore. Call a cab. If you drive home in your condition, I'll have the cops on you so fast you'll think you died and went to hell. Good night."

Dani couldn't stand up.

Richard didn't move.

Dr. Saunders raised his snowy brows. "Alcohol affect your hearing? I said, good *night*."

As soon as they were in the corridor, Dani looked for a rest room but didn't find one in time and vomited into a drinking fountain.

Dr. Saunders leaned out of his office and said quietly, "Get some paper towels and clean that up before you go."

3

The weather was changing.

Clouds were curling across the night sky, blocking the stars, and, finally, the platinum moon.

Dani stood on the sidewalk in front of their house and watched the night lights disappear from the sky as Richard paid the cab driver, her back to the idling car. She looked at the house; they'd left quickly and the lights were still on, making the windows glow.

So that's how it looks, she thought. *From the outside.*

Richard walked by her as if she weren't there, went through the gate, and up the front path.

She followed him into the house and asked, "What about the car?"

"What about it?"

"Well, if you take the Samurai to work, how will I pick up Jas—"

"Call April. Have her drive you." He crossed the living room, turning off the lights as he went, and slowed to step over the caked patch of vomit on the carpet. Climbing the stairs wearily, he said, "Clean that up."

Dani watched him, her gut seizing up. An unbearable weariness washed over her and she began to cry quietly although she fought the tears; she knew Richard would be annoyed if she cried, aggravated, maybe even angered, but she had to speak.

"Richard? Don't you think we should talk?"

"About what?"

"About . . . about what we're going to do."

"Do?" He turned at the top of the stairs and laughed at her coldly. "We're going to do exactly what the doctor ordered." He shuffled toward the bedroom.

"But . . . but—" She couldn't just drop it; they hadn't spoken a word in the cab and she felt empty, gutted. "—shouldn't we . . . talk? Richard? I'll pour us a drink." There was a long silence as Richard stood in the hall staring at the floor, then Dani whispered, "Please?"

"Come to bed. You've had enough to drink."

When she heard the bedroom door close, Dani muttered, "No, I haven't."

She had a tall glass of wine over ice before she cleaned up her sickness on the living room floor.

Shortly before dawn, Dani sat up in bed and choked back a scream.

It had happened again in a dream, the accident. But seeing Jason fall again was not what had shot her from her sleep.

It had been Richard.

He'd stood at the top of the stairs again, but naked and in murky shadows, groaning and shining with sweat as he did that thing . . .

That horrible thing.

4

The next morning, April drove Dani to the hospital to pick up the car. The cloudy sky was the color of dirty steel and the breeze was armed with a cutting chill.

Over coffee, Dani had explained about the roller skate and told April how terribly worried she and Richard were about their son. That was all she'd told her, all she'd needed to tell her. For now. If it was necessary later, she would come up with some explanation for this Dr. Kru . . . Dr. Krusa . . . whatever his name was.

"He'll be fine," April assured her. "Kids bounce back fast, you know. You just watch. But you . . . you seem a little, you know, upset about something else."

Dani shrugged, heaving nonchalance from the gesture with constipated effort.

"Richard and I had a fight. You know, just before . . . the accident." *Careful*, she thought. *Don't tell one you can't cover later.* "I think it upset Jason. You know, made things worse."

"I'm telling you, don't worry about Jason. He'll be fine. Kids're tough. Like Timex watches. Remember last year

110

when my little Kenny fell off the monkey bars and broke his ankle? He hardly noticed it. Even enjoyed it, I think. All the attention, you know? They're like TV evangelists, kids," she giggled. "They keep coming back for more. Wish I had a little of what they've got in 'em."

April pulled into the hospital parking lot and stopped in front of Dani's car.

"How about I park and go up with you?" April suggested.

"Oh, no, hon, that's okay. I know you're busy."

"Busy? Hell, I'm bathing the dogs today, f'Christ's sake. I'll park the—"

"No, no. I can't stay anyway. I've gotta go pick up his schoolwork."

"Oh. All right," she conceded. "See you later today? Got some wine coolers in the fridge."

"This afternoon. Thanks for the ride."

Dani smiled until April's station wagon was out of the parking lot, then she leaned against her car and sighed, looking up at the gray hospital building.

She couldn't go up and see Jason. Not yet. She wasn't ready.

Dani could not get out of the parking lot fast enough.

5

Jason was groggy, but not too groggy to laugh. He was propped up in bed, the new cast on his arm resting in his lap as he watched a Donald Duck cartoon on the Disney Channel. He'd never seen the Disney Channel before and was nearly happy enough to jump out of bed when he learned the television in his room had cable.

Dr. Saunders had said his arm wasn't as bad as they'd thought and would probably heal nicely. He'd told Jason to rest in bed until his mom came to get him.

Jason didn't want to think about that. He hoped she was late.

Ramona, his nurse, a squat woman with big smiling eyes and a musical voice, bustled into the room; she held a Styrofoam cup with a straw sticking through the lid.

"Here you go, sweetie pie," she said, handing it to him. "Chocolate, just like you asked."

"Thank you, Ramona."

"Not supposed to have milk shakes this soon after breakfast, but I smuggled it outta the kitchen for you."

Jason was laughing at the cartoons again.

"You gotta roommate coming in a coupla hours. But your momma'll probably be here by then, I'm sure. Bet you can't wait to get outta here, huh?"

Jason's laughter crumbled as she fluffed his pillows. He sipped his shake, frowning, and whispered, "I can wait."

6

The fourth-grade class at Millhouse Elementary School was at recess when Dani arrived and the teacher, Miss Carmody, greeted her on the playground.

Miss Carmody was a tall, svelte woman with a pleasant face but a timid, breathy voice. She clicked her tongue sympathetically as Dani told her of Jason's accident.

"We'll have to work on that boy's coordination," she said good-naturedly, walking to the classroom. "He seems to fall a lot."

Inside, Miss Carmody gathered up the week's remaining assignments, put them in a folder, and gave them to Dani.

"You can take this, too," she said, going to a long table in the rear of the classroom. On the table were several stacks of large rectangular sheets of heavy-duty paper; they were rumpled from dried watercolors. Miss Carmody lifted a sheet with a red ribbon taped to the cover and held it before her. "Too bad you missed last night's art show," she· said. "Jason won second prize."

Dani clung to her smile as if for life as she stared at her son's painting. Acid began to sizzle in her stomach.

She knew, suddenly, why Jason had kept the art show a secret.

Miss Carmody said hesitantly, "He's very . . . imaginative. Don't you think?"

"Oh . . . yes. He is. Imaginative."

"You know, some of the other faculty members found this very interesting."

"Yes, interesting." Dani stepped forward and took the painting, clumsily rolling it up on the table.

Miss Carmody joined her hands before her, fingers fluttering like moths. "We thought there might be . . . well, some . . . significance to Jason's painting. We thought maybe you'd—"

"I have to go to the hospital now, Miss Carmody. Thanks for your help." She started for the door, dropped the folder, and papers hissed over the floor.

Miss Carmody hunkered down beside her to help gather them up and said quietly, nervously, "If you ever need to, Mrs. Campbell, you can come talk to me. Or the school counselor. He's—"

"Thanks again."

In the car, Dani wrung her fists around the steering wheel until she caught her breath, then she unrolled the painting again.

It *was* very good, bright with colors, even dark with shadows in most of the right places.

A pretty green long-necked bottle stood in the center of the picture with fire and smoke bursting from the top. Peering from the flames were two hideous, monstrous faces. On the left, a scaled reptilian face glared with fiery eyes, a gaping mouth lined with needle-like fangs, and, on the top, a tuft of wavy curly brown hair. The fangs dripped with red-black blood. The other face seemed softer, somewhat feminine, more human, with gold worms coming from the head instead of hair. A big black padlock pierced the thin lips, locking the mouth shut, and, worst of all, the creature had no eyes.

Written at the bottom in red pencil was: THE MONSTERS FROM THE BOTTLE.

Dani almost tore it up into small pieces. She knew she'd have to sometime because if Richard ever saw it, he would . . . he would . . .

She didn't want to think about it.

She wanted a drink.

Dani rolled the picture back up, started the car, and drove away.

7

Dani stopped a few feet away from the open door of Jason's hospital room when she heard an unfamiliar sound. She stood in the busy corridor and listened, took a cautious step forward and craned her neck to peer into the room.

At first, she thought he was in pain, then thought perhaps he was crying because he'd been left alone in a hospital.

She was wrong.

Jason was laughing.

Dani started into the room but spun around when someone touched her shoulder. She looked into the stern face of Dr. Saunders.

"Dr. Krusadian will call you at two this afternoon," he whispered. "Don't let me hear you weren't there. Understood?"

He went into the room ahead of her.

"Well, Jason," he said, smiling, "ready to go home?"

Jason turned his smiling eyes from the television.

"Your mom's here."

When he looked at Dani, Jason's smile disappeared as if

it had never been. His eyelids dropped halfway and his brow creased slightly.

"Yeah," he said in a low monotone. "I'm ready."

Once again, he was the Jason Dani knew.

8

They drove home in complete silence.

Jason usually spoke little anyway, but his silence in the car was a nervous one, cautious. He kept eyeing the rolled-up painting on the seat between them.

When they got home, Dani said, "Your teacher gave me this," handing him the painting as she sat down on the sofa. "Jason, is there anything . . . well, would you like to talk about this picture?"

He stared at his cast silently, reading some of the nurses' inscriptions. Finally, without lifting his eyes, Jason shook his head.

"It's . . . well, you know, it's *good*, but—"

"Thank you."

"Um, look, Jason, there'll be a man coming here tonight. A doctor. He's coming here to . . . to talk with us."

"Is he gonna talk about my arm?"

"Well, sort of. See, this doctor might be able to fix it so . . . so your dad . . . doesn't get so mad . . . you know, like he does? He's . . . I don't know, he's just gonna talk to us, that's all. To your dad and me. I think he might want to talk to you, too, okay?"

He nodded.

She looked at him for a while, waiting for him to look at her, just lift his head, anything. But he didn't. Dani touched his chin with a forefinger and he raised his head first, then, a moment later, his eyes, and looked at her.

"You're . . . you're so pale," she whispered. "You wanna go to bed, sweetheart?"

He nodded again.

115

"I'll bring you a bunch of pillows. And how about a popsicle?"

Another nod as he started up the stairs, holding the rolled-up painting.

"Um, Jason? Um, your painting . . . well, just for now, could you, um, you know . . ."

"I'll put it away," he said without looking back.

Before getting the pillows and popsicle for Jason, Dani went to the car for the groceries she'd bought earlier. She took them to the kitchen and opened the day's first bottle of wine.

It was one of her last.

9

The phone rang at exactly two o'clock that afternoon.

Dani's hand trembled as she reached for the receiver; her other hand was wrapped around a glass of wine.

"Hello?"

"Mrs. Campbell? Dr. Krusadian calling."

His voice was deep as an arthritic ache and curled by an accent of some kind. Jamaican, perhaps, but she wasn't sure. He was definitely black.

"Um, yes, this is Dani Campbell."

"Good. I'm calling about this evening. I will be there at seven. I wanted you to know so I wouldn't interrupt your supper. I'm very prompt."

"Well, Doctor, I appreciate that, but . . . well, it would be much easier if we could come to your office."

"I don't have an office."

In the dead silence that followed, Dani wondered about Dr. Krusadian.

"I see," she said. "Well, if you don't mind my asking . . . if you don't have an office, what kind of doctor are you? Exactly?"

"A very good one, Mrs. Campbell. I'm calling to verify your address."

After he recited their address succinctly, Dani said, "That's right. Do you know where that is?"

"Exactly. Seven o'clock. Good afternoon."

He hung up.

10

Richard didn't say a word when he came in from work that evening. By that time, rain had begun to fall outside and, occasionally, thunder rolled in the distance. Dani had gotten to the bottom of a large cheap bottle of chenin blanc and was relaxed on the sofa watching *M*A*S*H* when he arrived. She'd managed to stack the newspapers by the fireplace and do the laundry, but she hadn't quite made it into the backyard for firewood.

After changing his clothes, Richard opened a bottle of wine, got a glass, and sat in front of the television to drink and read the paper during the commercials. He did just that for a long time without saying a thing or even acknowledging Dani's presence.

When she could take the silence no longer, Dani said, "Dr. Krusadian's going to be here at seven."

"Mm-hm."

"Do you think he'll want to talk to Jason, too?"

Richard made a little humming sound, like saying *I don't know* without bothering to open his mouth.

"Richard?"

"Hm?"

"You . . . you're making noises. Why won't you talk to me? What have I done?"

"Nothing. Just don't feel like talking. Been talking all day. We'll do plenty of talking later, probably. When he comes. He say how much this is gonna cost me?"

"No," she sighed. "He didn't say."

117

"Probably plenty. What's for dinner?" He didn't look up from the paper.

"Soup and sandwiches. Is that all you can think about? How much it's gonna *cost*? I mean . . . Richard, I'm *scared*."

"So'm I. I just don't want to talk about it."

They didn't.

11

The ringing of the doorbell mingled with the growl of thunder.

Richard seemed not to notice; he was still reading the paper.

Dani leaned forward and ran a hand over her hair, patting. She took one more drink of wine and her hand froze with the glass halfway back to the coffee table.

My God, she thought, *we're drinking. He's here and . . . how much wine have we had?*

There were two bottles on the floor beside Richard's chair. Empty.

"Richard, put those bottles away. Please?"

"Why? I'm not drunk. I have nothing to hide. S'only wine, for Christ's sake. Answer the door."

Dani walked through ankle-deep mud to get to the door. It sucked at her feet, making each step an ordeal as the doorbell rang again. She looked down, actually expecting to see the mud, but there was only carpet. She stood with her hand on the doorknob for a moment, took a deep breath, and pulled the door open.

Dr. Krusadian filled the doorway. Only a small amount of light from the porch light squeezed past him over his shoulders. Below that, there was only Dr. Krusadian in the doorway from side to side all the way down to the threshold.

He wore a black raincoat, open in front. Beneath that, a

118

black suit, narrow black tie, white shirt, and, on his head, a black fedora tilted forward slightly.

His face was as black as his clothing, coal black, so black it was like looking into a night sky that held only two glittering stars: his eyes.

Dr. Krusadian smiled; his lips pulled back to reveal a bit of their chocolate brown and pink undersides and two rows of enormous pure white teeth.

"Hello, Mrs. Campbell. I am Dr. Krusadian."

Dani realized she was nibbling on a knuckle nervously and dropped her hand suddenly.

The thick meaty fingers of his left hand were wrapped around the handle of a black bag, a doctor's bag, just like in the movies. His right hand held what looked like an overnight bag.

Dani covered her mouth to hold in a nervous giggle; it surprised her, bubbling up from her chest like an unexpected belch.

"My goodness," she said, "it looks like you're moving in."

He was still smiling as he said, "Only for the night."

Dr. Krusadian moved forward, turning his bulk slightly and easing through the doorway shoulder first.

Horrified by the thought of being in his way, Dani stumbled backward, gasping so suddenly she choked and coughed.

Dr. Krusadian put his bags down, took off his coat and hat and handed them to her, then closed the door behind him.

And locked it.

Without taking her eyes from him, Dani draped his coat over a chair and put down his hat.

"And where is Mr. Campbell this evening?"

Dani stammered before she finally got her reply out of her mouth; she was suddenly very, *very* uncomfortable.

"He's in the living room."

"Well, why don't we join him." He gave a little half-bow as he picked up his bags and said, "After you."

She was reluctant to turn her back on him but walked quickly and didn't stop until she was standing beside Richard's recliner.

Richard folded up the paper and started to stand but froze with hands on the armrests, elbows jutting and shoulders hunched, frowning at the doctor's suitcase. He muttered, "What . . . what're you . . ."

"Mr. Campbell? I am Dr. Krusadian." He put his bags down again, filling the room with his smile. "I've come to help."

12

Dr. Krusadian lifted his cup of Cafe Mocha from the kitchen table to his lips, which were waiting, stuck out and puckered, as if he were about to whistle. He sipped carefully, loudly, eyes closed and sausage pinky delicately cocked.

Richard stood by the refrigerator, hands in the back pockets of his jeans, gawking at Krusadian as if the man had just come up through the floor.

When Richard realized earlier that Krusadian was planning to stay the night, he'd begun to show signs of smoldering anger that had set off alarms in Dani's head. She'd quickly suggested they go to the kitchen for coffee, hoping to hold Richard's anger back a while longer.

Now Richard was setting off alarms again by the way he looked at Krusadian. He stepped forward and leaned against the table.

"Look," he said, "if you don't mind my asking, I'd like to know—"

"Many things, I'm sure, Mr. Campbell. But first, why don't you sit down and let me explain what we'll be doing

120

together and perhaps that would answer some of your questions."

Dr. Krusadian's voice was creamy, rich, and his accent covered his words like a dark chocolate coating.

Dani stood by the counter watching both men. Richard didn't move and Dr. Krusadian rolled his eyes slowly upward to him.

"Sit down," he said, his big lips moving slowly around the two words and coming to rest in an expression that was almost, but not quite, congenial.

Dani and Richard each took a seat at the table.

Dr. Krusadian's cup disappeared between his mitt-like hands as he began, his words accompanied by distant thunder and rain on the windows.

"You have a problem. Both of you. *All* of you. Three people with one single problem. I am here to help you deal with it. I am here to help all three of you, but my foremost reason for coming is Jason. I will focus on your son. Through working with him, a solution will most likely . . . reveal itself. That has been my experience."

He sipped his drink and savored it a moment before taking it down. "You may think this presumptuous of me because we've never met, but I'm quite confident that I know exactly what you've done to your boy, Mr. and Mrs. Campbell. Oh, I'm not sure what you've done to him physically, but here—" He tapped his forehead. "—I know what you've done to him up here.

"They are such amazing people, children. So . . . *sturdy*. They have to be. They must endure so much, don't you think? Or—" He grinned. "—do you give any thought of that sort of thing? Probably not. Like so many people, you are probably too wrapped up in your own many problems to concern yourself with such a little, insignificant person. We *all* have problems. Demons, they are. Build up inside you like a sickness until you must, *some*how, expel them. But too often, they are expelled onto . . . *into* . . . the children."

Lightning flashed in the window, shining like inspiration on Krusadian's broad face.

"But they have demons, too, you know, the children," he went on. "Demons we know nothing about. We had them, too, back then, but adulthood has a way of sweeping them up and putting them away. Or dressing them up and calling them nostalgia. We remember the school bully and we smile. We forget that, back *then*, that bully was the stuff of nightmares, a dreadful monster waiting around the next corner with his fists clenched. We forget that, and the children, then, must endure it alone. And they *do* endure.

"But they must also, too often, deal with *our* demons because we *can't* endure them, we've forgotten how. So we pour them into the children, beat them in, as if we sense their strength and wish to exploit it. But, strong as they are, the children, they are not *that* strong. No one is.

"And yet, they endure somehow. For a while. Until they can no longer. And they . . . they change. It becomes too late. They grow up with their demons—so *many* demons— from their childhood, from their parents. And *those* demons must be expelled. So those children turn to *their* children. And it goes on and on."

He smiled at Richard warmly, sympathetically. "Perhaps you're like that, Mr. Campbell. Perhaps you've had too many demons pounded into you for too long, and now you are continuing the chain." He turned to Dani. "You, too, perhaps. I don't know yet. If that is the case, you have my sympathies. I grieve for your pain. But." His smile evaporated and his face became stern, hard. "That is irrelevant. You are *adults* now. You're all grown *up*. You should know better. My concern now is with Jason. Which is why I am here. The chain breaks with *me*. Here and now."

Dr. Krusadian sipped his Cafe Mocha, put down the cup, and sat very straight and stiff.

Dani chilled.

Suddenly, Dr. Krusadian meant business; the small talk

122

was over and he seemed to be rolling up his sleeves in his mind.

"My job," he said, "is to remove from Jason all of the demons you have inflicted upon him. They are ugly, I promise you. Hideous. Once I have removed them—if I *can*, that is, but I have confidence—once I have done that, do you know what I'm going to do next?" He smiled, tapping a thick finger on the table and turning looking back and forth between the two of them. "After I have removed your son's demons, I am going to *show* them to you. And I promise you this: you will learn from them." He took another loud sip. "It usually takes only one night, but each case is different and I will work at whatever pace I deem necessary. During that time—by the way, Mr. Campbell, what is your occupation?"

"I'm . . . uh, I'm a contractor. My company, we, uh, built this neighborhood. Galaxy Heights."

"How nice for you. And you?" He turned to Dani and hiked one thick eyebrow high over his right eye.

"Nothing. I mean, um, I'm a housewife."

"Fine. Tomorrow is Saturday. If it will be necessary for you to go to work tomorrow, Mr. Campbell, you will have to make arrangements to be away from the office. Until we are finished here, neither of you will go anywhere or see anyone. Is that understood?"

"Hold it," Richard said, raising his palms. "Just . . . *hold* it." He stood and began to pace.

From the way he was chewing on his lips, Dani could tell he was trying very hard to temper his words, and she was somewhat relieved.

He said, "I was willing to cooperate with whatever, uh, counsel Dr. Saunders saw fit. Whatever problems we may have, I don't think they're as serious as Dr. Saunders makes them out, but I figured it couldn't hurt to, you know, talk to someone. Besides that, Saunders didn't give me much choice. But . . . Jesus, this is just . . . you can't just barge into my house, just move *in* like this, and tell me I can't even go to work—I mean, that's our *living*. How do you think I'm gonna *pay* you? I'm . . . well, I'm sorry, Dr. Krusadian, but I don't like the way you work. I'm very uncomfortable with you. I'd like to cooperate, I really would, but . . . I can't. Not like this. I'm gonna have to ask you to leave."

Dani was moved. She knew how difficult it was for Richard to remain so calm and speak so eloquently. She found herself actually feeling proud of him and thinking that maybe things weren't so bad after all, maybe they *could* change.

Dr. Krusadian had listened carefully to Richard, sitting straight in his chair, one hand over his cup. A few seconds after Richard stopped talking, the doctor said, "Are you finished?"

"Yes. As far as I'm concerned, this *conversation* is finished."

Dr. Krusadian nodded. "First of all, unlike Dr. Saunders, I take no payment for my services. None. This is not my business. It is my calling." He looked beyond Richard and eyed an open bottle of wine on the counter. "Also unlike Dr. Saunders—" He scraped his chair backward and stood and the room seemed to darken. "—I am giving you no choice whatsoever. You will cooperate with me fully."

The doctor moved forward and Richard, wide-eyed, scooted quickly out of his way.

"If you do not," Krusadian continued, lifting the bottle and sniffing with disapproval, "I will notify the proper authorities. I will not waste my time with the police or the county or the state, nothing like that." He turned the bottle over and wine gurgled into the sink. "I will notify . . . the *proper* . . . authorities." Holding the bottle, he turned to Richard. "I will, in fact, Mr. Campbell, come down upon this household like the iron fist of God and you will regret the day your mother opened her legs for your father."

Richard clenched his fists, eyes darting between the

empty bottle and Krusadian's face, as if trying to decide which outraged him more.

"Dani," he growled, "call the police."

"If you call the police, Mrs. Campbell, they will come. But when they leave, it will not be I who leaves with them. They will take away your husband, I assure you, accompanied by flashing red and blue lights that will attract the attention of everyone in the neighborhood." He turned to Richard. "Within hours, everyone you know as well as God knows *how* many total strangers will be aware of your dirty little secret. That does not, of course, include all of the newspaper articles and court appearances. All very public. And, if your luck is especially sour, perhaps Geraldo Rivera will decide to do a live prime time special on child abuse, and one night after you're out on bail, he will burst into your bedroom with cameras and—"

"All *right*, Jesus Christ, all *right!*" Richard screamed, hitting empty air with downswinging fists. He went on quietly, taking shallow staccato breaths between his words. "All right, all . . . right, all . . . right . . ."

"That *is* what concerns you most, isn't it, Mr. Campbell? That others might find out? What you do? In your home at night?"

Dani was shocked to see Richard's shoulders hitching with sobs. He turned his back to her and leaned his forehead against the refrigerator door and cried quietly.

Dr. Krusadian put his hand on Richard's back; the hand engulfed an entire shoulder blade. The gesture was sympathetic; his voice was not.

"Do it my way," he said, "and no one knows. No one but us."

Richard did not respond, but Dr. Krusadian nodded as if he had.

"First," the doctor said, "under no circumstances are either of you to question anything I do at any time. Ever. Now, we will empty all of these." He handed the bottle to

Dani. "Every swallow of alcohol you have in the house goes into the sink. We don't need it."

Numbed and walking through a stranger's dream, Dani took the bottle, went to the wine cupboard, and removed all the others.

Dr. Krusadian asked Richard, "Do you have a basement?"

Richard moved away from the refrigerator rubbing his eyes. "What . . . what has that got to do with—"

"I believe you are about to ask a question, Mr. Campbell. Don't. It is against the rules, remember? Now. A basement?"

Richard led him to the back of the kitchen to the basement door.

Opening the door, the doctor reached in, flicked on the light, and peered down the stairs. "Mm-hm. Fine." He closed the door and smiled at them. "Just fine. Now, why don't you introduce me to Jason?"

Dani stepped away from the sink, suddenly on guard. It struck her all at once; they weren't going to get rid of him, this strange and frightening man was going to *stay*, and worst of all, he was going to be alone with Jason. She was about to protest when Richard spoke.

"Is there . . . anything else you want to tell us? Doctor?"

Krusadian grinned. "One more thing. If either of you raise a hand to the boy while I'm here I'll kill you. Both of you if necessary. Now." He gestured gallantly toward the kitchen door and took one step backward. "After you."

13

He'll terrify Jason, Dani thought as she followed the boy downstairs.

Jason wore his ALF pajama bottoms and a T-shirt Dani had cut to fit over his cast.

126

DR. KRUSADIAN'S METHOD

Dr. Krusadian was standing at the fireplace, hands joined behind his back as he looked down his broad nose at the pictures on the mantel.

The gurgling of bottles being emptied into the sink came from the kitchen.

In the living room, Dani said, with the slightest tremble in her voice, "Jason, this is Dr. Krusadian."

The doctor turned quickly, spread his arms, and grinned enormously.

"Jason!" he said as if greeting an old friend. "How nice to meet you. I see you've been to the Land of Disney." He waved toward the picture. "You must tell me all about it. I've never been." He quickly moved to Jason's side and leaned forward, putting his arm around the boy, leading him to the sofa.

Dr. Krusadian seemed a different person suddenly, sparkling and animated, almost . . . child-like. As far as Dani could tell, there was no fat beneath his black suit. Nothing shifted or jiggled when he moved; his body was concrete.

"Wait right here for me, Jason," he said. "I'll be with you in a moment. I have something for you. We'll have a grand time together." Krusadian lifted his head, dropped his smile, and bellowed, "Mr. Campbell? Time to go upstairs."

Richard came from the kitchen. "What?"

"Come." Krusadian went to his black bag and removed two things: a golden box the size of an average alarm clock and a small metallic object that chittered when he dropped it into his suit-coat pocket. He went up the stairs and, after exchanging a quick, unsettled glance, Dani and Richard followed.

"You listen to the doctor, honey," Dani said over her shoulder as she climbed, not really meaning it. Tears were burning in her throat and she wanted to tell Jason he didn't have to listen to a goddamned thing that black monster said, but—

—*I'll kill you. Both of you if necessary*—

—she knew she couldn't do that.

"You listen to him," she repeated, stopping on the stairs to look at her son, so small on the big sofa below, "but . . . if you want me, honey, you . . . you just holler. 'Kay?"

He nodded and looked away.

Dr. Krusadian stopped outside their bedroom and faced them, gestured to the door and said, "After you." He didn't look inside to see if it was a bedroom; he just . . . knew.

He followed them in.

Richard leaned on the dresser with both hands, watching Krusadian in the mirror.

Dani sat on the bed, craving a drink. But the bottles were all gone, every drop. She remembered some Valium in an unmarked bottle in their bathroom medicine cabinet and turned her eyes to the door, to the rectangular mirror over the bathroom sink, deciding to take one of the pills when Krusadian left them alone, even if she had to chew it dry.

The doctor stood before her, swallowing her field of vision, and said, "Mrs. Campbell, will you please give to me all of the pills and any other consciousness-altering drugs you have in this room." It was not really a request.

Dani said, "But I don't . . . well, we don't keep any—"

"Don't make me look for them." He looked around the messy room distastefully. The bed was unmade and clothes and underwear were strewn over the floor. "I wouldn't particularly care to do that."

She went to the bathroom shaking, still fighting tears, and got the pills. She considered keeping a couple—just a couple—even dropped them into her quivering hand, but—

—*I'll kill you*—

—she knew she couldn't do that, either.

Dr. Krusadian dropped the little bottle into his pocket and held out his hand again, saying curtly, "The cannabis. I can smell it."

"The-the-the—"

"Mari-juanaaaa."

Vision blurring, she went to the dresser, nudged Richard

aside, opened the top drawer and got the little plastic bag of grass, muttering, "My God, Jesus, Jesus Christ . . ." It was just a little bit, not even an eighth, and they only smoked on the weekends, not even *every* weekend, and it was so *old*, hardly had any aroma at *all*, how could he *possibly*—

"Thank you." Into the pocket. He put the gold box on the corner of the dresser. "A music box, in case you would like some music. I am going to work with Jason for a while." He went to the door. "You two . . . work with each other."

They stared at him blankly.

"In other words, Mr. and Mrs. Campbell . . . talk." He grinned. "Just . . . *talk* for a while." After he pulled the door closed, there was a brief insect-like chittering sound on the other side, metallic, as if he were tapping two spoons to the door.

Then he was gone.

Richard looked at her as if to say, *What the hell was that?* then crossed the room and tried the door. The knob turned, but the door wouldn't budge.

"Jesus Christ!" he barked, pounding the door with a fist. "He locked the—" He spun on her, glaring. "—can you believe this? He locked the goddamned door!"

"Richard . . ."

He began to pace. "We're locked in our own goddamned bedroom!"

"Richard . . ."

"How did he *do* it? He must've put a—"

"Richard, maybe we should—"

"Shut up. Just shut up, okay? I don't want to talk. I just . . . I just want . . . I want a *drink*, is what I want." He turned on the nine-inch color television on his nightstand and first sat on the bed, then lay back, hands locked behind his head. "I just . . . don't want to talk," he sighed.

Dani went to the bathroom to find the Maalox; her

stomach was rebelling, shooting great bursts of flames up into her throat. She heard the roar of a crowd coming from the television; Richard was watching some sports event. She wished she could lose herself in something so easily.

When she found the Maalox, the bedroom door burst open and she quickly left the bathroom to find Dr. Krusadian in the room again, staring with burning disapproval at the television.

"This will never do," he said, crossing the room. He picked up the set, jerked the cord from the wall, and started back out.

"Son of a bitch!" Richard shouted, shooting to his feet. "That's it. I mean, that is really *it!* You can't—"

The television flew across the room. Dani did not see Dr. Krusadian throw it, just saw it miss Richard's head by spare inches and hit the wall with a thick pop. Glass shards sang together in chaotic harmony as they scattered and fell. The back of the set came off when it hit the floor.

Richard stood swaying in the middle of the room, then lowered himself to the bed.

Dani blinked again and again, hoping she'd imagined it. She hadn't.

"Do you have a question, Mr. Campbell?" Dr. Krusadian's voice made Dani's teeth vibrate and ache as if they were being drilled.

Richard stared, swallowing frantically again, as if something had caught in his throat.

"There is much to be done," the doctor said. "You have no time for television."

He pulled the door closed.

Locked it from the other side.

Dani heard the soft thumps of his footsteps on the carpet fade down the hall.

From downstairs, she heard him laugh. "Jason, my boy, alone at last!"

In the bathroom again, Dani didn't bother with the small measuring cup she usually used; she took three generous swigs of the thick chalky liquid straight from the bottle and waited for it to douse the fire in her gut.

Before it had the chance, she threw it back up.

14

Jason heard the television implode.

He remembered a man who spoke on career day at school last month, a television repairman named Buddy. He talked about all the things a television repairman is required to know and do in his work and Jason remembered Alicia Brandstetter—a mean, sour-faced girl—asking what would happen if you kicked the television screen really hard, like she wanted to do last week when a newscaster came on to show pictures of the President going on some stupid trip to Russia right in the middle of *Thundercats*. Buddy said it wouldn't just crack or break open, it would implode. That, he explained, was the opposite of exploding; the picture tube would blow inward on itself instead of out because it had a vacuum inside.

At first, Jason was confused, wondering how anyone could possibly get a clunky old vacuum into a television screen, but Buddy explained that a vacuum wasn't something Mom used to clean the carpet.

A vacuum was nothing.

Absolutely nothing.

A television's picture tube, according to Buddy, is so empty that the emptiness is *hungry*, so desperate to be filled that, if its shell were cracked, it would collapse on itself, violently sucking in as much air as it could take.

Jason often imagined himself inside a giant picture tube. He imagined that he actually *was* a vacuum, not just inside one, because that would be impossible. No one—nothing— could be inside a vacuum.

A vacuum was nothing.

Absolutely nothing.

He sometimes wondered what an implosion would sound like. Somehow he knew—he wasn't sure how or why, he just *knew*—that the sound from upstairs was exactly that.

Someone had thrown his dad's little television set.

Probably his dad.

But in front of company? That was odd.

He didn't think about it, though. Instead, he thought about picture tubes and vacuums and implosions as thunder purred like a jungle cat and lightning peeked in the windows.

"Jason, my boy! Alone at last. Forgive my tardiness," Dr. Krusadian said as he came slowly down the stairs shaking his head. "You must never listen to people who criticize you too harshly for occasionally breaking or forgetting the rules. Even parents sometimes, I'm terribly sorry to report, forget them. Break them. Ignore them. No one is perfect."

Never in his life had Jason seen a human being so big. Or so black. His cheeks shone like black apples.

He effortlessly pulled the recliner around so it faced Jason and sat down, leaning forward.

"Jason, do you know why I've come?"

Jason didn't know exactly, but he knew it was big and important. He'd heard shouting when he was upstairs in his bedroom. When he finally realized that it was a stranger shouting—well, not shouting, exactly, but speaking in a very loud, threatening voice—at his dad, and his dad wasn't breaking things up in the living room, he knew something was up. But he didn't let on that he knew; he was afraid his dad would get angry about it later if he did.

"To talk about my arm?" Jason replied.

"Yes, to talk. With you. I've come to talk about lots of things. Like that picture." He turned to the Disneyland picture on the mantel. "I'd like to talk about that. Yes . . . yes, I would." Dr. Krusadian looked at the picture as if he were looking out a window at something beautiful and a smile spread over his face like warmth over a cold window-pane. "Must be a wonderful place, Disneyland."

"I had fun," Jason lied.

"Is it big?"

Jason nodded.

"A place where everyone can be a child. Mmm. Must be absolutely delightful."

Jason nodded again, only slightly this time, lowering his gaze to his broken arm. He could feel Dr. Krusadian looking at him.

"But there's one thing I don't understand, Jason. About that picture. How is it that a boy like you could go to such a place—a gigantic land made up of fairy tales and pirate ships and trips to outer space—and spend one tiny little second without a joyous smile on his face. You're not smiling, Jason."

There was another cavernous silence.

"You don't look like you were having fun."

The silence of a vacuum.

"Were you? Having fun?"

No reply.

"I don't think so. But if you don't want to talk about it yet, that's perfectly all right. Do you like music?"

"Uh-huh."

"Good. I have something for you." Dr. Krusadian went to his black bag and removed a white cardboard box shaped like a big cube. He sat down again and put the box on the coffee table. "Powerful thing, music. *Magic*. It can make you happy, make you cry. Some makes you angry, some relaxed and soothed. I don't know what I would do without music. How about you?"

"I like music."

"Of course you do. All children do. They have to. Because sometimes it isn't easy to be children, is it?"

Jason didn't speak, but he looked up at Dr. Krusadian

finally. He could tell by the darkness in the man's eyes that he already knew the answer to that question.

He *knew*.

"Music has always been my refuge," the doctor said. "I turn to music for comfort, for protection. I put music into my life the way one puts a bandage on a wound so the wound can heal. Like that cast on your arm. It's there to protect your arm while it gets better. Sometimes," he whispered, "I wrap my whoooole life in music. Like a broken arm in a great big cast." He spread his arms before him as if embracing a huge cast. "Have you ever done that, Jason?"

Jason gave that careful thought and realized he'd never done anything of the kind. It made him feel bad, that realization, because he'd *felt* that way before, lots of times: like a great big wound that needed bandaging.

"No," Jason said, "but . . . I know what you mean."

"I thought you might. What is *your* refuge, Jason?"

He chewed his lip while he thought about it.

At first, he was going to say his bedroom, but that wasn't true. When his door was closed, his dad just came in anyway, sometimes even kicked the door open without bothering to turn the knob. He'd broken two locks that way.

Jason had a lot of books in his room and sometimes turned to them for comfort and diversion. He didn't have as many as he used to, though, not enough to call them his refuge. If his dad ever caught him reading when he wanted Jason to pay attention to his shouting and hitting, he usually swiped the book from Jason's hands and ripped it into three or four pieces.

Feeling lost, Jason looked up at Dr. Krusadian and, sounding surprised, whispered, "I don't have one."

The doctor's face fell. "I am truly sorry to hear that, Jason. But—" He held up a finger. "—that is why I am here."

Dr. Krusadian reached into the box and removed what looked, at first, like a gold-colored ball with fascinating intricate designs carved into its smooth surface.

But it wasn't a ball because it had a little stand attached to the bottom with tiny legs to stand on.

When he spoke again, Dr. Krusadian's voice was quiet, secretive.

"Different music does different things, Jason. Some music is meant to make you dance, while other music will put you to sleep." As he spoke, the doctor opened his other bag and removed a heavy black tarpaulin folded into a square. Standing, he pulled the coffee table back a few feet and began spreading the tarpaulin over the carpet in front of the sofa. "Music like that—dance music, lullabies—fills you up. It puts something inside you. Do you understand, Jason?"

"I think so," Jason said as Dr. Krusadian took a long sturdy rope from his bag and began threading it through brass rings in the corners of the tarpaulin.

"Some music, however, does the exact opposite." He sat in the recliner again, still speaking softly, his twinkling eyes holding Jason's attention. "Instead of filling you up, some music lets *you* . . . fill *it* up . . . with anything you wish. Does that make any sense to you, Jason?"

It didn't, really, and Jason frowned at Dr. Krusadian.

"Perhaps it would be best to simply show you." The doctor touched the globe gently with a fingertip. "This is a music box. Of sorts. A very *special* music box. This music does not give you anything. Doesn't make you want to dance or sing. This music . . . *takes*. It takes whatever you need to get rid of, Jason, whatever you need to let go of. But before I play it for you—and this is important—I must tell you that it is to remain our secret. Ours alone. You must never tell a soul. Not even your parents. Promise?"

His eyes wide with fascination, Jason nodded.

"Now," Dr. Krusadian whispered, placing a big hand on the globe, "listen."

When he lifted his hand, the globe began to turn very slowly and Jason noticed something startling.

There was another globe inside, turning in the opposite direction.

And inside *that* globe was *another*, turning in the direction of the first.

Each had minute designs carved into them, as the outer globe did: wiggly openings, round ones, triangular ones, all passing one another with each revolution, giving the illusion of movement.

The openings seemed to blink like eyes . . .

The globe appeared to breathe with life . . .

And its music began to play . . .

For a moment, it sounded nothing like music at all. It sounded instead like the cracking of wood, the slow falling of a great tree in the distance. Then other sounds joined in: a high, wistful pinging, a gut-deep thrum, a hollow, mournful whistle . . .

They blended, the eerie sounds, locking together like cogs until they were one single, unified sound. Achingly beautiful music bled from the rotating globes and embraced Jason, held him like a guardian angel . . .

Stroking him . . .

Rocking him . . .

"Isn't it beautiful? Dr. Krusadian asked.

His deep resonant voice reached Jason's ears as if from a long distance. The boy's gaze was held firmly by the spinning globes but, peripherally, he could see Dr. Krusadian rise to his feet and walk to one of the room's four shining lamps.

"The music is forever changing," he whispered as he clicked the lamp off.

The room dimmed slightly.

"And the globes never remain the same . . . do they?"

Click.

Dimmer still.

Lightning fluttered in the windows like playful ghosts.

"The music is waiting, Jason. Waiting for you to decide

what to give it. If you listen carefully . . . if you'll watch closely . . ."

Click.

". . . sometimes you'll . . . *see* things . . ."

Another click and the murky darkness fell unnoticed around Jason.

". . . pictures . . . some pretty . . . some not. Lie down, Jason."

He did, still watching the globes. He wasn't sure, but . . . Jason *thought* . . . he saw something inside . . . something glowing, pulsing, blinking a bluish white inside Dr. Krusadian's music box.

Sitting down again, the doctor whispered, "Watch closely. Look inside, Jason . . . *deeeep* inside . . . and perhaps you'll see them, too . . ."

As Jason stared intently, he began to feel sleepy, groggy, like he had just before having his tonsils removed.

Then the pictures began . . .

15

After the volcano in her stomach began to subside, Dani drank some more Maalox and fought to keep it down.

Richard was sprawled on the bed staring at the ceiling. His eyes appeared glazed, dead.

Dani listened for noise from downstairs, but heard nothing.

"He's gonna pay for that fucking set," Richard croaked. "He doesn't *know* it yet, but he's going to."

When Richard wasn't talking and the thunder was still, the room was so silent Dani could hear her blood flowing.

"We won't say anything right now," Richard went on. "We'll just go on with him while he's here. Cooperate quietly."

Dani stood in the bathroom doorway looking around the

room for something. A book, a magazine. Anything to take her mind off . . . *everything*.

The music box caught her eye.

"But as soon as that son of a bitch is gone, I'm gonna sue his fat nigger ass from here to the goddamned Second Coming, you just *wait*."

She ignored him. He wasn't talking to her, anyway; he was talking to himself, the way he so often did.

Dani sat in her chair at the dresser and studied the box, frowning.

There were holes in the gold-colored cube, finely carved holes of all difference shapes and sizes.

The more she looked at it, the more beauty she saw in its patterns and the more she realized that—

—there was something *inside*.

"We'll call that other doctor—what's his name?—Saunders. Find out a little more about this asshole. Not gonna throw *my* fuckin' television at me and get away with it." He was beginning to sound sleepy. "Honey, turn the light off, will you?"

Dani didn't hear him. She was trying to figure out the shape of the object inside the cube. It looked like . . . maybe . . . a pyramid carved with more intriguing curlicues and squiggles . . .

"Dani? Dammit, Danielle, will you turn the god—" He got off the bed. "Okay, I'll get the goddamned light."

The sudden darkness startled Dani from her concentration. A small yellowed night-light in the shape of a daisy was plugged into the outlet above the dresser, always there, glowing day and night. It came alive in the darkness, shedding a pool of dull yellow light onto the dresser.

Onto the cube.

It shone a hazy gold, like sunlight filtering through heavy, dirty clouds.

"I'm gonna take a nap," Richard said. "Wake me up when that bastard comes back." He rolled onto his side and mumbled into his pillow. "Locking us in our bedroom . . . moving into our fucking house . . . Jeee-*zus*."

Dani's stomach began to burn again. It had eaten the Maalox, sucked it up, and now was chewing on itself again like a mad animal caught in a trap. She leaned forward, hugging her stomach, and belched sulphur as she looked at the box.

Thinking . . .

That was her problem; she couldn't stop thinking . . .

About Jason: one year old and giggling in his high chair, pink round face splotched with applesauce.

That image came often, always turning up the fire in her gut, fueling it with . . . what? Sorrow? A feeling of loss? Both of those, she knew, and something else, the worst of all.

Guilt.

Because that was the last time she could remember Jason laughing, really laughing through a genuine grin. She'd tried to remember others, but couldn't. That was the last.

It was easy to think Jason's laughter stopped when their drinking—their *nightly* drinking—started, but maybe not. Maybe the drinking came after, in an attempt to silence the constant shouting.

That, she decided, *is when Jason's laughter went away. When the shouting started.*

The shouting was one thing, but the *hitting* . . . It was the hitting that had done so much damage.

No, a voice said, a guttural fiery voice in her stomach, *the damage came when the hitting didn't stop. And why didn't the hitting stop?*

She scrubbed her face with her hands, trying to reroute her thoughts.

Why, Dani? Why didn't it stop?

"I tried," she breathed into a curled fist.

Coward.

"No."

Coward.

139

"I tried . . . once . . ."

Once wasn't enough, was it?

"But . . . I did . . . *try* . . .

Her head dropped heavily and she put both hands on the cube and—

—it came alive.

Dani gasped and jerked her hands away.

But it was too late . . .

16

"Do you see the pictures, Jason?"

"Mmm . . . hmmm . . ." His eyelids were stones and his body was turning to warm smooth milk and soaking into the sofa. But he never took his eyes from the globes within globes . . . from the tiny pictures that flashed from the holes and were magnified for an instant in his head.

"Can you see the pictures, Jason?"

"Uh . . . huh . . ."

"Good. I . . . I would like you to do a favor for me, Jason."

"Wha . . . ?

"I'd like you to look for particular pictures for me. Will you do that for me, Jason?"

" 'Kay."

"Find for me the last time you remember being happy. Truly . . . *truly* happy. Can you do that?"

He looked. Searched. The pictures flashed through his mind like a side show being projected on the side of a moving roller coaster until—

—*there.*

Jason willed the picture to stay in his mind, in focus.

The globes stopped turning, just held, and the picture grew bright, vivid, *real,* and—

—Jason slipped his right thumb in his mouth.

"How old are you, Jason?"

He started to reply, but speech was now a distant memory that took a moment to recapture.

"Don't . . . know . . ."

"Can you hold up fingers for me?"

Jason's fingers wagged slowly, stopped, then disappeared, tucked beneath his chin, giving up.

"Where are you?"

"Kitchen."

"What are you doing?"

"Eating. Nummies. App . . . applesau . . . ap . . ."

"Applesauce?"

He nodded. "Mommy's . . . laughing. Feeding me."

"Mommy's happy?"

Another nod.

"Where's Daddy?"

"Work. Home soon."

"Find Daddy in the picture, Jason."

Jason frowned, listened.

He heard the front door open, heard Daddy's footsteps.

"Daaa-*eee*!" he cooed.

"Is he home?"

"Just came in."

Jason's smile disappeared; he pulled his thumb from his mouth.

This, he knew somehow, was the bad part, like the monster finally coming into the light in a scary movie. He didn't want to look, but the picture remained inside his head, held by the globe, vividly superimposed over the dark living room.

"He's . . . he's gonna . . ."

Goddamned son of a bitch Steevers . . . at work . . . fucking idiot doesn't know what the hell he's doing . . . we got any wine?

"He's mad," Jason said.

"Mommy said, *But it's only five—*

I don't give a damn what time it is, goddammit.

A fist slammed the table.

Jason started, bumping the little jar with the baby's face on it.

The jar shattered on the floor, sending small gobs of applesauce through the kitchen.

Daddy's foot crunched some glass.

Son of a bitch, *that little—*

Daddy's fist flew—

—hit Jason's chair—

—and the world tilted.

"Falling! Daddy h-hit . . . the ch-*chair! Falling!*" Jason screamed.

"Not really. It's okay, Jason, it's—"

His body jolted on the sofa when he—

—hit the floor, bumped his head, and screamed—

—Jason! Oh, God, Richard, what did you—

—*Well, look at this, it went right through my goddamned* shoe, *the little*—

"Daddy's . . . hurt. Glass with . . . blood. He's showing me . . . screaming because . . . I hurt Daddy. I cut him." Jason's arm flew up in front of his face. "No, Daddy, no, *nooo!*"

The entire sofa jerked with each invisible blow as Jason screamed . . .

. . . then cried . . .

. . . then whimpered as thunder growled.

Jason tried to focus on his faint, dark surroundings, tried to look through the images projected over them, but something else directed his attention away from them. He felt something leave him, felt a pull, then a silent, internal fear, like a tooth being pulled slowly from its socket and—

—something moved beside the sofa between Jason and the doctor with a thick, liquidy slushing sound, making the tarpaulin on the floor crackle softly.

"It's all right, Jason," Dr. Krusadian whispered as lightning X-rayed the room. "It's gone. You've let go of it. Gotten rid of it. It's gone. Just close your eyes for a while and relax."

He did, and for a few honey-thick moments, Jason slept . . .

The pyramid inside the cube began to turn and something inside glowed softly and Dani shook her head whispering, "No . . . I tried . . . I *did* try . . ." The dark bedroom became a ghost and she was suddenly on the stairs hurrying down to the living room where Richard sat in his recliner, bottle between his thighs, the newspaper crumpled on his knees.

You hurt him, she hissed, *goddamn you, Richard, you* hurt *him.*

He ignored her.

Dani rounded the chair and faced him, her eyes tearing with fury.

Did you hear me, Richard? You hurt his head! He's just a baby, for Christ's sake, you could've killed *him!*

Did I?

But you could've—

I didn't, did I?

I can't believe you're—

Just drop it. I had a shitty day and—

If you ever do that again, so help me God, I'll—

Richard's face caught fire and he exploded from the chair and swung the bottle. Wine rained over them and the bottle stuck her neck. Dani went down and he began to kick her.

She clutched the edge of the dresser, feeling herself slipping from her chair. Dani *knew* she was still in her bedroom, could still *see* it, but—

—she was reliving the beating that had made her pray for death, that gave her such a clear vision of her family's future. It was the first time Richard raised a hand to her and she decided as she bled that it would be the last, if she could help it.

Richard screamed at her as he kicked and slugged and jerked on her hair, but she heard none of it. There was a strange calm inside her as she smelled her own blood, a calm brought on, perhaps, by the inevitability of it. So many times, she'd caught a glimpse of Richard's potential for violence—temper tantrums, broken dishes, a crack in the bedroom wall where he'd struck out with a fist one angry night—but she'd always turned away from it, ignored it.

She couldn't ignore it that first horrible evening he'd beaten her until death seemed a good idea.

She couldn't now, either.

Dani fell from the chair to her knees, still holding the dresser, eyes still gripped by the cube, now only faintly visible through the pictures it was showing her. She vaguely felt the floor come up and hit her in the back when she fell and her breath exploded from her lungs, but that wasn't important as the fact that—

—Richard's fist was plummeting toward her face, a knuckled flesh-colored meteor that filled her vision and finally struck, bringing blackness and pain.

His knuckles chipped a bottom tooth and cut both her lips badly. He broke two of her ribs, the middle finger on her left hand, and cut the back of her head with his shoe, sending blood dribbling down her back.

But he wasn't finished.

Don't you ever . . . ever . . . talk to me like that again! he screamed. His face was the color of blood and his entire body quaked as he began kicking her some more. *Ever! Ever! Ever!*

Dani vomited onto the living room carpet.

You don't know anything, hear me? he screamed, circling her with clenched fists. *You don't know what's going on with me, at work, in my head. You don't know shit!*

The beating went on for an eternity; Dani passed in and out of consciousness, sometimes forgetting who was beating her. But even when confusion washed over her like fevered chills, a part of her brain remained detached from her situation and processed a series of orderly thoughts. They were thoughts about what she would do when Richard was finished and she was able to walk. She would go into Jason's room, gather him up in some warm clothes, maybe get a few things of her own, and go—

—where? She had no idea, but she couldn't stay with him. *Could* she? It would only happen again, maybe in a few days or weeks, maybe next year or the year after that, but it *would* happen again, she had no doubt. She might go to April's. Or maybe her mother's. Anywhere. And she would file for divorce immediately. And then she would—

—what? Get a job? Doing what, waitressing? Working in a 7-11? A Burger King? She had no skills. She hadn't gone to college; in fact, she'd barely gotten through high school. She and Jason would have to live on mere scrapings. Richard had always supported her well. His business was not always good—in fact, it frequently became quite rocky, and that was usually the reason for his tantrums and shouting fits—but he was a very good provider and kept her comfortably surrounded by both necessities and luxuries.

So. Maybe they could see a counselor. Weren't there shelters for battered women and children? Maybe they could go to some group therapy, or whatever people did when they had problems like this. Maybe. Maybe not.

Maybe not.

As Dani writhed on the bedroom floor and Richard slept a few feet away, she felt something move inside her, twist and turn, as if trying to . . . come out. It was not unlike the sensation of giving birth, but without the pain. She couldn't tell if it was something she was actually felling, or if it was a part of the vivid, frightening vision she was having.

The sensation stopped.

The beating stopped.

She sensed Richard standing over her, heard him . . . *groaning*. It was the same wretched groan that had come from him after he'd kicked Jason down the stairs . . . the same groan that had come from him as he stood on the landing doing that horrible *thing* . . .

145

She remained on the living room floor, pain dancing over her body like some vile fanged elf, as Richard went downstairs, his miserable groan fading down the hall, finally silenced by the slam of the bedroom door.

Except she wasn't *in* the living room.

She was on the bedroom floor hugging her knees.

Dani lifted her head and looked for the blood she'd been shedding, but it wasn't there.

The room was dark and Richard was snoring.

Dani hugged herself and lay still on the floor, awaiting the return of the numbness she'd worked so long and hard to perfect, the numbness that enabled her to go on. But without alcohol, it had abandoned her.

In the stillness of the dark bedroom, Dani listened to her nerves scream.

The foggy half-sleep that fell over Jason reminded him, vaguely, of the lead blanket the chubby man in the hospital had spread over him before taking X-ray pictures of his arm. It was heavy and cool but felt protective and safe. He managed to lift his eyelids a fraction of an inch during his odd rest; along with the room's darkness, his vision was smeared with murky film that made the room seem filled with smoke. Even the lightning, which was actually becoming brighter and more frequent as the weather grew fierce, was dimmed to a mere flickering of pale light from outside.

Through cotton-stuffed ears, Jason heard sounds: a wet, snotty sucking, like Jell-O being scooped from a bucket; heavy plastic crackling with movement; Dr. Krusadian's puffs of exertion; the hush of something being dragged over the carpet. With a great heaving effort, Jason opened his eyes and lifted his head an inch from the sofa. Through the clouds in his eyes, he saw Dr. Krusadian pulling on the rope he'd threaded through the tarpaulin's brass rings. The dark plastic was gathered around something squat and bulbous and heavy that slid with each pull of the doctor's big arms.

And within the plastic, something moved.

"Rest, Jason," Dr. Krusadian whispered. "Just close your eyes and rest."

Jason was far too weary to ask the question that wriggled just behind his lips. He let his head fall back on the cushion and felt himself disappear into the air like a rising cloud of vapor.

17

When Jason opened his eyes again, he was aware that some time had passed, but had no idea how much.

The room was still dark. Dr. Krusadian was at his side once again, hands joined between his knees, elbows resting on his thighs. His teeth gleamed within the broad frame of his smile and he asked, "How do you feel, Jason?"

"Fine, I guess." He wasn't sure. Of *anything*. He scanned his memory for something—he wasn't sure *what*—but came up with only fleeting blurred images and the vaguest of sounds. When he saw the globe, though, something fell into place, dousing his apprehension.

Dr. Krusadian put his hand on the globe and whispered, "Ready?"

He nodded, even though he couldn't quite remember what he was ready for.

The music began.

Haziness overcame him.

And the pictures returned.

Dani moved her arm first, sliding it over the carpet to push herself up, and her hand slipped through a thin coating of cool, slimy wetness.

Did I throw up? she wondered, rising to her knees and brushing her palm over the carpet again. The glow from the daisy night-light above the dresser wasn't enough for her to see what was on the floor, so she reached up and flipped a switch on the wall. The light in the walk-in closet before her came on; the louvered door was open a crack and light striped the carpet.

Dani squinted down at the glistening strip of moisture and reached for it again to touch it, smell it, but something moved within the closet and she jerked her hand back and slapped it to her chest, staring openmouthed through the two-inch opening.

The doorjamb was wet; a drop of clear gelatinous fluid dribbled down to the carpet.

Dani leaned closer to the closet and peered inside, her eyes wandering below the hanging clothes to the dark places where tennis racquets and shoe boxes and rolls of decorous wrapping paper leaned in the shadows.

And something else.

Something wet and puffy, the color of drying semen.

It moved with the sound of phlegm being sucked through a straw, sloshing out of the shadows toward her, and Dani threw herself forward, slamming the door and holding it shut with her weight as she screamed.

"Where are you now, Jason?"

"My bedroom."

"What are you doing?"

"Hiding. Daddy's screaming again."

"Why is he screaming?"

"I don't know."

"Where is he?"

"Downstairs. He's . . . no, wait he's . . ." Jason's voice became a trembling whisper as he listened to his father's bitter, drunken shouting growing louder. Closer. ". . . he's coming *upstairs!* Up *here!*"

The bedroom door slammed open and Jason saw his father standing in the doorway holding a G.I. Joe action figure in one hand and a toy Jeep in the other.

You know where I found these? he bellowed. *On the living room floor, that's where. You know how I found them? I nearly broke my goddamned ankle, that's how!*

148

He stormed across the room toward Jason, dropping the toys, and Mom appeared in the doorway behind him. She leaned heavily against the doorjamb, her head falling to one side like a rag doll's.

Jason was relieved to see her, certain she would intercede, hoping she would be able to somehow dampen his father's anger. But the sadness and utter helplessness in her face told him otherwise. She looked at Jason with a pain in her eyes he'd never seen before but would see many times after that, a pain that made him ache; then she turned her gaze to her husband and Jason saw surrender.

She disappeared down the hall and his father's fists began their work.

Jason began to scream pleas for mercy as his body jolted on the sofa, bouncing on the cushions as if receiving electric shocks. He felt no actual pain, but seeing his father's fists falling on him again and again filled him with such terror that he screamed and writhed as if in agony.

Through his father's roared epithets and battering fists, through his own ragged cries, Jason heard two things: the messy slurping sound he'd heard earlier and his mother screaming from far away, "Let me out! Let me out of here, please! Plee-heeeze!"

They were screaming in the Campbell house again . . .

When the music stopped and the brutal vision faded, Jason opened his sleepy eyes to see Dr. Krusadian once again dragging the bulky tarpaulin out of the living room.

"You just relax, Jason," the doctor said as the thing in the tarpaulin squirmed wetly. "You relax and . . . back in . . . few minutes . . . we'll . . ."

His voice faded as Jason slept. But even in his sleep, he could hear his mother screaming.

18

"Jesus *Christ*, Dani, what're you screaming about?" Richard rose clumsily from the bed as Dani slammed a chair against the closet door. "What the hell is—"

"There's something in the closet."

"What?"

"Something's in the *closet*, I *saw* it, it *moved!*"

"Oh, Christ, Dani, you're drunk." He started for the closet, reaching for the chair.

"No! Please, Richard, don't open it!" She stepped in front of him and put her hands on his chest, closing them over his shirt desperately. "Please."

He rolled his eyes and pushed her aside.

Dani gripped his arm and pulled hard, snapping, "*No!*"

With the speed of the lightening that brightened the windows, Richard spun and slapped her face hard, knocking her onto the bed as—

—something clattered in the closet, rattling the door against the chair and—

—with a brief metallic clicking, the bedroom door opened and Dr. Krusadian glared at them in an electric flash of lightning and the thunder that followed could have been his voice.

"What is it?" Dani screamed at him. "What have you done? *What the hell is it?*"

"Leave the room," he said, his voice level but deadly. "Now. No questions."

Dani ignored his words and shouted again, "What is it? What have you—"

Dr. Krusadian's lips pulled back over his teeth and his voice hit the walls of the room like a wrecking ball.

"Leave! This! *Roooom!*"

The thing in the closet threw itself against the door and the wooden chair crackled weakly, preparing to give way.

Dani stopped breathing and wrung her hands at her chest as she looked at Richard. His face was blank.

Dr. Krusadian gave them room to pass and Richard left the room first with Dani behind him, not wanting to be separated. A tightly rolled length of barbed wire was unrolling itself in her stomach, slicing her insides to shreds.

In the hall, she could still hear the closet door being rammed from the inside and she wanted to run screaming from the house.

Krusadian stopped outside the bathroom between Jason's room and theirs. He opened the door and gestured for them to enter.

They did so without question.

Krusadian closed the door and locked them in without comment.

Richard sat on the edge of the bathtub, loudly grinding his teeth; anger was alive in his face now, like maggots beneath the decaying skin of a corpse's face.

"What the fuck did you do?" he growled.

"I-I-I didn't d-do *anything*, Richard! I . . . didn't do . . . anything."

He looked into her eyes and for a moment she thought he was going to hit her. Then he turned away, stood, and began to pace in the small space.

"Richard?" she whispered.

He said nothing.

"Richard?"

Impatiently: "*What?*"

Dani leaned over the toilet and threw up.

The bathroom seemed to grow much smaller as Dani and Richard waited for Dr. Krusadian to return.

Richard said nothing and, although she wanted to speak, just to break the funereal silence and cover the endless steady dripping of the sink's faucet, she said nothing, either.

With no clock in the bathroom, their stay was timeless

151

and Dani feared, after a while, that Krusadian might leave them there for the night.

Maybe he's left the house, she thought, realizing there were no sounds in the hall or from downstairs. Then the worst thought of all: *Maybe he's taken Jason with him.*

Richard sat on the tub's edge with his face in his hands, occasionally murmuring into his palms, but only to himself.

Sitting on the toilet, Dani watched him, willing him to look at her. She needed to be touched, held, reassured, but knew better than to expect those things from Richard in a time of crisis, or any *other* time. She could not remember what the touch of Richard's hands felt like; she was now only familiar with the pain of their blows.

There was a sound from their bedroom, muffled through the wall, and Dani lifted her head to listen. She recognized the rattle of the closet's louvered door being opened. Objects clattered, something thumped the wall.

"What's he doing?" she breathed, knowing she would be ignored. She stood, listened.

He left the bedroom and moved into the hall. Slowly.

Dani went to the door and cocked her head.

Dr. Krusadian was dragging something past the bathroom.

Unable to resist, she asked, "What are you doing?"

"With you in a moment," he replied, dragging . . . dragging . . .

Until he was gone.

A few minutes later, she returned to the toilet and waited, only to stand again when she heard the door being unlocked from the other side. It opened and Dr. Krusadian grinned at them.

He said, "Let's take a break."

19

In the kitchen, Dani put a mug of water in the microwave for tea as Richard drank a Coke silently at the table.

Hushed voices drifted from the living room where Dr. Krusadian was talking with Jason; he refused to let Dani or Richard see him until Krusadian had a word with Jason.

The rain sounded like battle outside.

The microwave beeped, Dani removed the mug and began dipping a tea bag in the steaming water.

"What the hell is *that?*" Richard asked, firmly but quietly, glaring across the kitchen.

Dani turned in the direction of his stare and the tea bag plopped into the mug.

There was a lock on the basement door. *Two* locks, she realized as she looked below the doorknob. They were padlocks, *enormous* brass padlocks twice the size of a man's fist, locked through hasps that had not been there earlier that evening.

Richard went to the door, jerked on the upper lock, and whispered, "Son of a bitch."

At his side, Dani touched the lock's perfectly smooth, cool surface. There was no brand name written on the lock, nothing to suggest it had been purchased in a hardware store. It was perfect and spotless, the biggest padlock she'd ever seen.

"Son of a *bitch!*" Richard repeated, louder, pounding the lock with a fist. "What the hell are these for? The *basement,* for Christ's sake."

"Remember, Richard, what he said about questions. No questions. Let's just leave it alone for now and get this over with."

"Yeah, for now. But I'm gonna sue him. Sue his black ass." He returned to the table and his Coke.

Dani looked down at the bottom lock and a glistening

153

wetness on the floor caught her eye. It was just a thin strip on the tile, flush with the door and disappearing through the crack beneath it. She hunkered down and gingerly touched it with two fingers.

Cold and slimy. Thick.

Just like the clear sheen of gelatinous fluid on the closet doorjamb in the bedroom.

Dani wiped her fingers on the cold floor, grimacing with disgust at the feel of the substance, about to point it out to Richard, when—something moved deep within the basement.

Something heavy and slow.

Something that made a sound like that of a person climbing out of a bathtub full of lard.

Dani felt her insides roll over and she stood, whimpering, "Richard? Rich—"

Dr. Krusadian entered the kitchen as Dani turned and her mouth shut so suddenly that her teeth clacked together.

"Jason will be here in a moment," he said. "He may seem lethargic, quite a little . . . *different*. Don't be alarmed. My method is swift and covers a lot of ground in a short time. It can be exhausting. One negative word from either of you will force me to have him removed from this home. Do you understand?" he asked, grinning.

Richard nodded.

Dani moved her head loosely, as if she had forgotten exactly how to nod.

"Good, then. You both look very tired. Not used to being held powerless and against your will in your own home, are you? Well. Think of what Jason has endured these past nine years. Perhaps you should put on some coffee, Mrs. Campbell." Over his shoulder, Dr. Krusadian called, "Come on in, Jason."

Jason shuffled into the kitchen in the middle of a jaw-cracking yawn. He smacked his lips and said, "Mom, can I have some chocolate milk?"

Dani knelt before him and touched his pale face, whispering. "Sure, sweetheart. How are you?"

His eyes darted to Dr. Krusadian and back. "Fine."

Looking up at the doctor, Dani ached to ask what he'd been doing with her son, but his narrowed eyes and cold razor-blade smile told her not to.

"Chocolate milk coming up," she said, going to the refrigerator.

Dr. Krusadian cleared his throat. "Excuse me while I use the facilities. Ehhh, the sooner that coffee is ready, Mr. Campbell, the better. We're all going to need it."

When he was gone, Dani knelt before Jason again and whispered. "Jason, listen to Mom. Does Dr. Krusadian scare you?"

He shook his head.

"Is he . . . well, what has he said to you? What has he done?"

"Talked. Just talked, is all. And played his music box."

"Mu . . . mu . . ." Her tongue froze. She thought of the golden cube on her dresser, the music it had played, the things she'd seen as she listened to it, and, worst of all, the thing in the closet.

Dani spun her head toward the basement door so quickly, her neck popped.

Light from the overhead fluorescents glittered reflectively in the strip of slime beneath the door. She noticed more of it streaked on the doorjamb just below the knob.

Demons . . .

The word passed through her mind like a ghost and Dani closed her eyes a moment, searching for it again. It was something Dr. Krusadian had said earlier that evening— although it now seemed days ago—one of his annoying melodramatic proclamations.

My job is to remove from Jason all of the demons which you have inflicted upon him.

Demons . . .

155

She opened her eyes again and looked at the substance on the floor.

Demons . . .

Something roiled up inside her; it was not quite guilt and not just fear, but a thick acidic mixture of both that bloated her stomach and gushed through her entire body until she could smell it clogging her nostrils.

"Richard," she hissed, rushing to the table, trying to ignore her sudden dizziness. "Richard, we have to get out of here!"

His heavy-lidded eyes rolled to her slowly and he mumbled, "Shut up, Danielle."

"But Richard, he's—"

"I *told* you, I'm gonna sue his goddamned—"

"*No*, we have to get out of here *now*. Before it's too late."

"Too late for what?" His voice was heavy with contempt and annoyance.

"I . . . I don't know, Richard." Dani fought back a sob; her trembling hands fluttered up and down his arm pleadingly. "I don't know yet, but I'm telling you he's doing something horrible, I'm telling you whatever was in the closet is—"

"How is that coffee coming, Mrs. Campbell?"

Dr. Krusadian put his black bag on the table, reached in and removed a small notebook and seated himself across from Richard, opening the book with a slight flourish of his arm. Taking a pen from his breast pocket, he began making notes, reading over the pages, and acting as if he were alone in the room.

Dani rose and got Jason's chocolate milk, unable to hold the carton or glass steady in her quaking hands.

Standing in the middle of it, Jason turned round eyes from Krusadian to his dad to Dani and back to the doctor again, the seat of his pajama bottoms sagging, the nails of his right hand scratching nervously over the scribbled inscriptions on his cast.

When Dani gave him the chocolate milk, he whispered, "Thank you, Mom," in a voice so soft and hollow that tears stung Dani's eyes and she reached out to embrace him, but he was drinking, eyes closed, head tilted back, and a part of her heart shriveled.

She hurriedly put some coffee on, then waited for Jason to finish his chocolate milk. When he went to the sink to rinse his glass, she glanced at Dr. Krusadian, saw that he was still involved with his notes, and leaned toward Jason's ear. "Come upstairs with Mommy, sweetheart," she whispered, slipping an arm around his shoulders and leading him out of the kitchen.

She'd made a decision; she would call Dr. Saunders and, if she reached him, would tell him she thought her family was in danger at Dr. Krusadian's hands, and if any harm came to them, she would see that the blame would fall on Dr. Saunders for forcing them to take the strange doctor into their home. She wanted Jason with her when she made the call; she'd also decided that she would not let him out of her sight until Dr. Krusadian was gone.

Before either Dani or Jason could step out of the kitchen, Dr. Krusadian said casually, "Jason stays with me at all times."

Dani turned to find that he hadn't even looked up from his notes. She said, "I . . . I was j-just going to—"

"At all times, Mrs. Campbell. You may go if you wish, but Jason does not leave my sight." He sounded distant, preoccupied with the notebook, then he looked at her and smiled. "Go on, Mrs. Campbell, it's all right. I'll let you know when it's time to go back to your room."

Dani couldn't let go of Jason; she looked down at him through her tears and saw, to her horror, that he was smiling at her."

"S'okay, Mom. I like Dr. Krusadian."

She pulled her hand away from him slowly, turning to Richard, who was staring blankly out the window at the stormy night, then Dani hurried from the kitchen and up the stairs.

In her bedroom, she looked up Dr. Saunders' number in the telephone directory, placed the call, and reached his answering service. After a few minutes of trying to impress the woman at the other end of the line that her call was urgent, Dani said, "Listen to me, please, this is not a medical emergency, it's *personal*, do you understand? If Dr. Saunders doesn't call me back immediately, he could be in a *lot* of trouble." She left her number, hung up, and sat on her bed, waiting.

The phone rang nearly ten minutes later and Dani picked up before the ring died.

"Hello?"

"Mrs. Campbell? Dr. Saunders."

"Oh, thank God. Dr. Saunders, please, you've got to help me, you've *got* to."

"What's wrong? Is it Jason?"

"No. Well, *yes*, in a way. It's actually, it's that man you sent over here, that horrible man, Dr. Krusadian. Dr. Saunders, he locked us in our *bedroom*! My husband and me, he locked us in our bedroom and just *left* us there for, Jesus, I don't know *how* long, but he was alone with Jason all that time, down in the living room, and he left his music box with us and, and—"

"Mrs. Campbell, please, hold on, just calm down, now. Okay? Just calm down."

Tears flowed freely and she sobbed loudly before she covered her mouth and took several long deep breaths. When she regained some composure, she said, "Yes. Okay. Yes."

"Now, Mrs. Campbell. What are you talking about?"

"Dr. *Krusadian*. He got here about . . . well, I don't know what time it is now, but he came at seven, so I guess he's been here for about—"

"Dr. *who*?"

Dani pressed the receiver to her ear so hard it made her

head ache. "Kru . . . *sadian*. The doctor you sent, the doctor you *made* us see."

"Well, Mrs. Campbell, you're certainly free to see another doctor regarding your son, but if you've done so, it hasn't been at *my* recommendation."

She couldn't find her voice for a moment. "What? *What?*"

"I don't know who you're referring to, Mrs. Campbell. I've never heard of the man."

"But . . . but you . . . you-you-you—"

"Sounds like maybe you need some rest, Mrs. Campbell. If you'd like, I could prescribe some—"

"Why are you doing this?" she sobbed.

"Um, Mrs. Campbell, I'm sorry, but . . . look, I don't really have time for—"

"You son of a bitch, why are you *doing* this? He's here now, in my *house*! With my *son*!"

Silence.

Then: "Goodbye, Mrs. Campbell."

Dr. Saunders hung up.

Screaming behind tightly clenched lips, Dani slammed the receiver into its cradle and lay on the bed sobbing for long minutes before she picked up the telephone again. She clumsily punched 9-1-1—

—but the dial tone would not go away.

Dr. Krusadian's voice bled through the endless hum: "No phone calls, Mrs. Campbell." He was speaking on the kitchen phone. "I'm leaving the telephone off the hook."

The dial tone went on and on and on . . .

Dani threw the receiver down and bolted from the room, descending the stairs in a staggering run, stumbling to a halt at the front door, no longer trying to hide her sobs. They echoed through the house with the thunder as she turned the doorknob.

Only after a moment of blindly throwing herself against the sturdy door did she see it.

A padlock.

An enormous shiny brass padlock . . .

20

Later—Jason had not idea how long—after his parents had been sent back to their room, Jason lost count of the times Dr. Krusadian started the globe spinning and played the music that never sounded the same twice. He lay on the sofa, the plaster cast heavy on his chest, and passed in and out of a heavy sleep each time the music stopped. Under Dr. Krusadian's gentle guidance, Jason relived incidents he'd tried so hard and so long to forget that when he experienced them again, it was like returning to an old forgotten nightmare that had disturbed his sleep long ago . . .

The time his dad made him sweep up a dish he'd dropped and broken in the kitchen, then beat him with the broom . . .

The Christmas Jason accidently broke an ornament on the tree and his dad stripped all the ornaments from the branches, cornered Jason in the living room and pelted him with the brightly colored bulbs, shattering them on his head and face and hands, inflicting small cuts that opened like new eyes and cried tears of blood . . .

The weekend his dad got *really* drunk, even drunker than usual, and decided Jason was being too pampered by his mother—"pussified," he called it—and spent all of Saturday and most of Sunday teaching Jason what it meant to be a man, getting drunker and drunker as he tried to make Jason cry; he pinched him and poked him and stuck him with pins, burnt him with cigarettes, plucked his eyelashes with tweezers, stomped on his feet and pulled his hair, and the moment Jason so much as allowed his lip to quiver, his dad beat him mercilessly, screaming, "This's what my pop did to *me* when I cried, and I'll be goddamned if I'm gonna do any different with you! Pussified, your mother's *pussified* you, and by Christ, I won't *have* it!" Jason was never able to stop crying that weekend and the tears lasted through the first part of the following week. The beatings stopped only because his dad finally got too drunk to stand up and make a fist . . .

There were others, *countless* others, and Dr. Krusadian gently led Jason through each one, touring his young past like a museum of pain and fear with exhibits that screamed, bled. And through it all, one image returned again and again: the sight of his mother cringing in the shadows or peering around a corner, looking, at first, as if she might step forward and scream for her husband to stop, might pull him off Jason and bring an end to the violence. But that look lasted only a moment and, each time, she retreated, backed away, disappeared silently to find a bottle and turn up the volume on the television set until the laughter and applause of a studio audience blanketed Jason's screams.

Always she was there, silent and watchful, looking numbed, then she was gone.

Always.

Except once . . .

"Can you hear me, Jason?"

"Mm-hm."

"Are you relaxed? Comfortable?"

"Mm-hm."

"Good. Now. I've noticed, Jason, that your mother is always *watching* when your father becomes violent. Is that right?"

"Al . . . ways."

"She never does anything else?"

He did not respond.

"Never?"

Still no reply.

"Tell me, Jason. Has your mother ever hurt you?"

Nothing.

"Ever?"

"Yes," he finally whispered, and the music began . . .

21

Dani no longer felt she was in her own home. It was a replica, a decoy meant to fool her, holding in its deceptively familiar shadows and corners the things of childhood nightmares.

When they returned to their room, Dani cautiously approached the closed closet and found that slimy substance on the doorjamb was gone.

"It was here," she muttered.

Richard sounded impatient and annoyed when he snapped, "What?"

"I swear to God, Richard, *something* was in this closet."

"You're still drunk."

"I'm *not*. Look, the carpet is still damp."

"Okay, so you threw up again. Jesus, Dani, will you give it a rest." The bed squeaked under his sudden weight and he groaned as he squeezed his head between his hands. "You said you called Saunders. What'd he say?"

"He denied it. Said he didn't *know* a Dr. Krusadian."

"What?"

She turned from the closet and faced him, hands fluttering. Her voice was a quiet midnight breeze, her sentences punctuated with quick breaths. "He's done this to us, Richard."

"Done what, Dani?" he sighed.

"Sent this man. This Krusadian. He's not a doctor, not really, I'm *sure* of it. I don't know *what* he is, but he's *not* a therapist, not like we thought. He's . . . wrong, Richard, there's something *wrong* with him, something *not right*, and he's come here to . . . to, yes, to punish us. Yes. That's it. He's come here to *punish* us, Richard."

"Punish us for *what*, for Christ's sake?"

"For what we've done all these years. For all the horrible things we've done . . . things I *haven't* done."

"Will you take a couple Valiums and shut—"

"There *are* no Valiums, Richard. There is no wine and no pot. Don't you see, there's *always* a Valium or a drink or a joint, but they're gone now. They've always been our answers to every problem and now they've been taken away from us. We're being *punished*."

Richard got to his feet, fists clenched, and growled through his teeth, "Goddammit, will you shut the fuck up. We're not being punished because we haven't done anything wrong. We're just like everybody else in this neighborhood, this town, this whole goddamned *country*. We've got problems, we have bad days, we fight, just like everybody else, you hear me? There's nothing *wrong* with us, we just had an accident that looked suspicious to one doctor, one miserable fucking doctor, and if he denies siccing this black bastard on us, I'll sue *his* ass, too, by Christ. So shut up. We're *not* being punished. There's nothing *wrong* with us." He paced as he spoke and, when he was finished, he sat heavily on the bed, breathing as if from a run, and spoke quietly to the floor. "I'll go into the city and get a really good lawyer. Top drawer. A Jew. Somebody who'll—"

"We're not going to sue anyone, Richard. Can't you see that we're *trapped* in this? Because we're guilty. We're dirty. Filthy." Tears rippled calmly and quietly down her face. She went to the dresser and leaned on it, staring down at the music box, afraid to touch it.

"Christ, Danielle, you talk about us like we're pornographers, or something! This . . . this is just insane! *You're* insane if you think we deserve to be—"

"You know it as well as I do, Richard. You most of all."

He clutched her shoulders and spun her around, spitting, "And what the fuck does *that* mean?"

"I let it go on. I watched. I said nothing, did nothing. Because I was afraid of what you would do to me. After you beat me that first time—"

163

His face twisted. "You lying bitch, I've never laid a hand on you and you know it, I've never so much as—"

"Stop!" she cried. "Please stop, Richard, it's making me sick, physically *ill*, this . . . this selective memory we've developed."

"I may have a temper, but—"

"No, Richard. You have more than a temper. I let it go on because I was afraid of you, so that makes me dirty, too. But you *did* it. You were the one who always *did* it, kicking him, hitting him, throwing him—" She stopped for an instant as a sob hit her in the midsection. "—throwing him around like a beanbag doll. The way you always—"

He was on her in an instant, fingers digging hard into her shoulders as he shook her back and forth, his face darkening with blood, eyes pushing from their sockets like a toad's, his mouth spraying her face with spittle as he roared, "That's bullshit, that is such *bullshit*, goddamn you, I was *not* always the one, was I, Dani, *was* I?" He slammed her back against the dresser, then quickly moved away from her, pacing, *"Was* I?"

She knew the answer, but she could not say the word . . .

22

"How old are you now, Jason?"

"Seven."

"And where are you?"

"My . . . room."

"Where are your parents?"

"Dad's in . . . his room . . . dressing, I think. Mom's in the . . . hall bathroom. They're . . . going out, I guess."

"Who will stay with you?"

"Probably Tracy. From down the street. Or Mrs. Royer."

Jason was silent a while, lying on the sofa, eyes half

open, but not seeing the living room ceiling, not really. He was, in his eyes, leaving his bedroom and going down the hall to the bathroom, where his mother was curling her hair. He stood in the doorway and watched her, unnoticed.

The phone rang and Jason heard his dad answer in the bedroom. Moments later, the curses began.

"Goddammit. Son of a *bitch*!"

Jason turned to hurry back to his room, but it was too late; his dad was coming down the hall, shirtless, a blue and red tie held in his fist.

"Forget it," he said angrily. "Just forget it. She can't come. Tracy can't come. Dammit." He pushed Jason aside and stepped into the bathroom. "She just called. No sitter. I'll call and cancel the reservations."

Jason ached when he saw the shattered disappointment on his mom's face.

"Can't we get someone else?" she asked hopefully.

"This late? *Who*, for Christ's sake?"

"But . . . but I've been looking forward to . . . you *promised* we'd—"

"Well, what the hell am *I* supposed to do? We're sure not gonna take him *with* us!" He spun and returned to the bedroom.

Jason stepped toward the doorway again but collided with his mom, who shoved him into the doorjamb and snapped, "Dammit, Jason, *get-out-of-the-way*!" Hurrying down the hall, she called, "April's gone tonight, but maybe Ken would watch him for us."

"Christ, Dani, he's not gonna want to—"

"Well, just let me call and ask."

Jason regained his balance, went into the bathroom, and stared at himself in the mirror as his parents shouted at one another.

"No," his mom said, "we *never* go out, we haven't been out in over a *year*, and now that we've actually made plans—"

"Well, don't bitch at *me* about it, *you're* the one who

wanted to have kids so bad, what the hell'd you think, they come *equipped* with babysitters?"

"Just let me call and ask Ken—"

"You're not calling to ask him anything."

When Jason heard his mom begin to cry, he decided to go back to his room and read a book, stay out of the way, but as he turned around, his arm caught on something—a cord—and when he pulled his arm back, his mom's curling iron slid away from the sink and fell to the floor.

Jason stared at it.

He knew he should pick it up, but Mom had always told him never *ever* to touch her curling iron and he was scared he'd make her angry.

So he stared, thinking about it, trying to decide what to do—

—as smoke began to curl upward from the blackening carpet.

The smell was awful and, terrified, certain of the punishment that would come, Jason bent down and picked up the curling iron, but—

—the smoke alarm in the hall began to scream and the noise so startled him that he dropped it again.

He was trembling now, quaking uncontrollably with fear, but he tried to pick it up again before too much damage was done and, as he bent down, he felt the presence of someone behind him as the smoke alarm wailed on.

When fists began to fall on his neck and back, Jason knew that it was his dad, knew that his mother would be standing in the hall, watching, her eyes dead, until she could take it no longer.

But he was wrong.

"Goddamn you! Goddamn you!" his mom screamed again and again, her fists pounding in turn with each syllable. "How many times? How many times have I told you not to touch it? How many times? Don't you know it's hot? It's *hot!*" She slammed him against the sink, clutched his wrist and pressed something into his hand, screaming, "Here, *Here!* Feel this? Feel it? Didn't I say it was hot?"

When Jason felt his skin melting, he began to scream, "No, Mommy, no, don't, *noooo—*"

"Why don't you do what you're told? All you do is make trouble! *Trouble!* All the screaming and crying—"

"doooon't, Mommyyy—"

"—because of *you!* Now we can't even go *out!* Because of *you!* Everything's turned to *shit—*"

"*noooo!*"

"—because of *you!*"

The alarm stopped.

His mom fell away from him, staring with disbelief at the now messy curling iron held in her fist, her knuckles as white as her face.

Jason could not get enough breath to cry out loud; he simply shook with muffled sobs as his mom began touching him, caressing his face as she cried, "What have I done? What have I done?"

And from the hall, there came a groaning, long and deep and tremulous.

"Oh, dear Jesus, what have I done? What have I done?" his mom sobbed as his dad stood moving oddly in the hall, blurred by Jason's tears.

Groaning . . . groaning . . .

Jason clutched the sofa cushions beneath him, grinding his teeth.

"Relax, Jason," Dr. Krusadian whispered as the thing that now hunkered beside him shifted its gelatinous bulk. "Just relax. Take deep breaths."

Jason did, took them in deep and let them out slowly, gradually relaxing, feeling his body sink into the cushions.

Dr. Krusadian stood and gathered the tarpaulin together. As he began to drag it, full and heavy and shifting, from the room, Jason spoke.

"What's that?"

Dr. Krusadian stopped, smiled, and replied, "Something for your parents."

23

As Jason lay on the sofa reliving the relentless punishments of his seventh and eighth years, working his way to the previous night's fall down the stairs, the shouting upstairs continued without pause. They had been shouting in long uninterrupted circles, and by the time Jason had forgotten all about his mom's curling iron and was into the next torment, they had come around to the beginning again.

"It only happened once," Dani gasped, "and I hated myself for it, I *still* hate myself. I've never done it again and you know it, but I've let *you* do it and that's just as bad. You do it constantly. Every day, sometimes. You don't have a *temper*, Richard." She spat the word "temper" through a burst of bitter, hateful laughter. "You have a *prob*-lem, Richard."

Veins stood out on Richard's neck and his hands opened and closed over the pockets of his tan chinos; his lips tore back over his teeth, then bunched into a rectum-like hole through which he puffed bursts of air as he slowly advanced toward her a step at a time.

"You're *sick*, Richard," Dani went on, not caring that his anger was stretched over his face like thin transparent plastic, transparent but disfiguring and suffocating. "You're sick and you *know* it, and that just makes you worse, doesn't it? Knowing that you're so *sick*, that you're such a *monster*."

He was closer, actually tearing his pockets from his pants now with fingers hooked into claws.

"Know that you *enjoy* beating up on children and women. That you actually *get off* on—"

He struck. His arm whipped through the air and his palm connected with her face with the sound of cracking ice.

"That's bullshit!" he hissed, cheeks quivering as they deepened in color. He repeated "bullshit" again and again, striking her each time, driving her backward until she fell against the dresser. The back of her head cracked the mirror and shards of reflective glass rained over her, dancing together musically like blood-speckled wind chimes. He dragged her away from the dresser by her hair and threw her to the floor, then swept his arm through the perfume bottles and powder puffs and lipsticks and jewelry, sending it all to the floor with her in a clatter of plastic and glass. A dozen different perfumes mingled and rose in an eye-watering cloud, filling the room with flowers and spices and sexual promise. Richard stood over her and dropped to his knees, straddling her chest. He began to beat her shoulders and face and head, spitting "*Bull*shit! *Bull*shit! *Bull*shit! Nothing's wrong! There's *nothing* wrong, goddammit, nothing's *wrong!*"

Dani tried to scream for help, certain that Dr. Krusadian, however sinister he might be, would not allow this to go on while he was in the house, but the fists were coming too fast and hitting too hard and she was afraid she would lose consciousness soon and—

—then she felt it. Against her. Pressing between her breasts.

Through the thunder in her skull, Dani heard the music box begin to play. It had fallen from the dresser to the floor with all the other things and lay beside her head, so close that she could hear its insides moving again, coming to life, turning slowly with soft clicks and whispers and—

—Richard struck her cheek and her head snapped to one side and her eyes, swelling and blurred, locked onto the box and held and she saw it, Dani saw—

—that horrible *thing*.

She'd seen it so many times before and each time she dragged it from the center of her attention like some bloated, incriminating corpse, and she'd buried it, hidden it away in one of the many secret compartments of her

169

memory, compartments she kept locked and covered so no one—including Dani herself—would notice them.

She'd seen it and ignored it.

That horrible thing.

And she saw for the first time once again. And the second and the third, countless times, on and on through the nine years they'd had Jason. She saw it pressing and throbbing against the wall of its small prison, trying to expose its one glistening eye so it could watch, first hand, the pain and violence that inflamed and excited it so. The images rushed through her mind with painful dizzying velocity, sickening her, inflating her with such hatred for herself that she felt she would burst and then—

—they were gone.

And she was left with only one.

Richard had stopped shouting, had even stopped beating her, but he was still on her.

Groaning.

Moving against her.

Pressing his sickness between her breasts.

He pulled one bloodied hand away from her face and placed it over the bulge between his legs, smearing his crotch with her blood and squeezing his erection, letting his head flop back, mouth gaping to make way for the dreadful groan that slithered up from deep in his chest and rose to become a trembling cry as his hips began to convulse on her and a dark wet spot appeared over the bulge and spread slowly like a soggy cancer as his back stiffened and he gulped air and sputtered, "Nuh-nothing's wruh-wrong! Nuh-nuh-nothing's *wrong!*"

Richard's body quaked for several seconds, then calmed to a brief shiver, and finally became still as he stared forever at the ceiling without even taking a breath. Then he lowered his head and blinked his wide confused eyes, looking at Dani, then his hands, then his soiled pants. His hands trembled as he dragged himself off Dani and crawled on all fours over broken glass to the bed against which he leaned as he sat and stared at his hands. They were imbedded now with tiny shards and slivers, but he didn't seem to notice; he dropped them in his lap, gasping suddenly for breath as he whispered, "There's . . . nothing wrong . . . is there? *Is* there? Please. There's nothing . . . wrong . . ."

"Yes there is," she said, spitting blood. "And I'm going to fix it."

A clatter at the door signaled Dr. Krusadian's entrance.

He stepped into the bedroom and, silently and without expression, surveyed the mess. He went to Dani's side, bent down and retrieved the music box, then studied the two of them closely before saying, "My work with Jason is finished. It is your turn now. Please clean yourselves up and come downstairs."

24

Jason sat up slowly on the sofa, feeling as if he'd taken a long nap filled with muddled dreams. He looked around the darkened living room and recognized Dr. Krusadian's bags beside the recliner. But there should be something else . . . the music box and tarpaulin; they were gone. He was alone and the only sound was the rain falling outside. When he tried to stand, Jason felt very dizzy and wondered why; he'd been doing nothing more than lying on the sofa talking with Dr. Krusadian and listening to the music box.

Hadn't he?

Jason tried to think back over the past few hours but could come up with nothing clear or solid. Just music. Beautiful, restful music. He couldn't even remember where his parents had gone.

There were voices upstairs, so he wasn't alone in the house, but that didn't quell the fear growing inside him, brought on by his confusion and disorientation.

"Mom?" he called, quietly the first time, then again, louder and with urgency.

"What, sweety?" she cried, her footsteps thumping down the hall. "What's wrong? I'm coming! It's all right!" She hobbled down the stairs, clinging to the banister with both hands, and knelt before him.

In the shadows, she was an obscene clown; one blackened eye was swollen into a ghastly lingering wink and blood smeared her pale face like dark red greasepaint.

"What is it, honey?" she whispered, clutching his small knees.

He was inclined, at first, to ask about her face, but didn't because he knew she would lie and he already knew the truth, anyway.

"I was . . . scared, is all."

"There's nothing to be scared of, baby. Not now. Not anymore. I promise." She leaned forward and embraced him, pressing her bloody face to his chest and crying softly. "Your mom's not gonna let anything happen to you anymore."

Voices shouted upstairs; Jason recognized Dr. Krusadian's rising like flames to the very top of the house. He sounded much the way Jason had always imagined God to sound.

"Is Dr. Krusadian angry?" Jason whispered. "Did . . . did I do something wrong?"

"No, honey, nobody's angry at you. You haven't done a *thing*."

The shouting stopped. Dr. Krusadian came down the stairs, turned on the lights, and put something in his black bag.

Jason watched his dad descend to the living room one heavy step at a time, shoulders wilted, head sagging forward. He was wearing different pants.

Jason squinted at the sudden light and rubbed his eyes.

Dr. Krusadian said, "Mr. and Mrs. Campbell, if you would come with me to the kitchen, please."

Jason opened his eyes when his mom pulled away from him and said, "I'd like to talk to you, Dr. Krusadian."

172

"We will talk."

"Alone," she whispered, glancing at her husband. "Please."

"In the kitchen, Mrs. Campbell." He took a step backward and gestured with his arm. "After you."

Jason watched his parents go, his dad first, his mom following reluctantly. She stopped in front of the doctor and whispered, "Look, whatever you've done—"

"The kitchen, Mrs. Campbell."

"—I've decided this has got to stop and I'm going to take Jason out of here. Tonight. Now. He . . . my husband . . . is sick. I can't let it go on anymore. I'm getting out."

"That's very noble of you, but out of the question for two reasons. It won't solve the problem, first of all. And secondly—" He grinned. "—I'm not through with you yet. Now, Mrs. Campbell. After you."

Dr. Krusadian turned to Jason, gave him a wink, and followed them into the kitchen.

When they were out of sight, Jason stood, crept to the kitchen entrance, leaned his back against the wall, and listened.

25

"Please sit down," Dr. Krusadian said, seating himself at the table.

Reluctantly, Dani pulled up a chair but she did not want to sit down; she wanted to take the doctor aside and explain that she had finally, after so many years, come to her senses and wanted to take Jason away from the house immediately. She had no idea where she would go or how she would support herself and her son, but she'd decided upstairs, only a few minutes before, that poverty—even *homelessness*— would be preferable to living on in the nightmare her family had become.

Along with that, she was afraid—*terrified*—of what Dr. Krusadian was going to do.

"It is time, Mr. and Mrs. Campbell, to face what you have done to your boy."

"Dr. Krusadian," Dani said, "if you'll just listen to me for a—"

"There will be plenty of time for listening afterward."

Dani flinched. "After . . . ward? After what?"

He simply looked at her with a gentle smile.

Richard sat at the table with his face in his hands, looking at neither of them. He jerked to attention when Dr. Krusadian spoke to him.

"I'm curious, Mr. Campbell. Can you explain this? Your wife's face? The cuts and bruises?"

No reply.

"Teaching her a lesson, were you?"

"We . . . had . . . an argument. That's all." His hands trembled noisily against the tabletop.

"Ah, an argument. You enjoy them, don't you? These arguments."

"It was just an argument. *Everybody* has arguments."

"Then you don't think this is a problem?"

Richard steeled himself, stopped the trembling, and leveled an icy glare at the doctor.

"Only because you're *making* it a problem. We were fine. Before."

"We were *not* fine," Dani hissed. "We've *never* been fine."

Dr. Krusadian asked, "When was the last time you two had sex? Together?"

They turned to him, but neither spoke.

"I say *together* because it's quite obvious that Mr. Campbell has been sexually active for some time on his own. Not what *most* would think of as sex, but it's sex to you, isn't it?" He turned to Richard, still wearing that smile. "You drink heavily, so I would imagine you're

174

impotent. Alcohol does that, you know. But you have found something *else*. Haven't you?"

Richard's face turned crimson, twisted painfully, and he turned away.

"And you," Krusadian went on, looking at Dani, "have closed your eyes to it all. Even joined in the fun."

"Wait, wait just a sec—"

"Do you still use a curling iron, Mrs. Campbell?"

She gasped and, seconds later, tears followed.

"I know what I've done," she sobbed. "At least I *admit* it! And I'm going to *stop!* Right now. Please. Let me go. I'll take Jason. I'll never let him near Richard again. I'll—"

"Like *hell* you will," Richard growled.

Dr. Krusadian lifted a hand. "Please. Let's not do this. Now, I believe, Mrs. Campbell, that you are *aware* of what you've done. I think both of you are, although one of you won't admit it. But I don't think either of you truly *knows* what you've done." He pushed his chair back and stood, taking a key from his pocket. "Do you remember what I said earlier about removing the demons you have inflicted upon your son?"

Dani wanted to scream. She had never in her life wanted so desperately to empty her lungs into the air and run as fast and far as she could.

"Dr. Krusadian, puh-puh-please . . ."

He ignored her. "Well, I have done that. Even from you, Mrs. Campbell. You had a demon of your own that needed release."

"Please, duh-doctor, I-I-I don't . . . want to . . . duh-do this . . ."

"But you, Mr. Campbell, are a rock."

Richard did not even look at him.

"You refuse to let go of whatever monsters you have locked inside. And I *know* you have them. Your life, I suspect, has been a tragic one. Your father was a hard, cruel man, am I right?"

Richard's teeth crunched together dryly and tears sparkled in his eyes, unfallen.

"Your childhood was violent and cold. Did your mother look away, too? I suspect. Surely there had to be one moment in your life—one isolated redeeming moment—when you vowed that *your* children would never have to endure such cruelty. Hm?"

Richard clenched and released his fists between his knees again and again.

"I suspect. But you let it pass unheeded. Instead, you went on to kick and beat your son through the same hell from which you'd come, denying it all the while. In fact, you've wallowed in denial. For the past several hours, you've had the opportunity to break, to cleanse yourself, but even *now* you remain unmovable. That is unfortunate, Mr. Campbell. For your family . . . and you."

Dr. Krusadian went to the basement door and slipped his key into the upper padlock, releasing it with a loud, solid . . . *clitch*. He unlocked the lower one and placed them both on the table, then faced them and said, "Come. I've something to show you."

Dani felt herself coming unraveled. She stood, but her knees threatened collapse, making her wobble rather than walk backward away from the door.

"Please," she whimpered, finding little voice in her throat, "don't do this. I said I was sorry. I said I would stop. *Please*."

"Not now. It's too late. Being sorry isn't enough," Dr. Krusadian said, offering his hand, "until you know precisely what you are sorry *for*. Come. I'll hold your hand. It will be all right. I promise. You, too, Mr. Campbell. What have you to lose? If you are so certain there is no problem, you have no worries. Do you?"

Richard looked around, blinking, as if coming awake, and sat up straight. Something dawned in his face as he turned to Dani. He seemed to be considering the possibility that her talk of punishment earlier had not been the ramblings of a drunk.

"Dr. Krusadian," Dani whispered, *"please* let me go. I-I'm sorry for what I've duh-done and I swear I'll make it all up to Jason, but please for Christ's sake let me—"

"Enough!" the doctor roared, then said with quiet threat, "if you do not comply, your son will be taken from you and all of this will be made public. If that appeals to you, then so be it. If not . . . then come let me show you something."

Dani watched the familiar anger creep into Richard's face, even into his posture. He stood, took a deep breath, and swallowed his fear.

"All right. You son of a bitch, all right," he whispered. "Come on, Dani, let's get this over with."

"No. No. Please."

"Goddammit, Dani, come on. How bad can it be, for Christ's sake? It's *our* basement."

Dr. Krusadian nodded, smiling, and said, "That is precisely the attitude I expected from you, Mr. Campbell. Now come." He pulled the door open and said, "After you."

Light from the kitchen spilled halfway down the narrow wooden staircase, halting at a wall of darkness.

"Dani," Richard summoned.

"No."

"Dammit—" He grabbed her wrist and pulled her hard toward the open door. "—come *on.*"

Dani shriveled up inside as he jerked her through the door, their feet clattering on the steps.

"Wait," she hissed, "wait, the *light*, it's dark, please get the li—"

The door slammed shut behind them.

The upper lock fell into place heavily and clicked.

Then the lower lock.

Blackness.

Dani screamed.

When he heard his mom's muffled scream, Jason hurried into the kitchen, frightened.

"Wassamatter?"

Dr. Krusadian held up his palms in reassurance and said, "Nothing to worry about, Jason."

"But I heard Mom—" He stopped and looked around the kitchen. "Where are they?"

"They are in the basement."

"The basement? Why?"

Dr. Krusadian gently covered Jason's back with one hand and led him from the kitchen. "Come to the living room and I'll set up my camera, Jason. I want to take your picture. And don't worry about your parents. They will be fine, just fine. They have a lot of thinking to do. And when they have have finished, things will be much different in this house." He patted Jason's back. "And much better."

Jason left the kitchen with Dr. Krusadian and the fearful shouting voices of his parents faded behind him.

26

Dani flipped the light switch up and down a dozen times in rapid-fire succession, sobbing uncontrollably, before she allowed herself to entertain the possibility that the light was not going to come on.

Richard's fists thundered uselessly against the door as he bellowed, "Open this fucking door, goddamn you, *open* it! This is kidnapping! I'll send you to prison for the rest of your fucking life, you son of a bitch!"

Pushing herself close to Richard, Dani clutched his arm and shook her whole body convulsively as if to toss the clinging darkness away from her.

"Get us out, Richard, please, you've gotta get us *out* of here!

"Stop it, for Christ's sake."

"Don't you see why he put us down here? I tried to tell you he—"

Something moved down in the dark.

It was a wet sound. Bare feet stomping through a sewer. A silent baby crawling through pudding.

It was coming toward the stairs.

"Oh, Guh-Guh-God," Dani breathed, then began pounding on the door, too, her elbow clubbing Richard's shoulder with each blow.

He ordered her to stop, but some of the fierceness had left his voice.

"The hell was that?" he muttered after a moment of still listening.

"That thing—I tried to *tell* you, Richard—that *thing!*"

It moved again.

Closer.

Richard took two steps down the stairs and Dani grabbed his shoulders, pulling him back and crying, "No, no, don't go down there, Richard, don't—"

He shook her off and snapped, "Will you leave me *alone?*" Two more steps.

Dani dug her fingernails into her palms and sucked her lips between her teeth, holding her breath.

"Who's there?" Richard shouted.

Silence.

Both were motionless for a moment and Dani found herself praying silently for the first time since she was a girl, when her grandmother told her again and again that Jesus was always waiting to help her whenever she needed him. Then Richard made a frustrated sound in his throat and muttered, "There's a flashlight here, somewhere."

She remembered the long black flashlight hanging from a hook on the wall over the stairs; Richard had hung it there years ago after the first time a fuse blew and he had to find his way down to the breaker box in total darkness. The thought of being able to see whatever was slopping around below made her insides wither and, when she heard his hand whispering over the wall in search of the flashlight, she reached out for him, groping until she found the top of his head.

"No, Richard, please."

He brushed her away, found the flashlight, and clicked it on.

The beam sliced through darkness and fell on the cement floor below, passing over boxes and bags and a few pieces of old dusty furniture. But beyond the bar of light, the darkness remained, heavy and fat.

"What's he done?" Richard whispered, sounding interested, perhaps even fascinated by the doctor's cleverness, then called, "Who's there?"

Dani clutched her own hair when he started down the stairs, unable to speak or even breathe.

Richard stopped, looked over his shoulder and said, "Well? Come *on*."

"Richard, please, don't make me—"

His face stopped her; it curled into that mask of threat that had held her prisoner for so long.

"If you don't come down here right now," he said, so quietly she barely heard, "I'm gonna come up there and *drag* you down here by your *hair*."

With her eyes only, she followed the beam of light downward again; she saw nothing, but she knew—as she knew the sun was coming up soon—that something awaited them down there, silent and with purpose.

"I-I-I'll just stay up here, Richard, really, I'm—"

"Get down here!"

Wiping a tear from her unswollen eye, Dani leaned heavily against the wooden handrail; she lowered her foot to the next step as if she were lowering it into boiling water. Then the next step . . . and the next . . . Then, under her feet, she felt something slick and sticky. She stopped, looked down at the step and, in the poor light, she saw a glistening strip of thick fluid that went all the way down the stairs, like the trail of a slug.

A very big slug.

With a dry, hoarse voice, she whispered, "Richard?"

Something slashed in a far corner of the basement and a

stack of boxes toppled over. One box spilled Christmas ornaments and a bundle of sparkling red and green garland over the concrete floor; some of the ornaments shattered and tossed freckles of reflected light over the walls.

Richard hurried toward the corner muttering, "What the hell?" and kicked two boxes aside, searching for the cause of the disturbance.

Dani quickened her pace down the stairs, reached the floor and called, "Richard, I don't think you should do that."

He spun to her, holding the flashlight down at his side so it spilled a puddle of light around his feet, and barked, "Well, what the hell do you *want* me to—"

Something rose quickly in the shadows behind him— something that looked like a hill of pus—then fell forward, wrapping itself around the lower half of his body.

Richard dropped the flashlight and groped the air as he fell forward, sputtering helplessly.

The light flickered as it rolled over the floor, finally holding on the thing that was engulfing Richard. It sloshed forward up his body, stopped, opened a black cavernous maw, then closed it with another quivering forward motion, like a snake devouring a kicking rat. One glaring eye bulged atop the creature, black, dead, and unblinking, like a shark's; another was positioned lower and to the side.

Dani stumbled backward, groping for the handrail, trying to scream, but unable to take in a breath; her lungs had turned to stone.

The glistening shapeless mass bloated with each gulp until only Richard's arms, shoulders, and head were visible. His mouth opened and closed, his hands clawed the concrete, and when his helpless eyes finally met Dani's, he screamed like a child.

"*Help meeee!*"

Her heel caught the bottom step and she fell back on the stairs and began scrabbling backward up the steps because—

—the boxes in the corner were being pushed aside, scraping harshly over the floor, to make room for another, this one black, like a great clot of cancer dragging a tail of cheerful Christmas-tree garland.

"Dani! For Chri—Dan—elp meeee!"

His arms waved and repeatedly slapped the floor until his hands left bloody smears on the concrete—

—until his arms had been swallowed up—

—until his head was gone.

But she could still hear him.

That was the worst of it—so far, anyway—hearing his muffled screams gargling from inside the creature as it bulged and constricted.

Finally discovering her breath again, Dani screamed, and once she started, she couldn't stop. The shrill cries came again and again like unmanageable sobs convulsing her lungs, and she kept crawling backward up the stairs as—

"—the creature that had swallowed Richard began to . . . *shrink*. The viscous snot-like mass began to take on a shape. *Richard's* shape. Even in her panic, Dani could make out the form of Richard's arm reaching upward inside the creature as it tightened around him, clinging to his body. She saw the curve of his shoulder, the lump that was his head, and the round indentation of his screaming mouth. The black eyes began to dissolve, run down the creature's sides like blood, and finally disappear as its size continued to decrease and Richard's body became more and more visible, writhing and groping for escape.

His clogged scream stopped.

Skin and tattered clothes became visible as the creamy slime began to disappear, as if evaporating.

Dani's back slammed against the locked basement door as Richard lay on his back down below, the middle of his body thrusting upward again and again, back arched, hands clawed; he stared blindly at the darkness above him, mouth yawning in a silent scream.

"Richard? Ri-*Richard?*" Her voice was raw meat and her

fingernails were breaking loudly as she clawed the door behind her, trying to pull herself up.

With great effort, he rolled on his side toward her, the flashlight inches from his face, which was a deadly shade of gray and trying so hard to speak. He made only a rasping sound in his throat as he reached out a hand to her; his soggy, tattered shirtsleeve dangled in strips from his arm and his fingers quivered as they closed over nothing as—

—the creature behind him drew nearer, slopping over the concrete as lumps rose from its black gelatinous surface and—

—the lumps took the shapes of hands with four fingers and a thumb each and—

—the hands closed into powerful fists that lifted and poised to strike as the thing closed the space between itself and Richard.

"Get *up*, get *up*, Richard, for Christ's *sake*, get *up!*"

But he didn't seem to hear her, only kept reaching out, mouth twisting, throat squeezing out small pathetic sounds, eyes rolling in his head like loose marbles.

When the thing poured itself over Richard's feet and began to make its way up his legs, he turned toward it, sucked in a loud breath that sounded like metal shavings filling his lungs, and found his voice in a long, bone-scraping cry as—

—the darkness in the basement began to come alive with them and they moved forward slowly, wetly, different sizes, different shapes, but all moving in with steady, confident determination and—

—Dani's hand found the doorknob and clutched it, pulling until she was on her knees, turning toward the door and pounding desperately, pleading.

Pleading . . .

They were screaming in the Campbell house again. But unless one listened very closely for them, the screams could not be heard from outside. They came from below. Had anyone heard, he or she would have known things were more unright than usual with the Campbells because these were not the screams with which the neighbors had become familiar.

But only Jason heard them.

He was in the living room with Dr. Krusadian, who had just finished setting up a camera on a tripod when the screams became words.

"I'm sorry!" Jason's mom cried. "I'm so sorry! I won't do it anymore, I *won't*, I *promise!*"

Jason froze and listened. At first, he'd thought it was just another fight between his parents, but now he knew better.

"Jason? *Jason!* Please help your mommy. *Please!* We'll go away! We'll go away and you'll never be hurt again, I *promise!* Don't let them get me, Jason, *please don't let them get meeee!*"

He turned to Dr. Krusadian, a chill working its way over his body, and asked, "What's the matter with Mom?"

"Don't worry about it, Jason. Trust me. Now, I'd like to get a picture to remember you by."

"Jason, I *love* you! Your mommy *loves* you! Plee-hee-*heeeze*, Jesus, get me out of here before, Oh Jesus *Christ*, before they get me, *please!*"

He turned to the doctor with terrified eyes and whispered, "What's down there?"

Dr. Krusadian studied Jason's face as he spent a silent moment with his thoughts, then knelt down beside the boy and put an arm around his small shoulders, pressing his mouth close to Jason's ear.

"Listen to me carefully, Jason. You must promise you will listen carefully."

Jason nodded.

"Think back over the years, over your life. Have you been happy? Have you ever been truly happy?"

No reply.

"Listen to your mommy, Jason, *listen* to me! I'll take you

away from him and he'll never hit you again, never, I promise, just *get me out of here!*"

"You are smiling in none of the pictures," Dr. Krusadian went on. "You don't *look* happy. I don't think you've ever been. Have you?"

A slight shake of his head.

Screams—such terrified, desperate screams—drifted in from the kitchen like foul smells on the air.

"There have been times you've *wanted* to be happy, haven't there?" Dr. Krusadian asked. "Times when others around you were happy and enjoying themselves. But you could not. Because there was something inside you . . . something fat and suffocating that would not *let* you feel happiness. Am I right?"

Another tentative nod.

"Open this door, Jason, *right now!* You open this goddamned door for your mother or so help me God . . . Oh Jesus, they're coming, they're *coming!* Jason, they're *coming!*"

The doctor gave him a gentle squeeze. "Well, Jason, that is gone. That thing inside you that kept you from being happy? I've taken it away. All this evening I've been taking it away a piece at a time. So you can be happy. Because I've taken it away. And I've given it to the people who put it there. I've given it to your parents."

"*Ja*-son! *Ja*-son! *Jaaaaa*-soooon!*"

"But," Jason whispered, "will . . . will they be okay? Will they be hurt?"

"They will be fine. Later. Things will be different. But they will be fine. Trust me."

Jason thought about that a while as the screams went on, growing into lung-bursting wails, then diminishing into raspy sobs. He thought about it and the frown on his brow slowly relaxed.

Dr. Krusadian stood and said, "Now. Come." He adjusted something on the camera and led Jason to the hearth, where he put his arm around the boy's shoulders. "Let's take a picture. Ready?"

He stood beside the enormous black man, expressionless and silent, still thinking about what he'd said. Then . . . slowly . . . Jason did something he hadn't done in a very long time.

With a click and a flash, it was recorded forever.

Dani wore her voice down to a hoarse croak as she pounded on the door, begging to be let out. The sounds coming from below were making her ill and she didn't want to look down the stairs, but when she felt she could scream no more, she looked over her shoulder against her better judgment and knew she was seeing her fate.

Richard was struggling in the grasp of the black creature that glistened like a big rotten peeled grape; the glutinous fists that protruded from it battered him relentlessly as it sucked him in, kicking and screaming Dani's name until her name was no more than a nonsense sound. And after it had devoured him whole, it, too, began to disappear around him like filthy water being sucked down a drain, until it left him lying alone on the floor, a sloppy quivering mess, naked now except for the gobs of fatty slime that clung to his body, as the others closed in. But before they reached him, Richard craned his head back until he was looking at her, his face upside down, hand reaching out again, lips battling with one another to form words as his body convulsed.

He hissed, "They're . . . inside me . . . now, Dani . . . puh-please . . ."

Then another was on him, this one purple as if engorged with blood, a long thick penis—tumorous and dripping fluids—jutting from its front, its throbbing head directed between Richard's trembling legs. He screamed again as it spilled itself over him, but his voice was losing its strength.

As Richard disappeared beneath it, Dani turned away, trying to pound on the door again, but was unable to clench a fist.

"I'm sorry," she rasped. "I'm sorry, I'm . . . so . . . sorry . . ."

Richard's weary screams were muffled, then swallowed, replaced by moist slurping sounds, then—

—silence.

A long silence.

Too long.

Her lungs clogged with dread, Dani turned her head slowly to look down the stairs again. Richard lay on the floor, the flashlight draping half his body in shadow, as another creature moved toward him silently, this one covered with long thin protuberances the size and shape of cigarettes, each with a glowing red ember at the end. It headed for him like an impossibly slow, malformed heat-seeking missile.

But there were three others, and they moved around Richard—

—coming toward the stairs.

With clumsy jerky movements, Dani turned her body toward them, pressing her back hard to the door and hugging her knees to her breasts. She ignored the others moving in the shadows at the far end of the basement as the three she watched oozed by Richard and into the glow of the flashlight. One came ahead of the others, the color of dead flesh, its bulk shifting this way and that as a hand—or the *shape* of a hand—reached out between the two bulbous eyes. Something grew out of the hand, something long and narrow, a familiar shape, with a long clamp running down one side. The clamp opened and closed as the fist squeezed the object's handle.

A curling iron.

The others advanced slightly behind, covered with eyes—*human* eyes—that were gouged and running with blood.

Blinded eyes.

Dani wanted to scream but didn't have the strength and saw no point to it anyway.

The creatures stopped at the bottom of the stairs. Waiting.

The most wonderful thought occurred to her then, as Richard began to stir again, surrounded by slime-fisted creatures with unfeeling eyes, his body clothed in slime. The thought made her so happy, so excited and hopeful, that she stood and grabbed the doorknob behind her, rattling the door as hard as she could.

"They can't come up the stairs," she muttered, then screamed it, pounding on the door again, her back to them, glancing over her shoulder every few seconds as she begged again for help—"They can't come up the stairs! Help me! They can't come up the stairs!"—until—

—the creature holding the curling iron out before it like a sword split open. Its enormous mouth gaped until it was a great black hole at the bottom of the stairs and Dani thought if she fell in she might never reach bottom. She stopped pounding, turned, and—

—a thick rope of slime shot from the mouth and up the stairs in a heartbeat, slapping around her ankle and pulling. Hard.

The world lurched and Dani found herself airborne, looking up at her feet until she hit the stairs and was bathed in sharp stabbing pain as the thing dragged her down over the hard wooden steps, closer and closer to the gaping cavern of a mouth that waited below, until she was plunged into the moist stale blackness and it closed around her and then—

—eternity began.

It was the first of three.

Jason stood in the kitchen doorway watching Dr. Krusadian. The big man stood at the rear of the kitchen, his ear inclined toward the basement door. The screaming downstairs had stopped some time ago, but the doctor listened carefully to the silence. Then he turned to Jason, stood straight and smiled, saying, "My work here is over." Jason followed him into the living room, where Dr. Krusadian picked up his bags and carried them to the front door.

"You're *leaving?*"

"I'm finished." He put his bags down, put on his coat and hat, and faced Jason. "When your parents come up later, they will be . . . groggy. A little confused, perhaps. And quite messy. Pay them no mind. They will clean up, get some sleep, and be fine. Wait for them in your room. And don't go into the basement. Jason, my friend—" He held out his hand and they shook. "—it has been a pleasure. I'm happy to know you."

"But . . . will I see you again? Can I call you? I mean, if I ever need you again?"

"You won't."

He touched Jason's head gently, then left.

27

Jason awoke on the sofa to the light coming from outside. He went to the window and watched the sun climbing into a cloudless sky. The storm was over.

A sound from the kitchen startled him and he spun around, watching the doorway anxiously. He heard their voices first as they came out of the basement.

"What time is it?" his mom mumbled.

Someone stumbled.

"Richard? Are you all right?"

"I'm . . . yeah, I'm . . . I think I'm . . . gonna be sick."

"Where's Jason? *Jason?*"

"Yeah, Mom?"

"Are you okay?"

He started toward the kitchen, calling, "Yeah, I'm okay."

"Don't come in here!" she blurted weakly, but firmly. "Just . . . why don't you just . . . go upstairs for a while. 'Kay?"

"Yeah. Sure, Mom."

But he didn't. As they continued muttering to one another, Jason crept to the kitchen doorway hoping to peer around the doorjamb without being caught. Then he heard a sound that he couldn't at first identify; it was like a wet, ragged cough.

No, not a cough. A sob.

His dad was crying.

"Richard," his mom soothed, "Richard . . . c'mon, Richard . . ."

Jason no longer wanted to look. He hurried upstairs to his room.

Dani stared at Richard, horrified and weakened by the sight of him. Naked and shivering, his body dripping slime, he appeared, for the first time she could remember, cowed and broken. He leaned heavily on the table, shoulders hitching as he cried quietly and fought to hold down his gorge. Beneath the dark wet streaks that striped his head, Richard's brown hair was completely white.

"My God, Richard," Dani breathed, "look at you. Did . . . did that really happen? What did he do to us?"

"Stupid question, Dani," he muttered, padding across the kitchen. "Stupid question." He leaned forward and vomited into the sink.

When she heard Jason's bedroom door close, Dani left the kitchen and carefully scaled the stairs, her body aching from head to foot. More than anything she wanted a hot shower, then crisp sheets and a long dreamless sleep. But as she trudged through her bedroom and into the bathroom on watery knees, she had a feeling there would be no more dreamless sleeps.

The rectangular mirror over the sink, framed by strips of glaring white lightbulbs, was unmercifully cruel. She stared at the stranger trapped in the flat glass and wanted to cry, but was too exhausted to shed any more tears.

The substance clinging to her made her look old and

190

lumpy. Lumpier than usual. Clots of it dribbled from her breasts, down her belly and over her face, and a string of it dangled from her chin.

And her hair . . .

Mingling with the honey blond were broad streaks of white. Old-lady white. Aged, decaying white.

She watched the reflection closely, half hoping it would change, or better yet, go away. When it didn't, she reached up, wiped the slime from her face and slopped it into the sink, revealing the deep lines that were carved into the flesh beneath her eyes.

Dani backed up three steps and sat on the edge of the bathtub, silently asking herself questions she couldn't answer.

What happened?

How much time has passed?

What were those things?

Closing her eyes, she tried to recall it all—

They're . . . inside . . . me now . . .

—but it was murky. She went back further to their conversation with Dr. Krusadian—

My job is to remove from Jason all the demons you have inflicted upon him . . .

—to the hint of smug threat in his voice before he sent them down into the basement—

It is time to face up to what you have done to your boy . . .

—and back further still to the fall that broke Jason's arm and brought the huge black doctor into their house—

No, she thought, feeling ill . . .

—and before that to the evenings full of screams and cries and the sounds of fists beating flesh—

. . . no, no . . .

—but the memories that stretched back almost a full nine years were somehow different, changed, as if someone had rummaged through her mind and rearranged them, and—

. . . please God no, he couldn't have . . .

191

—no matter how hard Dani tried to shift those memories in her mind, no matter how hard she tried to turn them this way and that and look at them from several different angles—

. . . *they're inside me now, sweet Jesus, they're inside me now!*

—those scalding memories of violent nights and scab-covered mornings would not return as the safe, padded memories they had once been and Dani slid down off the tub and curled into a sobbing, retching ball on the tile floor.

The memories were not hers. They were no longer viewed through *her* eyes, tinted by the filter of her own thoughts and perspectives.

They were the memories of a victim, not of an observer.

The memories were Jason's.

And they were there to stay.

Dani screamed into her hands until she lost consciousness.

28

They didn't scream in the Campbell house anymore. And things *did* change, just as Dr. Krusadian had promised.

Jason's parents stopped drinking. They didn't mention it, didn't even act as if they'd ever *touched* alcohol. The bottles that had been emptied at Dr. Krusadian's insistence had simply not been replaced.

Jason's mom kept busy around the house; she began to cook large delicious meals on the weekends and, during the week, they ate out more often than before, frequently at the restaurant of Jason's choice. His favorite was Chuck E. Cheese, where his dad always filled Jason's pockets with tokens and let him roam the game room while Mom and Dad sat quietly at their table.

Dad stopped reading the paper so much and spent more

time with Jason in the evenings. In fact, they *both* spent more time with Jason.

Yes, there was definitely something different about them, but—except for the way they *looked*—they were different in a good way. They were quiet and nice and they touched him softly, sometimes staring at him silently for a long time with a sad look in their eyes. But they looked tired and . . . older. Their voices were thinner; they spoke slower and walked slower, shoulders heavy and brows furrowed. And in the bathrooms, Jason noticed bottles of coloring with labels that promised to hide gray hair.

But that wasn't so bad, because things were better.

They traveled. Disneyland was much more fun the second time around, and at Marine World and Safariland, Jason had his picture taken with animals he hadn't even known existed.

They took lots of new pictures to replace the old. Jason laughed and waved from the back of an elephant; he and his parents stood with Goofy and Donald Duck; he smiled as he hugged his mom on the beach and laughed on his dad's lap on a picnic in the redwoods.

The new pictures were all very different from the ones they replaced because, in each of them, Jason looked happy. Very happy.

His parents didn't, though. They never smiled for the camera anymore.

Mom had arranged them all on the mantel in the living room, putting two on each side of Jason's favorite picture.

It was an eight-by-ten, framed in brass, and had arrived in the mail in a plain brown envelope addressed to Master Jason Campbell. There was no return address.

It was the picture that had been snapped immediately after Jason learned what had been done to his parents in the basement.

Jason stood next to the mountainous Dr. Krusadian in front of the fireplace.

And Jason was grinning joyously . . .

DEATH LEAVES
AN ECHO

by Charles de Lint

for Dean
who never tires of reminding us
that there's more
than just the darkness

and for Gerda
who taught him that

Our echoes roll from soul to soul,
And grow forever and forever.
　　　　　—ALFRED, LORD TENNYSON,
　　　　　　"The Princess"

ONE

1

If he hadn't been so tired.

If he hadn't been so angry.

There was time for recriminations and regrets, all the time in the world, just not enough time to brake before the Pinto's wheels hit the black ice and the car went sliding off the highway, heading straight for a bare-limbed elm tree standing there at the side of the road as if it were just waiting for him.

He'd passed it hundreds of times before along this stretch of road, never really giving it much thought. It was just there, greening in the spring, ass-bare in the winter. But now all he could think was, Why didn't the Dutch elm get you too, you smug bastard? Because the score was coming up fast: elm tree, one; Shiel, a big zero. End of story.

There was time to think of that.

All the time in the world.

We're into slo-mo now, he realized. A tacky video effect. The last scene of a *Miami Vice* rerun, everything slowing down until a freeze-frame, then "Produced by Michael Mann" spread across the screen. Fade to black. Commercial.

But there weren't going to be any freeze-frames here—just a fade to black, game over. He was going to ram that sucker, no question. All he could do was stare at it, his head a jumble of raw terror and the most inane extraneous thoughts a dying man could imagine. Aware of everything, but helpless to do a thing. Hands fried to the steering wheel, knuckles white, as the car took its own head like a runaway horse. A sudden cramp knotting the muscles of his calf as he pumped the brake pedal. Wheels locked, tires sliding on that black ice.

It wasn't like he hadn't known. The traffic report he'd just finished listening to as he left Ottawa had ended with a warning of black ice in outlying districts. But was he paying attention? Not likely. I'll just take the black ice, thanks, and maybe one of those little aperitifs when that elm turns me into pâté.

There was no flash of his life going past his eyes. But he did think of all the late nights he'd been putting in for the past couple of weeks, getting the store ready for Christmas, and then Anderson calling him, telling him he wanted an inventory done tonight after closing hours, no ifs, ands, or buts. The fat prick. It took five hours—four listening to his staff bitch about another late night while he went through the bins with them, another hour on his own tallying up the results and phoning them in.

And the reward? No overtime pay, because he was the manager and on straight salary. But we've got this nice elm tree, wrapped with a ribbon, and it's got your name on it.

The Pinto left the road, hit the ditch with a bone-rattling jolt, and kept going. Slo-mo time still holding fast. It took an hour for the wheels to lock. Another hour to slide the twenty yards or so toward the ditch. Maybe forty-five minutes in the ditch with that elm tree looming up.

All the time in the world.

No time at all.

I want that freeze-frame, he told the elm.

But then the bumper of the Pinto kissed its trunk. The slo-mo was gone now. Everything turned to a blur. Bark spraying. Headlights shattering. The front of the car folding in like an accordion—can you play "Lady of Spain"? The engine coming through the dash to sit on his lap. His head going straight for the windshield.

He had time to think of Annie. His wife. Waiting at home for him because she'd finished work hours ago.

Better me than her, he thought. If one of us had to go, I thank you God for picking me.

Because there was no way he could live without her. He could call up her features without even trying. The big dark eyes. The waterfall of dark curls, half of them going grey though she wasn't even thirty yet. The sweet quirky smile . . .

His face met the windshield. Skin broke. Blood sprayed. The windshield turned into a webwork just before it shattered. And then—

2

"Jesus!"

Michael Shiel sat bolt upright in his bed, eyes flared wide but unseeing, bedclothes clinging to his sweaty body like a second skin. His chest hurt and he was hyperventilating. A headache drummed behind his eyes as though he'd really hit that windshield. He could actually *feel* the glass embedding itself in his face for long seconds after he'd woken.

Just a dream.

Slowly he calmed his breathing, wiped the sweat from his face with an edge of the sheet. His head still ached—a sharp fiery pain like someone was digging around in back of his eyes with a dull knife.

"Jesus," he said again.

Softer now. Voice full of relief.

Still moving slowly, he swung his feet to the floor and padded across the room toward the door. He needed a painkiller something bad. His pace slowed as he reached the door, an abrupt sense of wrongness nagging at him. He turned and looked at the bed.

"Annie . . . ?"

The bed was empty.

He flicked on the light. Not only was the bed empty, it was just a double, not the king-size that he and Annie owned. There was no old housecoat of Annie's hanging on the back of the door. Her dresser was gone, along with the makeup always scattered across it, and her jewelry box, as well. The print she'd bought at the last Ottawa Christmas Craft Fair that hung over the bed was gone, too.

But it was still their bedroom. No question. It was the same room he'd gone to sleep in. What was changed was that Annie, and everything connected with her, was gone.

You're still dreaming, Shiel told himself as he leaned weakly against the doorjamb. The headache worsened. I've got to still be dreaming. Because how could she be gone—Annie and everything she owned? Maybe Annie could walk out and leave him—

(no way, absolutely no way, they were still in love after five years)

—but take everything with her without waking him? Exchange their bed for another while he was in dreamland, ready to say a too personal how-do to a great big frigging elm tree?

It was impossible.

He rubbed his face. His head pounded. Wake the fuck up, Shiel, he told himself. But he could close his eyes and nothing changed when he opened them to look around himself again. Annie was still gone, and everything she owned with her. Like she'd never been here. Like she'd never existed in the first place.

He slammed his fist against the doorjamb—the sudden sharp pain momentarily overcoming the raw ache behind his eyes—but all he got for his trouble was a sore hand to add to the headache as it kicked back in with renewed fury.

If I'm not dreaming, he thought, each word slow and

settling with frightening clarity in his mind, then I've lost it.
It's time for the men in their white coats to come and take
me away.

He pushed away from the doorjamb and slowly walked
around the bedroom, fingertips brushing the dresser top, the
night table, the end of the bed. He recognized the bed. It
was the one he used to have in his old apartment on Fifth
Avenue before he'd met Annie. The dresser dated from that
time too, but they hadn't traded it in on a larger model like
they had the bed.

And Annie's dresser was really gone. There weren't even
any indentations on the carpet to show where it had stood.

This was worse than the nightmare that had woken him.
A hundred times worse. It was his worst fear come true.

Everybody was afraid of dying. Nobody wanted to bite
the big one, though eventually we all did. Every one of us,
old and young, big and small, sick or healthy. Some sooner
than others, but like taxes, it wasn't something that would
ever go away. You lived with it, but it sat way back in your
head, on hold. You couldn't do anything about it, so to keep
you sane, your mind let you worry about other things
instead. Minor annoyances. Less final traumas. Like getting
stuck in traffic, gaining a few pounds, having an argument
at work, whether or not your relationship was going to
last . . .

Shiel sat on the bed and cradled his face in his hands.
Christ, Annie. Couldn't we have talked it out?

A dry sob shook him. One heave of his shoulders.
Headache burning at the back of his eyes. Hand still
stinging from where he'd hit the doorjamb. Slowly he raised
his head.

No way. No way she'd walked out on him. No way it was
possible for her to have taken all of her stuff while he was
lying here asleep. How the hell could he *not* have woken up
when the beds were exchanged?

(then what . . . ?)

Either he was crazy, or something weird was going

down. Something very weird. And since he didn't feel crazy . . . What was it Sherlock Holmes used to say? When you have eliminated the impossible, whatever remains, *however improbable*, must be the truth.

Right.

Eliminate the impossible.

Their marriage wasn't on the rocks. In fact, things just kept getting better between them. Maybe back when they first got married, when a hundred and one minor arguments came and went while they were still adjusting to living with each other, it could have been possible. But not now. Christ, he would have *known* if there was something wrong.

(wouldn't he?)

He wasn't dreaming.

(was he?)

He looked around the room, his gaze doing a slow pan. The way things looked—the *absence* of Annie's things—sure made it seem like a dream, but it wasn't likely. You didn't dream headaches like this, did you? You didn't—

Eliminate the impossible, he reminded himself.

So if she hadn't left him, and he wasn't crazy or dreaming, then what did that leave?

Someone fucking with his head.

Shiel stood up. Not Annie. He couldn't believe that of her. But then who? And for Christ's sake, *why*? It wasn't like he had any particular importance in the general scheme of things. He wasn't a nuclear physicist. He didn't have anything to do with national security. He wasn't important at all. Just an ordinary joe, managing a record store, trying to put the bucks aside to open his own store. Married, no kids, but happily married all the same. Wife worked for Statistics Canada, clerical work, nothing important.

So why would anybody bother to play games with them?

He left the room and wandered through the house they had bought and renovated three years ago. It was on Highway 4, between Franktown and Perth, which made for a forty-five-minute commute since they both worked in

Ottawa, but it was worth it to them for the feeling it gave them of living in the country. Not like it was anything particularly special, just an old place sitting on the highway, a nice lot behind it sloping down to pastureland.

He'd had friends whose family had a cottage near Perth where he'd spent a lot of weekends back when he was growing up. He'd passed this place coming and going he didn't know how many times, the whitewashed walls with the paint peeling, untidy lawn. But for some reason the old house had always appealed to him. When it came up for sale, he couldn't believe that all it was going to cost them was the back taxes and whatever it cost them to renovate the place.

He went from room to room, remembering the work they'd done on it—mostly just the two of them—but the place was like a crypt now, every trace of Annie was gone. From the knickknacks she'd picked up at some of the local flea markets, to her grandmother's wing chair that was supposed to be standing by the hearth. The chair sitting there now was one he could remember throwing out three years ago—another souvenir from his apartment on Fifth. It had been reupholstered—the pattern of the fabric the same as the one he'd considered for it before he decided the chair wasn't worth the trouble. Not when they had Annie's furniture, too.

(Annie)

Not a trace of her left. From the carpet in the dining room to her favorite cast-iron frying pan. Whoever'd done this number on him had been very thorough. He pulled aside the sheer curtain in the living room window and saw only the Pinto out in the lane. Her Honda was gone, too.

That was when he started to get the shakes—a trembling that began in his legs and arms, traveling all through him. He wrapped his arms around his chest, shivering, teeth chattering.

(Annie)

Eliminate the impossible.

207

Fine. Sure. No problem. But *this* was fucking impossible. People didn't just disappear along with everything they owned. How could anybody be that thorough in so little time? How could he not have *heard*?

He went into the kitchen and took a bottle of Jameson's from the cupboard, pouring himself a shot. The whiskey went down like a small fire, hitting his stomach and sitting there, setting up a dull warm glow. It helped ease the shakes. Not much, but it helped. He poured himself another shot.

Eliminate the impossible?

No can do. We're back to dreaming or the fruit farm, because none of this can be real.

He stared at the amber liquid in his glass for a long moment, then downed it and moved to where the phone sat on the kitchen table. Finger still trembling, he dialed up seven digits, then listened to the ringing on the other end of the line.

3

Back to slo-mo, Shiel thought. The pauses between each ring seemed to last a good ten minutes, the rings themselves were long klaxons that hurt his teeth, but finally the connection was made.

"Hlrmph?"

"Randy. It's Mike."

A long pause ensued, followed by, "You got any idea what time it is?"

"No, I—"

"Three-fucking-ayem, buddy."

Shiel had been working at pulling his thoughts together, wanting to sound sane in the middle of all this insanity. He was going to lay it out the way it had happened, nice and easy—

(slo-mo)

—but it didn't work out that way.

"She's gone," he blurted out. "Annie's gone, Randy. I feel asleep and when I woke up, she was gone—along with anything that ever belonged to her."

Another long pause, then, "Annie who, Mike?"

"Don't fuck with me. My wife, Annie. Look, I know it's late, but—"

"You don't have a wife."

Shiel was staring across the kitchen, looking at the Braun blender on the counter, seeing it, but it wasn't really registering. As Randy spoke, the blender blurred in his sight.

"Randy . . ."

He couldn't finish. The walls of the kitchen seemed to be closing in on him. His headache was a sharp whine of pain. The receiver shook in his hand.

You don't have a wife.

What the fuck was going *on*?

"Mike? You still there?"

"Yeah," he said dully.

He closed his eyes and could call up Annie's features without even trying. Met her in the late spring of '81, lived together a year before they got married. Church wedding and didn't she looked just like an angel coming up the aisle? Married five years.

You don't have a wife.

If it was a conspiracy, then not only Annie but his best friend was in on it, too.

"Hang on, buddy," Randy was saying. "I'll be right over."

The connection went dead, the dial tone harmonizing with the whine in behind the back of his eyes. He laid the receiver in its cradle, fumbling it before it went into place.

You don't have a wife.

I'm losing my goddamn mind.

209

4

"Who was that?" Janet asked sleepily as he hung up the phone.

Randy Sullivan turned to look at his wife where she was lying beside him, head turned away from the light on the night table on his side of the bed.

"Mike," he said. "Sounds like he really tied one on last night."

He drew back the sheet and got out of bed, body still feeling thick with sleep. Janet rolled over to look at him, eyes closed to slits against the light.

"What are you doing?"

"He sounds like he's in really bad shape," Randy said as he put on a shirt. "Said something about his wife walking out on him."

Janet sat up. "But Mike isn't married."

"I know that and you know that, but right now, Mike doesn't know that."

"He's a confirmed bachelor."

"We only report the news, babe. We don't make it."

He tucked in his shirt, zipped up his jeans. Janet shook her head.

"I didn't think he was much of a drinker, either," she said.

"He's not. So if he tied one on, it's probably hitting him harder than it would us confirmed alcoholics."

Janet laughed. Between the two of them they were lucky if they could put away more than a pair of beers each in an evening. Her smile faded.

"You be careful out there. The roads are supposed to be treacherous . . ."

Randy leaned over to kiss her good-bye. "Yes, mama. I'll take the pickup."

"And mind you don't wake the boys."

Randy chuckled. Tod and Benjy could sleep through an explosion. "That's a big ten-four," he said. "Don't wait up for me."

"Just be—"

"Careful. Gotcha."

He closed the bedroom door and walked down the hall, workboots in his hand, pausing only in the bathroom where he had a leak, then reached into the medicine chest and took down the little bottle of Valium that the doctor had prescribed to him the last time he'd had a muscle spasm in his back. Could be Mike would be needing something like this to calm him down. Though if he'd been drinking it probably wouldn't be a good idea to mix the two. Still . . . He put the pill bottle in his pocket all the same.

He waited until he was by the front door before sitting down on the stairs and putting his boots on. Despite the way he'd played things down with Janet, he couldn't shake a very serious worry about the way Mike had been going on. He'd never heard Mike sound quite so out of it before. And what the hell made him think he was married anyway?

Annie. Right. Maybe Mike had picked her up in some bar after work last night, brought her home, and now she'd taken off, grabbing herself a few bills from his wallet on the way out.

Only one way to find out.

Shaking his head, he shrugged on the heavy plaid workshirt that was hanging by the door, checked its breast pocket for keys, and headed out to the pickup.

5

The first thing Randy said when Shiel met him at the door was, "You look like shit, man."

Shiel grabbed his arm. "She's really gone—like she never existed."

"Okay. Slow down. Let's get some coffee brewing."

211

Randy led the way to the kitchen. His gaze fell on the whiskey bottle, then quickly slid away.

"Three shots," Mike said. "That's all I've had."

Randy shrugged. "I didn't say a thing. Grab yourself a seat, buddy, and I'll do the honors."

Shiel returned to the kitchen table while Randy put on some water, got filters out of a cupboard, ground coffee from the fridge. He brought the pot over to the table, along with a couple of mugs.

"Okay," he said. "Tell me about it."

Shiel began with his nightmare, then followed through. Randy listened, getting up once to fetch the kettle when it was boiling and some cream from the fridge. He poured them both a mug and shoved one across the table to Shiel.

"We've been friends a long time, right?" he said. "We go back—what? Ten, twelve years?"

Shiel nodded.

"And I've never shitted you, right?"

This time a shake of the head.

Randy sighed. "So I'm telling it to you straight now, Mike. I don't know any Annie. So far as I know, *you* don't know any Annie—at least not since I've known you. And you sure as shit have never been married."

All Shiel could do was put his head in his hands. The room had become a blur again. The whine behind his eyes sharpened.

"What . . . what is it, then?" he asked in an empty voice. "Am I going nuts?"

When there was no reply, Shiel finally looked up to meet Randy's gaze. There was pain in his friend's eyes, and a very real sympathy, but there wasn't what Shiel was looking for. There was no "April fool, man"—never mind it was the middle of November. No "Guess we can't pull a fast one on you, Mike ol' buddy."

"I don't know what's going on," Randy said.

Shiel bowed his head. "Jesus," he said numbly.

"I don't know what to say," Randy went on. "I can see

212

you believe what you told me, but Christ, Mike. I know you've never been married. Janet knows it. So maybe we're nuts. But I look around this place and I don't see anything different. And like you said—how the hell could anyone switch beds on you while you're fast asleep on one of them? It just doesn't work that way."

Shiel nodded slowly. "You're . . . I guess you're right."

"Maybe if you get some sleep . . . ?"

Sleep. Shiel felt hysterical laughter building up inside him. Sure. My nonexistent wife's disappeared, I'm not playing with a full deck anymore, and I'm supposed to get some sleep? Like it's going to change anything? Like I'm going to wake up and everything's going to be normal again?

"Sure," he managed. "I'll try to get some sleep. Listen, Randy, thanks for coming over."

Randy fumbled the pill bottle out of his pocket. "You're not supposed to mix this with alcohol, but if you took one it probably wouldn't hurt."

Valium. Right. Veg out.

"Thanks," he said again, taking the bottle. He set it down very carefully beside his coffee mug. "You should probably get yourself on home, Randy. Sorry to get you up with all this . . . you know . . . all this craziness."

"That's what friends are for."

"Well, I sure appreciate it."

Randy finished his coffee and stood up. "You sure you're going to be okay?"

You don't have a wife.

(like fuck I don't)

"Yeah. I'll be okay."

He walked Randy to the door and stood there, watching until the pickup's taillights faded in the distance. Then he slowly closed the door.

6

He didn't take any of the Valium. He didn't have any more of the whiskey, either. He put the bottle away, poured himself another coffee, then cleaned up Randy's mug and the pot. He felt like he was working under remote control. One part of him trying to put a damper on the screaming fear that whined through his head, wailing on the same frequency as the ache behind his eyes; the other part a handy-dandy robot, compulsively cleaning up table and counter.

Yo! Get yours today. No muss, no fuss. A little screwed up in the head, sure, but hey. It's only a robot.

He sank into a chair in the living room, sloshing coffee on the rug as he started to get the shakes again. He managed to put the mug down before he spilled the rest of it.

Oh, Jesus. What was he going to do?

There was a book he remembered reading not too long ago. *Communion.* All about how little spacemen, or elves, or who-knew-whats, were experimenting on humans. Taking them away to some shiny place—a spaceship if you went the UFO route, elfland if fairies were more your thing—and checking them out. To fill in the blank time when you were under their control, they pumped up your head with fake memories so that you wouldn't remember where you'd really been, or what they'd been doing to you there.

Guy who wrote it claimed it was true.

But then so did the old ladies who saw Elvis at a seance.

Except what if there really *were* UFOs? What if they'd taken him away and fucked up when they were laying in the new memories they'd left him? Or what if they'd taken Annie and then given everybody else fake memories—like that she'd never existed in the first place?

And they'd just forgotten him.

The scariest thing, he realized as he was thinking about all that, was that he was actually giving it some serious consideration.

You are gone, he told himself. Right off the very, very deep end, pal, and maybe you're never coming back. But then he thought of—

(Annie)

—and he knew that real or not, there was no way he'd give up his memories of her. Or stop looking for her. Because she *had* been real. And if she wasn't, then nothing else meant shit anyway.

TWO

1

He fell asleep in the chair, waking up the next morning, stiff and with a crick in his neck. But at least the headache was gone. Only so was Annie. Still gone. And that was because—

(*You don't have a wife.*)

He squeezed his eyes shut and counted slowly to ten. Backward. Breathing deep and slow. Trying to calm himself. When he opened his eyes again, he checked the time—just going on nine—and went into the kitchen to use the phone. She'd have been at work for about twenty-five minutes by now.

He knew the number by heart and dialed it quickly. The receptionist answered, saying good morning in both English and French.

"I'd like to speak to Anne Shiel, please," he said.

There was a moment's pause as the receptionist went through her directory to track down the name.

"I'm sorry, sir, but we don't have anybody by that name working here."

Shiel swallowed thickly. "Try Anne Lancaster," he said, using his wife's maiden name.

"No one by that name either, I'm afraid," the receptionist replied after another look through her directory.

That shaky feeling returned to Shiel as he sat there at the

kitchen table, grip tightening on the phone receiver. He wanted to scream at the voice on the other end of the line, but he kept his voice as level as he could.

"Thanks . . . thanks very much for your time."

He hung up before the receptionist could reply.

Stay calm, he told himself. It had been a long shot anyway. If Randy couldn't remember her, why would he think they would where she'd worked? But he'd had to give it a try. Nobody said it was going to be easy.

In the back of his mind a voice whispered. Stop playing around, Shiel. Check yourself into the Royal Ottawa now. Let the doctors handle your problems, because your mind's gone, solid gone.

He called the store and got his assistant manager, Sarah Talbot, on the line. Dedicated Sarah. She looked like she'd stepped straight off the cover of a Sex Pistols album jacket with her spiked black hair, five earrings to an ear, her leathers and studs and torn T-shirts, but she had an overachiever's sense of responsibility that went straight against the grain of her image. He told her he wouldn't be in today, hung up and dug out his address book.

The number for Annie's parents wasn't in it anymore.

He looked the number up in the phone book—J. Lancaster, still at the same west end address that he remembered—and started to dial, then cut the connection and cradled the receiver. No, he'd see them in person, not try to deal with this on the phone. He wanted to see their faces when he asked them about Annie, not give them the chance to just hang up on him.

He rubbed his cheek. Shower and shave. Put on some fresh clothes and get out there. Right. Just as soon as he collected the energy to get up.

His gaze traveled the kitchen. So familiar, but everything was changed. Like a well-loved picture that someone had taken an airbrush to, erasing something here, something there, leaving gaps and holes that you wouldn't notice unless you were acquainted with the photo in its original state. Annie's set of *Country Living* magazines were gone from the rack by the window overlooking the backyard. The cookbooks on the sill had been reduced to only those he'd bought. Annie's collection of antique folk art—the wooden geese, cats and the like, all brightly painted, that had filled the walls, balanced in nooks and crannies . . . they were all gone.

Shiel laid his head on his arms at the table and stared bleakly into an unseen distance.

Jesus, Annie . . .

2

He could remember a couple of nights ago, sitting here at this same table with her. She was looking at the newspaper, reading an article about a national cemetery that the federal government was considering in the east end. A number of prominent Canadians had been polled on the idea—from Margaret Atwood and CBC journalist Barbara Frum to research scientist Dr. Gerhard Herzberg—none of whom expressed a great deal of interest.

Shiel hadn't read the article himself—the subject of death and dying always bothered him—but it had sparked a conversation between them about what they'd like to have done with their own bodies when they died.

"I guess I'd like to be cremated," Shiel had said.

"And what about your ashes?"

"Oh, you could put them in a jar and keep them by the bed." He laughed a little uncomfortably. "Naw, I'm just kidding," he added.

Annie had laughed with him, but then she'd asked, "Why do you say that?"

"I don't know. It'd be a little creepy."

"Do you think I'd be scared of your ghost?"

Shiel hadn't had an answer for that.

"If there really are ghosts," Annie said, "the best thing

that could happen to me if you died was for some part of you to come back and stay with me."

But I don't even get that, Shiel thought, still sitting there at the kitchen table, head cradled on his folded arms. I get zip. A big blank void.

You don't have a wife.

He felt like he was caught up in some shlocky AM tune. Woe is me. My baby's gone and I can't get her back. Except his baby only existed in his mind. How would that play on AM? A lot of you folks out there got the same problem? You wake up in the middle of the night and find out you imagined the last six years or so of your life?

He sat up and shook his head. It—

(Annie)

—wasn't a lie. His wife's features swam in his mind. No way the memories were a lie.

He got up to take his shower, glancing out the front window as he went by it. He caught a glimpse of something through the boughs of the tall scraggly cedar hedge that separated the highway from the front lawn. Sunlight flashed on something metallic. There was a car parked there. Somebody having engine trouble? Maybe a flat tire? But as soon as he opened the front door, the car pulled away.

He ran to the highway, but the car was gone before he could get a clear glimpse of it. Standing there in just a shirt and jeans, feet bare, shivering a little in the cold morning air, he realized that he'd just been handed the first tangible evidence that he wasn't losing his mind. Someone had been watching him, watching the house. There could have been a lot of reasons for it—everything from someone looking to buy a little rural real estate to a thief casing the place—but with Annie's disappearance, it didn't take much for Shiel to put it together.

Whatever the reason, no matter how crazy it made him feel, there *was* a conspiracy. Someone had stolen his wife. Taken her away, and along with her, everything that had belonged to her, right down to the memories that other people had of her. To have been so thorough they'd have to have been keeping tabs on him and Annie for a very long time.

I don't know who you fuckers are, he thought, or why you're playing this game with us, but I'm going to find her. And I'm going to find you. Don't ever think that I won't. And when I do, you're going to regret the day you ever started messing with us.

The anger that filled him as he went back inside to take his shower felt very good. A lot better than that shaky feeling that had been feeding on him ever since he'd woken up last night to find Annie gone.

3

"Yes?"

John Lancaster looked the same as ever, a tall salty-haired general practitioner who Shiel had often thought bore more than a passing resemblance to Albert Einstein. Annie's father. He hadn't approved when Shiel and Annie had first begun seeing each other and was only won over when he realized that whatever his own personal opinions of Shiel, this was the man his daughter had chosen to be her husband and nothing he could do or say would change that.

Standing on the porch of the Lancasters' west end home, Shiel hesitated for a long moment before replying to his father-in-law's brusque question. There was absolutely no recognition of him in Lancaster's eyes. The man deserved an Academy Award for the performance.

"I'm here about Annie," Shiel said.

"I'm afraid I don't follow you, young man. Annie who?"

Shiel shook his head. "It doesn't work, John. I *know* she's real, so tell me what's going on. For Christ's sake, will you give me something?"

"Give you something?" Lancaster asked, looking confused. "Are you asking for money?"

Jesus, Shiel thought. The man had it down aces. Not a flicker of give.

"Anne Lancaster. Your daughter. I want to know where she is."

"I don't have a daughter, Mr. . . . ?" His eyebrows rose questioningly.

"Shiel. Mike Shiel. Your son-in-law."

Lancaster shook his head slowly. "I'm not certain what you're referring to, Mr. Shiel. As I have no children, I certainly don't have any in-laws. I'm afraid I'm going to have to ask you to leave."

He started to close the door, but Shiel stepped forward, wedging his shoulder up against it. "Not so fast, John. I'm serious. I want some answers and I want them now."

"I don't know you and I don't have a daughter, Mr. Shiel."

"Bull!"

"I am trying to be polite, but—"

Shiel wanted to grab him by his lapels and give him a shake. "Look," he said, trying to maintain some kind of calm. "All I'm asking is for you to give me a break, okay? I've been going crazy ever since I woke up and she was gone. If I could just know that she was all right, it'd help. Not much, but it'd be something."

There was momentary sympathy in Lancaster's eyes, but it was the kind of sympathy one felt for a stranger. The victim of a car accident. Or a skid row bum looking for a handout.

"I'm sorry, Mr. Shiel, but I really don't know how I can be of any help to you."

"Just tell me where she is. Give me that much."

"I don't know who 'she' is. Now if you'll excuse me, I have—"

"Don't cut me off like this!"

Easy, Shiel tried to tell himself. Turn down the volume. But he knew it was all pointless. This officious bastard wasn't going to give him zip.

222

"You seem to be under some strain, Mr. Shiel," Lancaster was saying, "so I'll forgive you your outbursts, but I really must ask you to leave now."

Shiel stared at him. "Enjoying this, are you?"

"I beg your pardon?"

"Giving me the runaround. I'll bet you just about laughed yourself sick when they came around to put you up to this. You finally get to put the shaft to me."

"You've tried my patience too far. Remove yourself from my—"

"Will you cut the crap, John? I can buy there being some government connection, so that's why they played dumb where she works. I can maybe even buy Randy's stonewalling, though that hurts. But you're going to give me something. I'm not leaving until you do. I mean, don't you care? She's your fucking daughter!"

Lancaster drew himself up straighter. "I don't care for your familiarity, Mr. Shiel, or your crude language. And I certainly don't care to be harassed in my own home. Now either remove yourself from my property, or I'll be forced to have the police come and remove you."

"Fine," Shiel said, stepping back from the door. "Call the cops. I've got a missing person to report anyway. And it's going to look awfully funny when they find out it's your daughter who's missing—the one you claim you never had. So I'll just sit myself down here on your steps and wait for them to come."

"I don't think you'll find things quite so amusing once they arrive," Lancaster said before he shut the door firmly in Shiel's face.

Shiel stared at the door's brass knocker for a long moment, then turned and sat down at the top of the porch stairs. He looked out at the street. This wasn't going any better than it had with Randy, he realized. What was it going to take to break through to these people? What kind of a hold did whoever was responsible for it all have over them?

He was still working at it when the blue and white police cruiser pulled up to the curb in front of the Lancaster house.

4

Detective Sergeant Ned Meehan looked up as his partner approached his desk in the squad room at the main police station downtown on Elgin Street.

"Did you pull his sheet?" Ned asked.

Ernie Grier nodded. "No priors. Everything else checks out. He's the manager of the Hot Deals record shop on Rideau, lives out of town—on Highway 4, out near Franktown. Only thing that doesn't fit is his missing wife. He never had one—never been married."

"Psychiatric history?"

"Nada."

"Wonderful. What about the woman—this Anne Lancaster. Does she exist?"

"John and Frances Lancaster never had a daughter and none of the hospitals in town have a record of her birth. No record of public school attendance. Carleton U says no one by that name ever picked up a BA from them or even attended classes. If she exists, it's only in his mind."

"Only in his mind," Ned repeated. "Christ. What do you make of him?"

Grier pulled a chair over to Ned's desk and settled down in it. "I don't know. Seems normal enough except for this business with his nonexistent wife. I feel kind of sorry for the guy."

Ned tapped a pencil on the desk and nodded thoughtfully. "Yeah. I know what you mean." Sighing, he rose from his chair. "Guess I'll go talk to him again."

5

It hadn't yet registered on Shiel that he could be in a lot of trouble.

About all he had going for him was that he'd been polite, keeping his temper in check, when the two uniformed officers had arrived at the Lancaster house. But while it depended on the Lancasters as to whether or not there'd be charges laid against him, there was also the possibility that the detective who'd interviewed him earlier would suggest that he undergo psychiatric evaluation. And if whoever was behind this conspiracy continued to be as thorough as they'd been so far, there was a strong possibility that he'd find himself checking into someplace like the Royal Ottawa whether he wanted to or not.

That's where the crazies went. Off the street where they couldn't do any harm.

You don't have a wife.

Maybe that wouldn't be such a bad idea. Because if he *was* losing it, that'd be the best place for him.

He hadn't been booked yet, or put in a holding cell, but that wasn't to say it wouldn't happen. Right now he sat alone in a small cubicle of a room, somewhere in the labyrinth of Ottawa Police Headquarters. The only furnishings were the chair he was sitting on, a table, and another chair across from him. The detective who had interviewed him had brought him a coffee before he left. That was twenty minutes ago. Since then, nothing.

They were leaving him here to stew, he realized. Maybe they were watching him from some hidden camera. Maybe they were in on it—

He shivered. Don't even think about that, he told himself. Things were bad enough as they were, without letting paranoia dig its claws into him. Except was it still paranoia when everyone you knew *was* conspiring against you?

225

Because it was either that, or maybe the aliens *had* landed·
and for one reason or another, they just hadn't done a good
enough job in messing up his head.

Maybe the cops were calling them in right now to finish
the job.

Oh, Jesus. Give me a break.

Again, just like last night, what scared him the most was
that he was half-serious in considering something just that
flaky. He wondered if he should have told the detective
about the car he'd seen parked across from his house this
morning. All he'd seen then was a flash of red metal. But
he'd seen it again today. Just as the cops were pulling away
from the curb in front of the Lancasters' place. A red Toyota
followed them downtown. Same color of red as the one out
by his place.

He hadn't been able to make out much of the driver—the
guy was wearing a baseball cap with the brim pulled low
and shades—except that he was clean-shaven. But he had
memorized the license-plate number.

Should he give it to the cops? Or was he really pulling at
straws? Who was to say the person owning the Toyota
didn't just live down the street from the Lancasters and
happened to be going downtown at the same time?

Paranoia was saying it wasn't.

There's no such thing as coincidence, he remembered
reading somewhere once. Only connections you haven't
figured out yet. He wasn't sure if he bought that. Christ, he
wasn't sure of anything anymore.

When the door opened, he looked up sharply, heart
drumming, but it was only the detective coming in again.
Round two.

"So what's the verdict?" he asked, trying to keep his
voice light.

The detective sat down across the small table from him.
"We've checked out this Anne Shiel, née Lancaster."

"And?"

"She doesn't exist." *You don't have a wife,* Shiel heard in harmony to the man's words. "The Lancasters have no children. We checked with all the hospitals, plus the public school you said she attended, Carleton U, and Stats Canada. No one's ever heard of her."

"But *I* remember her," Shiel said. "I remember six years of being with her. Am I nuts?"

The detective studied Shiel's face. "I don't know, Mr. Shiel. What do you think?"

I think it's all bullshit, Shiel wanted to tell him. I think you're screwing me around just like everybody else is. I think maybe I am nuts. Christ, I just—

"I don't know," was all he said. "The memories seem so real."

The detective nodded sympathetically. Ease off, Shiel told himself. You don't want to be put away right now. Not until you know the truth. For Annie's sake, as much as your own.

"So what happens now?" he asked.

"The Lancasters aren't pressing charges and we've got no reason to hold you. But I want you to promise me you'll leave them alone—and that goes for Stats Canada and anybody or anyplace else where you might think to go looking for this . . . ah, woman. I don't want to see you in here again, you got me?"

What if she was your wife? Shiel wanted to ask, but he just nodded his head.

"I understand. I'll let it go."

"You do that." The detective rose. "Come on. I'll get you out of here."

6

The brisk November air felt clean in his face as he stepped out of the police station onto Elgin Street. Someone had brought his car here from where he'd parked it on the Lancasters' street. He got in, dutifully put on the seat belt since he was sitting right here in front of the copshop, and started it up. Looking back at the glass doors and windows that walled the Elgin Street side of the building's foyer, he saw the detective standing there, still watching him. Putting the car in gear, he gave the detective a nod and drove off. The detective lifted a hand, but his expression never changed.

Once he was on Elgin, driving north, Shiel realized he didn't know where he was going. Or what to do next. Forget it. That's what everybody was telling him. Randy, the cops, even a part of himself.

You don't have a wife.

"Shut up," he told the voice inside him that kept repeating those words. "Just shut up."

Not five blocks from the police station, he pulled onto a side street and parked. Getting out, he fed some change into a meter, then headed for the public phone he'd spotted on the corner. He'd promised not to go see anybody else looking for Annie, but he hadn't said anything about calling.

All the numbers he wanted were missing from his address book. They were all Annie's friends—or people he'd met through her. He looked them up in the phone book then tried them, one by one.

"Hello, Cathy? This is Mike here. Mike Shiel. Annie's husband. What's that? Annie Lancaster. What? Oh. I guess I got the wrong number. Sorry to have bothered you."

They all went the same.

He stood there, leaning his head against the glass, staring out at the street, trying numbers until he ran out of change. Finally he hung the receiver in its cradle and went back to his car. There was a parking ticket sitting under the wiper.

"Thanks a lot," he muttered as he stuffed it into his pocket. "I really needed this."

A woman walking by gave him an odd look. He nodded to her, but she quickened her pace and hurried by.

Right. Start talking to yourself like all the rest of the

loonies do. Is that how they end up in rags and on the streets? Part of their life disappears and they fuck up the rest of it looking for the part that went missing?

It could happen to him, then. All too easily. Because he couldn't see himself going back to work and serving customers like nothing had happened. What no one seemed to understand was that *everything* had happened to him. Nothing could be the same again. Not with Annie gone.

He got into his Pinto and looked around. No red Toyota. He hadn't seen one the whole time he'd been in the phone booth, either. He checked the time. Past noon. The bars were open.

Might as well start my new life out right and get plastered, he thought, because there sure as shit isn't anything else I can think of to do right now.

You don't have a wife.

Damn straight. Not anymore. But I had one, pal. I don't care what anybody says. I had Annie. Someone took her away. Someone's cleaned the slate on her life like she never existed. But I knew her. She's real to me.

Gaze blurring, he rubbed his eyes on the sleeve of his jacket and drove away, north again on Elgin, heading for the Market and all its bars.

THREE

1

Halfway through his first beer, Shiel realized that coming here had been a mistake. He was in the Lafayette on York Street in the Market. It was one of the oldest taverns in the area, a serious drinking establishment that bore about as much resemblance to the trendy singles bars that had been springing up in the area in the last few years as a mongrel dog did to a purebred prizewinner. They shared a certain genetic makeup, but you'd be as apt to find a yuppie in the Laf as you'd be to find one of the welfare cases in here sipping wine in any of the polished chrome and glass places over on William Street.

Yeah, Shiel thought, I fit right in. Just another loser. Except the people in here shared a certain camaraderie from which his sports jacket and clean jeans excluded him. And he wasn't a drinker anyway. Never had been. All sitting here was going to do was swap his AM "My Baby's Gone" blues for the twang of a Merle Haggard tune.

Oh, I'm a trucker cowboy and the spacemen stole my red-hot momma, uh-*huh*.

He played with his beer bottle, widening the circle of its condensation on the tabletop, and thought about the detective who'd interviewed him. The thing he hadn't been able to explain to the cop was, if he was making all this up, then how come he knew the names and addresses of all these people that Annie had known? It wasn't just a matter of picking names at random from the phone book. He'd *known* the people—never mind that they didn't know him. Knew where they lived, what they did.

So was he turning psychic as well as psychotic? What do you say, Mr. Policeman? You got a reasonable explanation for that one?

He couldn't blame the detective, though. The guy'd just been doing his job—and being very pleasant about the whole thing, when you came right down to it. If Shiel had been behind the counter of Hot Deals and someone came in off the street to lay this kind of a trip on him, he'd have ushered the guy out the door just as politely, but firmly. He'd have laughed about it with Sarah or whoever else was on the floor at the time, and then forgotten about it, only pulling the memory out the next time he and some of the other record people in town got together and started swapping loonie-tune stories about the weirdos they got in their stores.

And what about the guy? If it was real for him—what the hell would he do?

Come down to the Laf and get plastered, probably.

Shiel took another swig of his beer.

"Want a Penny for your thoughts?"

Shiel turned to the source of the voice and blinked. Standing beside him was a woman as out of place in the Laf as he'd be in a corporate boardroom. Long blond hair, deep blue eyes, with the kind of figure that would turn heads for two blocks down any street. Her features weren't classically beautiful—striking, rather. The kind that made a billboard model look too bland.

She was wearing a black flounced skirt and a cream camisole under a stylish red leather jacket, dark stockings and high heels. The sort of woman that the beer companies liked to pretend would fall all over you if you drank their brand of beer, but not the kind of woman you found in a place like this.

"I think you've got the wrong guy, lady," he said.

And besides, I never pay for it, he added to himself. Maybe he was being unfair, but what else would someone looking this good be doing in the Laf? No matter how hard city council and the cops tried to clean up the area, the Market was still hooker heaven.

She laughed and sat down at his table. "I know what you're thinking, Mike."

"How the—"

She laughed again—a nice warm laugh, deep and throaty. "You don't remember me, do you?"

I should, Shiel thought. How did you forget someone who looked like she did? But he shook his head.

"Nineteen seventy-three? Philemon Wright High School?"

This happened to Shiel all the time. People knew him, but he could never connect a name to their face, where he knew them from, *if* he even knew them half the time. It came from working in retail for so many years. You saw such an endless parade of faces that they all blurred together after a while. Usually he just played along—"Right, yeah, now I remember"—but he wasn't up to bullshitting today.

"Sorry," he said. "My mind's in neutral."

His lack of recognition didn't seem to faze her in the slightest. "I'm Penny Moore. I used to take the same North American Lit class as you did—with Mrs. Armstrong. We used to call her Phyllis Strongarm—remember?"

Penny's name still didn't ring a bell, but Shiel found a smile. "Yeah, I remember. She was a bulldog about homework. So what's—"

"A nice girl like me doing in a place like this, offering myself up for your thoughts?"

Shiel was surprised that she'd actually pulled a genuine laugh out of him. "Something like that."

"I was out shopping and happened to see you come in. I . . ."

She ducked her head for a moment, hiding a blush, Shiel

233

realized, behind that mane of blond hair. When she lifted her head again, she had a funny look in her eyes.

"This is going to sound really stupid," she said, "but I used to have a terrible crush on you back then, so when I saw you come in here a few minutes ago I— Oh, I don't know. I just wanted to say hello. To see how you were doing."

"I can't believe I don't remember you."

"Well, I looked pretty different back then. I guess I'm what you'd call a late bloomer. I was pretty dumpy looking, my hair was this stringy mouse-brown . . ."

Her voice trailed off. Shiel just sat looking at her, unsuccessfully trying to match her up to one of the kids he'd gone to high school with.

"God, you must think I'm really dumb."

Shiel shook his head. "No. I'm just . . . going through some weird shit lately."

"Oh. Well look, maybe this isn't a good time to be bugging you, then. I can just—"

Shiel caught her hand as she started to rise. "No, please. I could use some company." He let her hand go. "Only not in here. I thought I'd come in and drown my sorrows, but I'm not much of a drinker, and this place is just making me feel worse. Do you feel like having some lunch?"

"If you're sure I won't be getting in your way."

Shiel shook his head. "Like I said, I could really use some company."

Penny gave him a bright smile. "Where do you want to go?"

"I don't know. Why don't we just cruise up William Street and see what appeals to us?"

Shiel was startled when they reached the sidewalk and Penny took his arm. You've got a wife, he told himself. Someone stole her, but you've still got a wife.

Penny turned to him, a guileless look in those deep blue eyes. "What have you been doing all these years?" she asked.

234

2

"You were never the kind of guy I thought would ever have sorrows that needed drowning—at least you weren't in high school."

They'd found a place on William Street. Beating the lunch hour rush, they had managed to get a good table by the window and a waitress who was still running on her morning charm. Come two-thirty, after dealing with the chaos of the lunch crowds, it might be a different story, but right now they almost had the place to themselves and her undivided cheerful attention. The coffee they ordered came immediately, the sandwiches hot on its heels.

"I'm kind of surprised myself," Shiel said.

"Want to talk about it? I'm an expert on hard-luck stories that make good."

"You look good, but I still can't place you. Are you sure we were in the same class?"

"Oh, I'm sure." She pulled her hair tightly back from her face. "I used to wear this ponytail that was drawn back so tight it hurt. Plaid skirts way past my knees with white blouses. Carried a suck-sac. Brown plastic rims on my glasses . . ."

She let her hair go and it fell back around her neck in a thick wave the way hair does in shampoo commercial, but not before a younger image of her flashed in Shiel's mind. He remembered her now. Take away the contacts and makeup, lose a few years, and put those pounds back from the right places to the wrong ones, drop the dye job and perm, and you had her. Penelope Moore. The class lump. The only girl in school who never attended one dance in the company of a member of the opposite sex. Shuffling through the halls, clutching her briefcase of books, glasses askew, shoulders stooped and looking at the floor . . .

"You remember," she said dryly.

He glanced up, embarrassed. "Guess we gave you a pretty hard time."

Penny shook her head. "You never did. You never spent any time with me, but you never dumped on me, either. I had this fantasy back then that you'd ask me out, but . . ."

She gave a shrug that was meant to be nonchalant, but Shiel caught the tension in it. Some hurts you never lost, no matter what you made of yourself, no matter how things changed.

"Looks like you're doing pretty good for yourself now," he said. It seemed an inadequate thing to say, but it was all he had. Remembering her now, thinking about how it must have been for her, he could empathize with how she must have felt.

"Oh, I worked at it," Penny said. "Believe me. But back than I just . . . let myself go, I guess. It wasn't all my fault. I didn't have a father—did you know that? I mean, my mother was never married and I've no idea to this day who my father was."

Shiel shook his head. "I didn't know."

"Well, it's not such a weird thing these days, maybe, but back then it wasn't something you talked about at all. When we moved to Hull my mother just let on that she was a widow and you can bet I never told anybody about it. Didn't have anybody to tell. Anyway, she ended up getting some strange ideas—my mother. Didn't want what had happened to her to happen to me. So she made sure that I always wore clothes that weren't in fashion, wore the ugliest glasses she could get me, kept my hair back, fed me lots of sweets so that I'd put on weight . . .

"She meant well, I suppose. She just didn't want any guy to think I looked good enough to take out, much less make out with. What happened between her and my father, having me on her own—her parents basically disowned her—it left her very bitter, but very tough as well. She made do and she made sure that I didn't stray from the straight and narrow."

"Jesus."

Penny smiled. "I can handle it now—talking about it, thinking about it—but it was tough back then. I didn't help myself at all either because I ended up with this real lack-of-confidence problem. When it came to self-esteem, I didn't even know what the concept meant, much less try to build it up in myself."

"I'm surprised you're not more bitter."

"What good would it do?" Penny asked.

Shiel nodded. "What turned you around?"

Her face clouded for a moment, but then that bright smile was back again. "Had a moment of satori, I guess. I was finished high school, planning to go to university—in Ottawa, naturally, because my mother would have died if I'd left home to go live on campus somewhere. I was feeling probably the lowest I'd ever felt when I finally realized that the only way I was ever going to be happy with myself, with life, was if *I* did something about it.

"So I did."

"And very successfully," Shiel said. "I mean, looks shouldn't be everything, but—"

"If you can't be happy with yourself—and in this society, that means looking good as well—then nobody else can help you. I worked hard at it, Mike, but it was worth it. Not just because I could look in the mirror and be happy with the woman I saw looking back at me, but because I really did learn that we *are* what we make ourselves—nothing more, nothing less. It's easy to blame somebody else for your problems—like I used to blame my mother, or the kids that made fun of me—but when you get right down to it, you've got to start with yourself.

"I did go to college—in Toronto. I took up acting for a while, appeared in some commercials, then I got into journalism, worked on a few of the dailies in T.O. and now here I am, starting a new job with *The Citizen* on Monday morning."

She grinned suddenly. "God, listen to me. I must be boring you stiff."

Shiel shook his head. "Not at all. I'm just feeling guilty, I guess, for the way I was back then—ignoring you and everything."

"You and everybody else. But don't be, Mike. The change had to come from"—she laid her hand against her chest—"inside me first, I think."

"But if you'd had some friends, it wouldn't have been so hard."

"It's always hard." Penny said. "But enough about me. What have you been up to? Now that I've dumped the whole sad story of my life on you, I'd think fair is fair."

She looked at him expectantly and Shiel hesitated. Her frankness had startled him, but it deserved to be met with honesty. Only how was he supposed to talk about what had happened to him?

You don't have a wife.

"It's my wife," he said finally. "Annie. She . . ."

And then it all came out in a rush. The loss and his fear that he was losing it, how his memories felt too real to be false, but so far as the world was concerned, Annie Shiel—or Lancaster, take your pick—had never existed. Except in his mind. What was left of it.

3

"Maybe I can help you," she said when he was finally done.

"You *believe* me?"

Her lips formed a moue. "Well . . . I believe that you believe."

Shades of Randy, Shiel thought. *I can see you believe what you told me* . . . The difference being that Randy had known Annie. Should have known her. But he didn't.

Shiel shook his head slowly. "How can you help?"

"With the paper."

"You're going to do a feature on me? 'Man Loses Imaginary Wife'?"

Penny laughed. "I'm sorry," she said, touching fingers to her lips. "No. Nothing like that at all. I'm thinking of the Tombs—the records section."

"It won't do any good. I told you, the police have already checked everything—hospitals, schools, the works."

"Okay," Penny said. "But let's say somebody *is* erasing all evidence of your wife's existence—"

In other words, Shiel added, let's pretend you're not crazy.

"—they can only go so far. They can erase records of her birth and schooling, her job history, but the paper? How can they wipe out facts that are right there in plain black and white?"

"I don't know," Shiel said. "They've been doing pretty good so far."

"Still, it's worth a try. C'mon. Do you have a car?"

"Yeah."

"Well, let's take a drive out to Baxter Road and see what we can come up with."

Shiel paid their bill and led the way to where he'd parked the Pinto. The parking meter had run out but there was no new ticket under the wiper. What do you know, Shiel thought. A small miracle.

"Was your wife ever in the news?" Penny asked as she buckled up her seat belt.

"We're just ordinary folks," Shiel replied. "Ordinary folks don't get in the news unless they win a lottery or go head-on with a tree in a car crash."

Last night's nightmare flickered momentarily behind his eyes. Head-on with a tree. Right. He shivered, remembering. If Penny noticed, she made no comment.

"There'd be a birth announcement at least," she was saying. "Maybe she was in the Girl Guides and had her picture snapped at a parade, or some guy took a shot of

239

her with the year's first tulips or something like that. Filler stuff—you know? Human interest."

Shiel shook his head. "Nothing like that—not that I know of."

"We'll just have to see what we can come up with, then."

The conversation turned to her life in Toronto as Shiel took them up Nicholas Street, then onto the Queensway, heading west toward the newspaper's building in the west end. They arrived at Baxter Road, parked, and made their way down to the Tombs. Two hours later they came up for air and stepped back out into *The Citizen's* parking lot, no further ahead than they'd been before.

Shiel kicked at a crumpled-up coffee cup and watched it skitter between the cars.

"Nothing," he said bitterly.

He shoved his hands deep into his pockets and stared out across the parking lot. Over on the Queensway, the traffic whipped by. He felt as though each passing vehicle were taking another piece of his sanity with it. Someone got into a car a few rows over, started it up and drove away. Everyone had someplace to go, something to do—probably someone to do it with. They hadn't lost an imaginary wife. Oh, no. They lived in the real world.

Penny touched his arm. "I'm sorry, Mike."

"That's okay. It was a long shot, right?"

"You shouldn't just give—"

"Up?" he demanded. He turned to look at her. "Why not? Why the fuck not?" He tapped a finger against his head. "Something's wrong in here—that's the real bottom line. I remember Annie. I remember six years of living with her. But she never fucking existed, did she? I mean, how could she be real and there not be one single trace of her *anywhere*?"

"I . . . I don't know what to say."

Shiel's anger drained from him, leaving him with only an emptiness inside. He looked away again, back to the traffic on the Queensway.

"There's nothing to say," he said finally. "Listen, thanks for trying. I really appreciate it. Can I give you a lift somewhere?"

Penny looked as though she wanted to take it a little further, but finally she just nodded. "I left my car at home," she said. "Maybe you could give me a lift back to my place?"

"Sure. What's the address?"

4

"Do you want to come up for a coffee or something?" Penny asked when they pulled in front of her apartment building just off Elgin Street. "You probably shouldn't be alone right now," she added as he hesitated.

"You want to take a chance hanging around with a crazy?" Shiel asked, not really joking.

"You're not crazy," Penny said. "C'mon. The place is a mess—I'm still in the middle of moving in—but it'll be better than driving aimlessly around, which is pretty well the sum total of what you've got planned, right?"

Shiel hesitated a moment longer, then killed the Pinto's engine. "Not crazy, huh?" he muttered as he joined her on the sidewalk.

The world has taken on a surreal quality for him ever since they'd left *The Citizen's* parking lot. At first it was just a spacey feeling inside him. But now, getting out of the car, everything was beginning to lose its definition. There were no more sharp edges—just images bleeding into each other. Looking up the street, he found it hard to tell where one building began and another ended. Street signs were unreadable. Pedestrians were patches of color—all except for Penny. She was crystal-clear—the center of a camera's focus, everything blurring around her.

"You don't act crazy, anyway," she said.

How about deluded? Shiel wondered as he followed her inside the building. Paranoid might fit, too.

You don't have a wife.

Led astray. Hoaxed. Hoodwinked. Fucked over. Oh, Annie . . .

"C'mon," Penny said.

She stood at the door of her apartment and ushered him inside. The place was a mess. Shiel stood looking at the array of cardboard boxes and suitcases, some still sealed, others opened with their contents spilled around the room. The place was a blur of shifting colors and images.

"Here," Penny said. She led him to the couch and cleared off a stack of books so that he could sit. "I'll go put the water on."

It didn't seem like more than a moment—a flicker of time, no longer than that between one blink and the next—before she was back, pressing the handle of a steaming mug into his hand. He looked up at her. She was still perfectly in focus.

"It's funny," he said. "Every time I look at you, I think of commercials. Beer commercials, shampoo commercials . . ."

Penny smiled. "Should I take that as a compliment?"

"Definitely."

The coffee was hot going down, but it helped shift the room into better definition. Objects began to regain their edges.

"Well, maybe you're just remembering some of the ones I've done."

"Maybe."

Suddenly Shiel had nothing to say. What am I doing here? he asked himself. I should be out looking for Annie, trying to track her down . . . Sure. And where did he start? Christ, he'd done everything he could think of. Maybe he should just go home and wait for her. Maybe they'd be bringing her back. Maybe whoever had taken her was just borrowing her and if he just waited long enough at home, she'd come walking in the door, hair tossed back, wearing that funny little smile of hers.

But who was he kidding? She wasn't coming back.

You don't have a wife.

He couldn't face going back to the empty house. Couldn't face looking at all the empty places where her things had been.

Looking up suddenly, he found Penny's gaze on him and he wondered how long the silence had been dragging on.

"You want some help sorting this stuff out?" he asked, taking in the clutter with a wave of his hand.

Penny nodded. "That'd be great."

5

The afternoon got swallowed by the task. They ate micro-waved frozen dinners around seven, worked some more, and then all of a sudden it was going on eleven and Shiel knew he had to get going.

"Listen," he said, standing up from the bookcase where he'd been organizing Penny's hardbacks. "I really should be heading out. Thanks for everything."

"You don't have to go," Penny said. "I mean, you can sleep in here—on the couch," she added as his brow furrowed.

Shiel didn't want to go home—not to that empty house— but it didn't seem right to be staying here for the night, either.

"I've been taking up enough of your time," he said. "I'm sure you've got better things to do than to baby-sit a basket case like me."

"To tell the truth," Penny said, "I've enjoyed having the company. I don't know anybody in town anymore, and I certainly don't feel up to making the rounds of the bars just to find some company."

"Like the Lafayette . . ."

She laughed. "I *told* you. I just happened to see you going in."

Shiel held up his hands placatingly. "I know, I know. I was just teasing."

"Stay, Mike. You'll feel better waking up in a place that's not so . . . empty."

That doesn't hold so many memories, he thought. False memories, maybe, but memories all the same.

"Okay," he said. "Thanks, Penny. You've been a real lifesaver."

An odd look came over her features for a moment, then she smiled and gave her hair a shake back from her shoulders.

"Let's see what kind of bedding we can round up for you," she said.

Shiel stood by the bookcase and watched her leave the room. There was something going on with her, he thought. Something she hadn't touched on yet, for all that's she'd pretty much spilled her whole life story to him. She'd never really said why she'd left Toronto, he realized. Maybe she'd come out of a bad relationship. Maybe she was missing somebody, too. Not like he was—but that wouldn't make it hurt any less.

Just a couple of lost souls, he thought.

When she came back in, her arms laden with bedding, he tried to help her make up a bed for him on the couch, but she wouldn't have any of it.

"Go ahead and use the bathroom," she said. "I'll have this ready for you by the time you're done."

He borrowed her toothbrush, washed his face, and stared at his image in the mirror. Should've packed a razor, he told himself as he ran a hand along his cheek. Well, it wasn't like he and Penny were going to make out or anything. By the time he finished in the bathroom, the couch was made up.

They had an awkward moment when he returned, both of them standing there like a couple of kids saying good night on a first date, then Penny stepped over to him. She kissed him lightly on the cheek.

"Pleasant dreams," she said.

Then she was gone, the bathroom door closing behind her.

Right, Shiel thought.

He turned off the light and stripped down to his briefs, then climbed in between the sheets on the couch. He put his hands behind his head and stared up at the unfamiliar ceiling.

Dreams.

Dreams he didn't need, pleasant or otherwise.

But they caught up with him all the same.

6

He was in a hospital room—suspended up around the ceiling while spread out below him was a scene straight out of a hundred TV hospital dramas.

The room was a small windowless cubicle in an intensive-care unit. The bed took center stage, wooden planks at head and foot, metal bed rails lifting eight or ten inches up along the sides. Lying in it was the star of the show.

The patient was heavily bandaged—not just his body, but all around his face as well. In a coma. He was hooked up to a ventilator—two clear corrugated plastic hoses joining in a Y shape, than a tube going down his trachea. A green power light glowed steadily on the machine. It made a hissing sound as it pumped air through the tube.

Behind the patient's head, mounted on a wall to the side of the bed, was a monitor to ready his heartbeat. Wires ran from the monitor to circular leads that were stuck on his chest, the machine giving off a beeping sound in time with the patient's heart rate. The shelf at the head of the bed held swabs, suction tubes, and resuscitative equipment. Taped to the wall near the monitor was a tongue depressor.

CHARLES DE LINT

A bag on an IV pole fed him a saline solution through an intravenous site on his wrist. His drug dose was regulated by an IVAC pump that sounded like a mouse caught in a wall every time it started up—an annoying scratchy sound. Another bag filled with hyperalimentation—it looked the color of fluorescent urine—fed him through a larger catheter attached to his neck.

The clean antiseptic smell of a hospital filled the air.

That's me, Shiel thought, floating up there by the ceiling, looking down at the coma victim.

He saw the elm tree rear up through his windshield before it shattered, felt the engine fall out onto his lap . . .

If I hadn't been dreaming, if I'd survived that crash, this'd be me lying here.

And then he realized that he was dreaming again. A serial dream. *The Mike Shiel Show*. Last night, when we left our hero, he was going head-on with a great big frigging elm tree and it was game over, folks. But look, you tuned in tonight and our hero's doing okay. Looks like a vegetable, sure, but he's not dead yet. The ratings are still good, so why change the name of the show?

Dreaming. Jesus. But everything looked so real. The smells, the sounds, every detail crystal-clear . . .

Wake up, he told himself. Get out of here.

But then the door opened and Annie walked in. Not the Annie he knew—full of life and always ready with a smile. No, this Annie looked like the world had just dumped everything it had on her. Her shoulders were stooped, her face pale, eyes shot with red, heavy circles under them. She moved slowly as she took a seat beside the bed, bowed her head.

"Annie!" he called to her.

She never looked up. Didn't hear a thing.

"Annie!" he cried louder. "Jesus, Annie. Look up here!"

She didn't so much as blink.

"ANNIE!"

Now she looked up, but it was only because the door had

246

opened again. A tall man in doctor whites entered the room.

"Mrs. Shiel?" he asked.

Annie nodded.

"The nurse said you wanted to see me."

"I just wanted . . . she said you'd tell me if there's . . . if there was any news . . ."

"We're doing the best we can, Mrs. Shiel. All we can do is hope."

"But what's going to happen to him? What's the"—she swallowed thickly—"bottom line?"

The doctor hesitated.

"I have to know."

"We don't like to get into worse-case scenarios . . ."

"Please."

Shiel felt his own chest tighten, hearing the desperation in his wife's voice. That's not me, he wanted to shout at her. I'm up here, Annie. For Christ's sake, if you'd just look up—

The doctor cleared his throat. "We're not sure how much cerebral damage there's been. We've got the X rays, of course, but until he comes out of the coma, we can't really tell."

"And if there's no brain damage? What aren't you telling me?"

Again the doctor hesitated.

"Please. I have a right to know, don't I?"

"There's an almost ninety-five percent chance that he'll be paralyzed from the neck down."

The doctor launched into some medical terminology that Shiel didn't hear. The room was fading on him. He could feel himself being pulled away. A final flash of conversation rose up to him.

"I'm sorry, Mrs. Shiel," the doctor was saying. "We're doing the best we can, under the circumstances, but . . ."

"ANNIE!" Shiel cried.

But then the room was gone and Annie with it. He was out of that dream—

247

7

—and into another.

This time *he* was lying on that hospital bed, the tubes and wires connected to him. The same antiseptic smell in the air. The same hissing, beeping sounds. Not in a coma, but not able to move a muscle all the same.

Oh, Jesus, he thought, remembering what the doctor had said. Now he was going through the paralysis that the doctor had been telling Annie about.

Quadriplegia.

Wake up, he told himself. You don't need this shit. The real world's fucked up enough, without laying this on yourself.

But he might as well have been talking to one of those whitewashed walls that surrounded him on four sides. He lay there and time ticked away—slo-mo, molasses time—then finally the door opened. He turned his head, wanting it to be Annie, but it was a nurse. Long, blond hair, in clean starched whites.

No. Not a nurse. It was Penny. Dressed up in a nurse's uniform.

What the hell was go—

"And how are you today, Mr. Shiel?" she asked him.

Her smile was bright and chipper, her voice husky.

"A-Annie," he said. His mouth dry, with a chemical taste in it. "Where's my . . . ?"

"Oh, I don't think we'll be needing her right now—do you?"

She started to unbutton her blouse.

This isn't real, Shiel thought as the blouse fell to the floor behind her. She unzipped her skirt and stepped out of it, then undid the clasps on her bra, her breasts spilling free as she pulled it away from her body and dropped it on the floor as well. She wasn't wearing any panties—just a garter belt to hold up her white stockings.

"Did you ever wonder why they call this section 'special care'?" she asked him.

She had pulled back the sheets and was on the bed now, the blond hair falling free around her shoulders, her breasts bouncing with the movement as she knelt beside him.

"Annie," Shiel tried again. "I want my wi—"

Penny laid a finger against his lips. "Hush now," she said.

She pulled aside the blue smock he was wearing and stroked his penis.

I don't want this, Shiel thought. This is bullshit. Some teenager's clichéd wet dream. A hard-core fantasy that'd be called something like *Naughty Nurse* if it was up on the silver screen. He didn't need this kind of shit. But his penis swelled under her attention, betraying him. It seemed as though the paralysis hadn't stolen everything from the neck down.

Penny touched the tip of his penis with a long nail, drawing it slowly across the skin, then she lowered her head, taking its length into her mouth.

And Shiel couldn't move. He couldn't get away. He heard the heart-rate monitor quicken its beeping. He lifted his head to look down the length of his body. Penny turned to look at him, her tongue gliding the length of his penis. It glistened in the fluorescent lighting, wet with her saliva.

I don't— Shiel began.

The room flickered suddenly.

Snap.

He wasn't in the hospital any longer, but lying on the couch in Penny's living room. She was still there, tonguing his penis.

Snap.

He was back in the hospital. Now she was licking her fingers, bringing them down to moisten the lips of her vagina. He shook his head at her, but she only smiled.

Rising up on her knees so that she was straddling him, she drew his penis inside her and slowly lowered herself until she'd swallowed the whole of its length. She squirmed, then began a steady up-and-down motion, her breasts jostling, the smile never leaving her features.

Snap.

In her living room. He was still paralyzed, Penny still riding him. Her eyes were half-closed now, rolling back to show their whites. Her breath was quickening.

Snap.

In the hospital. She lowered herself so that the weight of her upper body rested on her elbows, one on either side of his shoulders, hands cupping his face, breasts pressed in close against his chest, the up/down motion quickening.

Snap.

On the couch. Penny pulling him out of her. Clasping his slick penis in her hands, she pumped it, up and down.

Shiel closed his eyes. Annie's features rose up in his mind.

I'm not a part of this, he told her.

But the orgasm was building up inside him all the same.

Snap.

On the bed. He ejaculated in a wet sticky shower all over his own stomach. Penny smiling. Putting her uniform back on.

"Sleep now," she said as she wiped him off and then pulled the sheets back in place. "You need your rest."

She stroked his brow, then left the room. Shiel turned his head, only his gaze able to follow her.

"Sleep," she repeated from the doorway, then she stepped through, closed the door, and he was alone in the room again.

He stared up at the white ceiling above him. Tears blurred his sight. All he could think of was Annie and his inadvertent betrayal of her. Guilt festered inside him, making him nauseous. She deserved better than him. She deserved somebody who'd remain faithful no matter what—dream or not.

He looked down the length of his useless body—brain still booted up, but all the body's motor workings on hold. Permanent hold. He couldn't feel himself. Couldn't turn the page of a book, if he'd wanted to read. Couldn't even take a leak by himself, not without it running all down his thighs and pooling under him, trapped between the plastic under-sheet and the flesh prison of his body.

You're dreaming, he told himself. This is just some bullshit dream.

But the hospital seemed all too real. And when he remembered—

(Annie)

The way she'd looked, all broken apart, sitting there by his bed. He knew what she'd been feeling. If that had been her lying there, and him looking at her—

Sweet Jesus. She deserved somebody who could walk. Not a slab of meat, lying here in a hospital bed where anybody could just walk in and help themselves to a serving. They could do anything to him that they wanted to, he realized. Anything. And he wouldn't be able to do a thing about it.

His helplessness rose in a blinding wave, a scream riding its crest.

FOUR

1

When Shiel woke, the only part of his body that he could move at first were his eyes. They snapped open and his gaze followed the plaster swirls on the ceiling directly above him. He had a momentary panic—it hadn't been a dream, it *had* been real—but then he moved his hand, his arm, his leg. Relief washed through him. He sat up slowly, the bedding bunched around his waist, and rubbed his face.

Jesus. He couldn't live like that—locked into a bed, his body a prison. No way he could live like that. And seeing Annie, hurting so bad . . . Her face filled his thoughts, but then the memory of the second dream spilled into the first—Penny stripping off her nurse's uniform—and he felt guilty all over again.

What the hell was happening to him? he asked himself as he unwound the bedding from around his waist.

That was when he saw that his briefs were lying on the floor. He'd gone to bed wearing them—he was sure of that. But now they lay on the carpet, staring up at him with what looked like an incriminating smirk in their bunched folds. His penis had a postcoital feel about it—a thickness, a certain satisfaction . . .

He turned to look at the hallway that led to Penny's bedroom. He'd been dreaming, hadn't he? Or had Penny come out in the middle of the night and he'd only *thought* he was dreaming?

There was something very weird going on here.

He retrieved his briefs and put them on, then his trousers. Barefoot, buttoning up his shirt, he walked down the hall to Penny's bedroom. The door was slightly ajar, silently opening wider at his touch. Penny lay on her bed, sleeping in the buff, the sheets pulled down enough so that Shiel could see most of her upper torso. His gaze touched, then held a beauty mark on the upper swell of her left breast.

He knew that mark. He'd seen it only inches away from his face. Last night. In a dream.

He backed slowly away from the room, closing the door until it was exactly the same as it had been when he'd entered. Returning to the living room, he sat down on the couch and held his head between his hands. He could feel veins pumping in his temples. His heartbeat accelerating. Unreasoning panic gibbering at the edges of the morass that had become his mind.

Was anything ever going to make sense again?

He took a few deep breaths, steadied himself. Think it through logically, he told himself. If you made love with someone as gorgeous as Penny—would you forget it?

But he didn't forget it. That was the problem. He'd thought he was dreaming, but in reality he'd only been half-asleep. Dreaming that they were getting it on while they really were.

He couldn't accept that. He felt guilty enough having dreamed he was cheating on Annie, without it being real. The birthmark had to be coincidence. But there were just too many frigging coincidences.

He remembered: *There's no such thing as coincidence— only connections you haven't figured out yet.*

He got up and began to pace back and forth. Okay. Connections. If someone was pumping him up with false memories, couldn't his thinking he'd made it with Penny be

254

another one of those same false memories? Possibly. Except that left him with the big one: Why?

Maybe he'd imagined that birthmark on Penny's breast. Well, he sure as hell wasn't going back into her bedroom for a second look. Who knew what she'd think if she woke up with him standing over her bed.

He found himself in front of Penny's bookshelf, the one he'd filled last night. Her high school yearbooks caught his eye and he pulled one down. *The Falcon.* Flipping through it brought back a hundred memories of Philemon Wright High School. Old faces, old friends. He stopped when he came to Penny's picture.

Yeah, he remembered her all right. But there was something about her . . .

He tried to snag the thought, but it wouldn't come. It had all been so long ago and he'd lost touch with pretty well everyone he'd hung around with back then, for all that he'd done little more than move across the river from Hull to Ottawa. Trying to remember much about someone he'd never really known was just an exercise in futility.

"Mike . . . ?"

He closed the book with a guilty snap and turned to find Penny standing in the hallway, looking sleepily at him. She was wearing a fluffy terry-cloth bathrobe and still looked like a dream. Nothing like the mousy girl in her yearbook photo.

Would you mind pulling that bathrobe down to your waist for a second so I can check you out for birthmarks? he thought.

"Do you always get up this early?" she asked.

"Well, you know," he said with a shrug. When you're losing your mind, it's hard to give it a rest, he added to himself. "Things to do, people to see."

He replaced the yearbook as he spoke.

"But it's seven-fifteen, Saturday morning," she said.

"I've got to get to work. Busy day, Saturday, what with Christmas coming and everything."

"Do you have time for breakfast?"

Shiel shook his head. Returning to the couch, he started to put on his socks and shoes. Penny sat down in a chair across from him, pulling the bathrobe around her legs when it began to fall open.

"What's the matter, Mike? You seem very . . . distant this morning."

"I . . ."

What the hell was he supposed to say? I had a wet dream about you last night—or at least I think it was a dream. Can you show me your left boob, or tell me if we got hot and heavy on the couch here a couple of hours ago?

"Just bad dreams," he said.

Fuck you, a voice spoke up in the back of his head. Back behind that sissy guilt, you were enjoying yourself.

"About Annie?" Penny asked.

He nodded. "Yeah. Partly. I dreamt I was in a coma and she was sitting by my bed in intensive care, crying her eyes out. Doctor said I was going to wake up paralyzed from the neck down."

"They go away," Penny said. "The dreams, I mean. It just takes a little while."

Shiel gave her a considering look. There was something odd about the way she'd phrased that.

"What do you mean, they go away?" he asked.

Penny looked confused for a moment, but recovered quickly. Was that a flash of guilt he'd caught in the back of her eyes?

"Bad dreams," she said. "They're supposed to be our way of working through daytime stress, and you've got to admit you're going through a lot of stress right now." She stood up. "Just let me make you something before you go—you can't head off for a day's work on an empty stomach."

Shiel watched her leave and slowly shook his head. Jesus, the paranoia cut deep. Here she was, just trying to

256

give him some moral support, and now he was starting to suspect her of Christ knew what. Lighten up, Shiel.

He followed her into the kitchen where she was breaking an egg into a frying pan. There was already bread in the toaster.

"Listen," he said. "I'm sorry if I'm spacing out on you. It's just all part of this bad-news weirdness I'm going through."

"That's okay. I understand."

"You're being a real good friend."

And let's not forget those hot dreams she's providing you with, that nagging voice in the back of his voice added.

Penny turned from the stove to look at him. "I want to be your friend," she said.

2

This is the perfect domestic scene, Shiel thought as he sat down to breakfast with Penny. Only problem was, he had the wrong woman sitting across the table from him.

It made him wonder . . . what would have happened if he'd never met Annie . . . if before that day he'd gotten together with Penny? Married her out of high school, maybe—that would make them a couple for going on to fifteen years now. Would he still be working at Hot Deals, or would he have gotten a straighter job? Maybe they'd be living in the suburbs, blanding out with their neighbors, their station wagons and two-point-four kids. Maybe they'd be divorced by now.

It was a ridiculous chain of thought, because it broke down right at square one. He'd never even paid any attention to Penny back then. And he *had* met Annie. He wouldn't be who he was today without her. The changes in him had been subtle, but he knew he was a much better person now than he ever would have been if he'd never known her.

That was why he *knew* she was real. He was here, the way he was, because of her. No matter how much the evidence piled up, he refused to accept that she was just some figment of his imagination. No way, pal.

He looked up to find Penny's gaze on him. The expression in her eyes was hard to read. There was an empathy present, but something else that wasn't as easily readable.

"I guess I must come off sounding like a real loser," he said, "the way I've been carrying on since we met yesterday." He found a smile to take some of the self-depreciation from his voice, but it wasn't one of his best.

The smile she gave him back had a bittersweet turn about it. "No," she said. "You just sound like you loved your wife very much."

"Love," Shiel said. The way she'd used the past tense sent an anxious pang straight through his heart. "I still love her."

"I know you do."

"Were you ever married?" he asked.

Penny shook her head. "I only ever cared—really cared—about one guy, but he went and married somebody else."

"And nobody since then? I can't believe you're not settled down with someone."

"I've just never met anybody else that was right. See— that's part of the problem with my big 'improve Penny' program. It was great for my self-esteem, but it makes me wonder if my mother wasn't partly right all along. All the guys who hit on me only want one thing. The nice guys, they just figure they don't have a chance because I've *got* to have a boyfriend, or I'm too glamorous for them . . .

"And it's all just nonsense. I'm not into glamour—not really. I keep in shape, I try to look my best, because I don't want to slide back into what I was like when I was a teenager, but what I'm really looking for is someone to settle down with, a guy that I can have some quiet times with. Good times. The kind that when you grow old together you can look back on and know that you didn't waste your life."

Like his life had been with Annie.

Her expression was so wistful that Shiel's heart went out to her. Wasn't it weird, the game plan that the world handed you? She didn't get anywhere as a kid because she looked like a lump; now that she looked like a million dollars, she still couldn't get anywhere. He knew that if he wasn't already married—

Something in her eyes stopped him cold. It was almost as though he could hear—

(*You don't have a wife.*)

—her saying it.

He pushed his plate to the center of the table. "I really have to get going," he said. "Sarah's never going to forgive me if I leave her to fend for herself another day—especially not on a Saturday. This close to Christmas it really gets to be a zoo in the store."

"I'll try to come up with something while you're gone," Penny said. "To find your wife, I mean. Would you like to have dinner here when you're finished work? Nothing fancy."

"I . . ." Shiel rubbed a hand along his unshaven cheek. "I really should get back to the house tonight." And get away from you for a bit, he realized. He'd been spending so much time with her that it was beginning to feel like they were having an affair. Especially after last night's dream.

"I'd like to see your place sometime," Penny said.

Shiel glanced at her. The opportunity for him to make the invitation lay wide open. No pressure. She wasn't pushing it. But it was there all the same.

He thought about the empty house. About being there by himself tonight while the hours dragged by. Weighing that against last night—

(it was only a dream—she's only trying to help)

"Okay," he said. "You're on for dinner. And after that we can take a run by the place."

And if it gets all hot and heavy? that nagging voice asked.

Screw you, he told it. I can control myself. She's just a friend.

That's how it always starts, the voice told him before he shut it off, refusing to listen to it anymore. Penny looked so happy—how the hell was he supposed to turn around and just tell her no again? No can do.

But he thought of Annie.

He hoped she'd understand. He just couldn't face being along. Being alone made it too easy to feel like he was losing it. Dropping off the deep end and there was no bottom.

"I've got to go," he told Penny.

3

With typical incongruity, Sarah was listening to CBC's *Morningside* when he arrived at the store. There she was, all decked out in her punker's gear—black jeans, a torn Jake Hamer Band T-shirt, spike heels, her hair a crest of black spikes—listening to Peter Gzowski talk about the intelligence of Guernsey cows. Shiel loved the show himself. Gzowski was laid-back and charming, interviewing anyone from politicians and movers in the business world, to authors and people dealing with social issues; always intelligent, but never highbrow. But Sarah and Guernseys?

When he came in she was leaning on the front counter, listening intently, lips dark with black lipstick shaping a smile as Gzowski read from a letter in which a Maritime farmer was talking about how his Guernsey was easier to train than his dog. Sarah looked up as Shiel stepped through the door.

"Hey, what do ya know? The prodigal son returns."

Shiel locked the door behind him. There was still a half hour before opening time, but Sarah already had the lights on, the cash float in the till, and was ready for business.

"How'd it go yesterday?" he asked.

Keep it normal, he told himself. If you keep things on an even keel maybe everything'll straighten out. Annie'll call up around noon for their daily phone chat, or maybe drop in to have lunch with him in the back.

Is that too much to ask?

"Wild times, Mike. You missed a lady who came in and got all pissed off because we don't carry vacuum cleaners."

With the bins and racks loaded with the latest albums, cassettes, and CDs, it was hard to miss what the store sold.

"You're kidding—right?"

"Uh-uh. Had to escort her out, still ranting away at me. We can, and I quote, 'expect a call from the Better Business Bureau.' "

"Wonderful."

Sarah gave a negligent shrug. "Ah, she'll never do it."

"Here's hoping. Are the orders ready to go out?"

"All except for the imports—I thought you'd want to do 'em yourself."

Shield nodded. "I'll go phone them in," he said as he started for the rear of the store. He paused at the door leading into the back with its Employees Only sign. Under it someone had scrawled "So keep out or die." "What's *Morningside* doing on today?" he asked. "It's Saturday."

"I was too busy yesterday morning to listen to it so I taped it up."

"Figures."

Shaking his head, Shiel went into the back room. He spent the next half hour until opening time on the phone with the Hot Deals warehouse in Toronto, then settled down to do yesterday's cash report and the bank deposit. Throwing himself into his work, he managed to keep his head clear of everything except for the tasks immediately at hand. When Sarah unlocked the front door, he joined her on the floor. Clipboard in hand, he stood by the counter and went over the import order with her.

The *Morningside* tape played on behind them, but Shiel wasn't really paying attention to it. It was only when Sarah went to help the first customer of the day that he actually heard what Gzowski was talking about. Teenage suicide.

Shiel felt as though a giant hand had slipped inside him and was tying his intestines into a knot. His legs went weak and he had to sit down on the stool behind the cash register. It was that or fall down.

Suicide.

Now he remembered.

4

He was ten months out of high school and already working in records, except he was just a clerk at one of the old Treble Clef stores—a local company that got swallowed by the big franchises that eventually moved in from Toronto and took over Ottawa's retail music scene. Round about then—at the front end of the seventies—there was nothing cooler than working for Treble Clef. He was at the Sparks Street Mall location, changing the sale prices on the weekend specials back up to their regular value, when who should walk in but Billy Simmons.

In high school, Billy had a real bad rep. Acting tough, talking tougher. He came from Déschenes, which had always produced the toughest kids around, and more than one teacher predicted that if—and it was a big if—he ever finished high school, he'd be in prison within a year. Instead, he'd ragged them all. Came out with top marks and ended up with a scholarship.

Shiel had hardly recognized Billy when he came in that day. The greased-back hair was gone; so was the leather jacket. He was wearing jeans still, but they were clean—not a grease stain on them—and a preppy Ottawa U sweatshirt.

"Jesus, look at you," Shiel had said. "What happened?

You look like someone dropped you in a tub of Mr. Clean."

"I'm moving up in the world, Mike m'man. Don't want to grow old in a record store, making minimum wage for the rest of my life, like some folks I know will."

"Yeah. Up yours, too."

Billy grinned—that shit-kicking look of his that Shiel knew so well. They'd hung around some in high school, enough so that Shiel took his lunch early to go shoot the breeze with him for a while. A lot can change in that first year after high school. With ten months behind him, they had enough gossip to catch up on to last them through Shiel's whole lunch hour.

"Ran into Patty down on Rideau Street the other day," Billy said. "Panhandling—can you believe it?"

"I thought she got accepted at Quelf. Wasn't she going to be a veterinarian?"

Billy shrugged. "Guess she just dropped out."

"Well, she's doing better than Andy Rothwell. He's become a Scientologist. Stopped me on the street the other day and tried to convince me to come in for a personality test."

"Yeah. Or what about Penny Moore?"

"Who?"

"The Lump—remember her?"

"Oh yeah. What about her?"

"Swallowed a bottle of her old lady's sleeping pills and bit the big one."

"She's dead?"

"That's what usually happens when you stop breathing. First time she was ever a success at something, I guess. And remember Candy?"

"I'm supposed to forget her?"

The conversation had gone on, Penny Moore's suicide just one more statistic, covered in a line or two, then forgotten.

5

Dead.

Swallowed a bottle of her old lady's sleeping pills and bit the big one.

Penny Moore was dead.

So who the hell had picked him up at the Laf yesterday and taken him home with her?

Shiel leaned weakly on the counter, his features ashen. He felt like there was a great pit opening up under his feet and he was tottering on the brink of it, ready to fall in.

"Mike?"

He lifted his head and turned slowly to look at Sarah, dimly realizing that she'd been calling his name for some time. Staring at her, seeing himself in her worried features, he could tell just how weirded out he had to be looking right now.

"Are you okay?"

Sure I'm okay. Just spent a day and a night with someone who's been dead for a couple of decades, my wife's—

You don't have a wife.

—vanished without a trace, like she never was. But yeah, I'm okay. It's just the rest of the world that's fucked up. I'm right in step.

"I . . ." He cleared his throat. If only things would stop spinning. "I've got to lie . . . down . . ." Before I fall down. Into that hole that's sitting there under me, ready to suck me away.

Sarah helped him into the back room and onto the battered old couch that they kept back there. Shiel stretched out, hugging himself to stop the shakes that were trying to pry him loose from the tenuous grip he had on reality and drop him down that bottomless pit.

"Mike, I . . . There's no one on the floor . . ."

He managed to lift a hand to wave her back out. "G-go on . . ."

"Do you want me to call an ambulance?"

He shook his head—almost couldn't stop, once he'd started. "I just need—to lie d-down . . ."

Plainly worried, Sarah backed out of the room. The store was filling with customers.

Oh man, Shiel thought, pressing his face against the back of the couch. *Who* is fucking with my head?

6

It took Shiel a half hour to get himself straight again. When he finally felt he could stand up without the world shifting too much underfoot, he went into the bathroom and washed his face, drying it with a paper towel. He stared at his reflection.

You're a mess, he told it.

But he was down now. The shakes were gone. His head wasn't spinning anymore. Not that anything made any more sense than it had previously, but he felt that he could face the questions once more without his body betraying him. Survival of the beast, he thought. That's what made the human animal so successful—given time, it could adapt to just about any situation.

Even this. Even losing it.

He went to his desk, pulled the telephone closer, and dialed 411. Once he got Penny's new listing from Information, he started to dial her number, then cradled the receiver.

Hang on, he told himself. Let's do this one step at a time. What's calling her going to prove? She was real. Flesh and blood. Maybe she wasn't Penny Moore—just someone who bore a certain resemblance to the girl they'd called the Lump in high school and was playing a game with his head—but she sure wasn't going to admit that. Not on the phone. Maybe not even in person.

He needed some facts. Something to back up his memory. Because his memory wasn't proving too reliable these days. Not as the evidence piled up to make a mockery of everything he believed was true. He remembered having a wife, but everywhere he turned that was denied. So why should it be any different with this conversation he remembered having with Billy?

Never mind that he *knew* he was remembering it right.

Never mind that he had a wife.

Let's play the game by its new rules.

Putting on his jacket, he stepped out onto the floor. There were a half-dozen customers looking through the bins—nothing Sarah couldn't handle until their part-timer Lawrence came in at noon.

"Mike . . . ?" Sarah began when she saw him.

"I'm okay. Really. Listen, I hate to do this to you two days in a row, but I've got some shit to work out. Do you mind holding the fort for a while?"

"Sure. Larry's going to be in soon and we've already got the orders phoned in. But Mike, you don't really look so good. Are you sure—"

"I don't feel so good, either."

"If there's anything I can do . . ."

"You're doing it already."

He gave her a shaky grin and left the store before he had to do any more talking, taking with him the chorus of the song playing on the store's sound system as he went. Toyah doing a version of the old Martha and the Muffins hit "Echo Beach." That line about it being far away in time followed him all the way to the public library on Laurier.

FIVE

1

Two hours of staring at a microfiche reader in the library's reference section on the second floor finally gave him something. Not what he was looking for, but something. It was buried in the local news section of a newspaper dating from the early seventies—just a paragraph with a small headline that read WEST QUEBEC GIRL ATTEMPTS SUICIDE.

Attempts.

That was the operative word here.

So maybe he hadn't heard Billy correctly. It was an old memory, after all. Years had gone by. Except, if he closed his eyes and concentrated, he could almost hear—

First time she was ever a success at something . . .

—Billy's voice.

Where do you draw the line? he wondered. The facts were there on the screen in front of him. Penny hadn't died—she'd only tried to kill herself. He'd met her, talked to her, spent some—

(carnal)

—time with her. What was real and what wasn't? What he remembered, or what he could see sitting there on the screen with his own eyes? Flesh and blood. He remembered the touch of her hand—

(stroking his penis)

—as she took his arm coming out of the Laf yesterday.

267

That was real. Those words on the screen in front of him—they were real, too.

Echo Beach. Far away in time.

If it wasn't for Annie . . . if it wasn't for this conspiracy that was spiderwebbing all around him, trying to convince him that she'd never existed . . . he wouldn't even be questioning this.

But there was Annie.

She was real.

He pushed himself abruptly away from the fiche reader, startling the two students seated on either side of him, and fled the reference room, the library.

But the questions weren't as easily escaped.

Walking the streets, with the first winter bite of the wind knifing through his thin jacket, those questions followed him, relentlessly dogging his steps, howling at the walls he was trying to build up in his mind to keep them out. He walked aimlessly, until he found himself outside of Penny's apartment building. He walked around back to its parking lot and found the red Toyota parked in a resident's spot. Same license plate number.

Had to be Penny's car.

Why wasn't he surprised?

Shoulders hunched against the wind, he set off eastward until he reached the canal and couldn't go any farther. He stood at the railing, hands deep in his pockets, and stared down at the debris and mud that had been left behind when the canal was drained for the winter. Pieces of people's lives. Cast-off things. Nothing important. Pop cans. Garbage. Things that were used once, then thrown away.

Something's using me, he thought. Right now, somebody's got a game plan and a scorecard, and I'm just a piece they're shuffling around the board. And when they're done with me, I'll be down there with the rest of the crap that gets thrown away when it's served its purpose and no one's got any use for it anymore.

Question was, when?

A better question was, why?

"Mike?"

He wasn't surprised to hear her voice come from behind him. He didn't turn around, didn't bother answering.

It was funny. He'd gone through a lot in the past few days—from questioning his sanity, through rage and a sorrow so deep that it couldn't even begin to be appeased. But right now he didn't feel anything. Just an emptiness inside, an emptiness so profound it sucked the meaning from words. It made all conversation pointless.

"Mike?"

But there was power in a name.

(Annie)

Too much power.

He turned finally, slowly. With his back against the rail he looked at her. How had she done it? How had she made his wife disappear—literally erasing Annie from existence?

There was no answer in her features. She stood a few feet away, still gorgeous, but her shoulders were hunched— the body language wailing defeat—and her eyes had a desperate haunted look about them that Shiel understood, though he couldn't have put it into words. It was a look of loss. Loss of hopes. Of dreams. Of meaning.

"We have to talk," she said.

What should we talk about? he wondered. Free trade? The new Eurythmics album? Holiday plans?

"Please," she said. "Come back to the apartment with me. It's too cold to stand here and talk."

Shiel regarded her for one more long moment, then he shrugged and pushed himself away from the railing. He fell in step beside her, hands still deep in his pockets, but there was a tingle in them now—an answering voice to the red rage that was slowly bleeding into his mind.

He thought of Annie.

He thought of what he'd been put through.

He thought of how it would feel to have that smooth white neck of Penny's between his hands.

Of squeezing her throat until her skin went blue and those pretty eyes began to pop from their sockets.

Of what she thought she could possibly say to make any of this any better.

So he let her take him home again.

In case she could bring Annie back.

But the anger continued to bleed into his mind until he was walking through a red haze.

And his hands ached, their muscles were so tense.

For the first time in his life he understood what it felt like to want to kill someone.

It was a kind of madness, that feeling. And the worst thing about it was that it felt so sane.

So terribly, terribly sane.

2

When they reached her apartment, Shiel sat down on the couch, not even bothering to remove his jacket. He slouched on the cushions, hands clasped on his lap, knuckles whitening. He watched Penny remove her coat, tracked her as she went into the bathroom. After a few moments, he heard the toilet flush. The water run in the sink. When she came back, the high-class model look was gone.

She sat down opposite him, slouching as well. She wore faded jeans and an old sweatshirt. Behind the glasses she was wearing now, her eyes weren't nearly the same startling blue he remembered them to be. Tinted contacts, he realized. But even without her makeup, in the old clothes and with her glasses on, she was still a knockout.

She could have anyone she wanted, he thought, so why was she messing around with him?

"Where's Annie?" he asked.

She just sat there, chin down, looking at the carpet.

"I said . . ."

She looked up and his words trailed off. She looked so

lost that his heart went out to her—never mind what she'd been putting him through.

"That's not so easy to explain," she said.

His empathy for her fled. Wrong answer, he thought. His gaze settled on her neck. The muscles of his hands spasmed slightly. He clasped them tighter.

"Don't dick around with me, Penny. Before we get into anything here, I want her back."

"It's not that simple."

Shiel half rose from the couch. What the hell had she done with his wife? All he could envision was Annie lying in a grave somewhere. The red haze grew stronger. His hands twitched.

"If you've—"

Her own hands lifted, palms outward. "Your wife's fine. No one's hurt her. No one's touched her. She's not even . . . involved in any of this, except peripherally."

Her words deflated him and he sat back down on he couch. Why should I believe you? he thought. But he did. Something in her tone, something in her face, told him that her plain statements were nothing but the truth.

Annie was safe.

She existed. He wasn't going crazy. Everything was going to be fine.

The red haze left his gaze. His hands stopped twitching.

But looking at Penny, he knew that however true it was that Annie was all right, nothing was going to be fine again.

"What the fuck's going on, Penny? Why're you playing around with my head?"

No anger in his voice now. Just weariness. He was so tired. After being wound up so tight, for so long, he was starting to unravel now.

"I never meant to," Penny said. "I thought it was all going to be so simple. I always loved you, Mike—back in school—but you never paid any attention to me. You didn't hurt me like the others, but I didn't exist for you, either."

"You sure picked a hell of a way to get my attention."

How come I'm just sitting here, talking with her? he asked himself. Like we're just shooting the breeze, going over old times. Like nothing's the matter. How come I'm not shaking her until she tells me what I've got to know?

"This," Penny said, waving a hand limply about the room in a gesture that took in more than their immediate surroundings, "isn't here to get your attention. I tried that before—right after high school—only I didn't do too good a job of it."

"The suicide attempt."

"It wasn't an attempt, Mike. I thought my mom'd come home and find me in time, but she was late from work that day. I thought she'd take me to the hospital and have my stomach pumped and I'd be okay. I thought you'd hear about it and know I was doing it for you and you'd come to me. I was reaching out for you, Mike."

Shiel heard Billy Simmons's voice in his head, underpinning what she was saying.

Swallowed a bottle of her old lady's sleeping pills and bit the big one.

"I really blew it that time," Penny was saying.

Billy hadn't been talking about attempts.

First time she was ever a success at something, I guess.

"I was reaching out," Penny said, "but in the wrong direction. Instead of getting you, I got this." Again that gesture, encompassing the apartment and more. "An echo of what I could have had if I hadn't been such a fool. If I hadn't been so scared to just do something with myself, for myself. If I hadn't been such an emotional cripple."

"What . . . what are you saying?" Shiel asked.

But he knew.

Swallowed a bottle of her old lady's sleeping pills . . .

She was saying—

. . . and bit the big one.

—that it hadn't been an attempt.

"This is bullshit," he said.

Penny shook her head. "I killed myself, Mike. I thought

it was all I had left. I didn't mean to die. I just . . . just wanted to make a statement, I guess. I was reaching out, but there was no one there to reach out to. I went too far. And then it was too late."

Shiel just looked at her. Things were becoming clear now.

Easy, he told himself. Don't spook her. You're not nuts, but she sure as shit is. He didn't know how she'd done it, but she'd managed to spirit away Annie, Annie and everything that gave evidence to the fact that she'd ever been real. He had to play her easy now, get Annie back. And then . . .

The anger was back, but it had no real focus. He pitied her too much to want to hurt her. He had to get Annie back and then get Penny some help.

"You don't believe me, do you?" she said.

Shiel didn't know what he was supposed to do in a situation like this. Did you play along, or did you try to talk some sense into them?

"You . . . you've got to admit—it sounds a little off the wall."

That sad smile of hers was back. "I know what it sounds like, Mike. I know just what you're thinking: This girl needs help. I've got to act real nice to her and get my wife back, and then see that she's put away in a nice padded cell where she can't hurt anybody else, herself included.

"I wish it was true."

Was he that transparent? Shiel wondered.

Penny was watching him, her eyes brimmed with emotion, the sad smile faltering. Shiel tried to swallow, but his mouth was too dry to collect any saliva.

"I . . . I don't believe in ghosts," he said finally.

Penny nodded. "Ghosts and phantoms—it all sounds so flaky, doesn't it?"

Shiel just looked at her. He couldn't believe they were having this conversation.

"But this whole world is a ghost," she said. "It's all a lie,

Mike. It's a world that's just like the one we came from, except your wife never existed in it. It's my world, the world the way it should have been."

"What are you saying? That you . . . created the world?"

She was in worse shape than Shiel had thought.

She nodded. "I had to wait until the time was right—until you could join me."

Shiel started to get an uneasy feeling. He remembered his car going out of control on the ice, the elm tree looming up from the side of the road as the car skidded toward it.

"I thought it'd be perfect," Penny said. "Nobody'd be hurt. We'd finally be together, just like I always knew we should be. But I forgot about you. I forgot that *you'd* remember her, even if nobody else did."

Looking at her, you'd never think she was this weirded out, Shiel thought. She looked sane. She delivered her lines so reasonably. But when he focused on what she was saying—

I'm not the only ghost here.

—when he remembered the skidding car and the tree. That stopped him.

"What the hell are you saying?" he asked.

"That car crash, the intensive-care unit you dreamed of?"

A sick feeling settled in the pit of Shiel's stomach. He closed his eyes and a vision of his Pinto sliding on the black ice shot into his mind. That great big frigging elm tree filling the windshield just before he hit . . .

"They weren't dreams, Mike."

The nausea spread, a cold unreasoning panic chittered in the back of his head. He could feel the ventilator hose going down his windpipe. He could hear the machine's internal hissing as it pumped air into his lungs . . .

"That was the real world."

An antiseptic sting in his nostrils. The scratchy sound of

the IVAC pump as it fed drugs into his bloodstream and the incessant beep of the monitor reading his heartbeat . . .

Bullshit. It was bullshit. He stared at her, slowly shaking his head, not even aware of the motion. For Christ's sake, he wasn't insane, *she* was.

"I waited and waited for the right moment to bring you here," Penny said, "here to my world."

"You're out of your—"

"This is the dream, Mike. But we can make it real. We just have to want to."

"I . . ."

"We're here because I wanted this . . . I wanted it so bad . . ."

3

Shiel stood up. He crossed the room to the window and stared out at the street below. When he shut his eyes, he could feel himself lying down in that hospital bed, connected to the life-support systems. Gibbering fears chewed at his reason.

It wasn't true.

He stared at the street. It was real. This apartment was real. The woman behind him hadn't committed suicide. He'd never crashed the Pinto. But Annie . . .

He could hear her voice, coming as though from a great distance. The sadness, the pain in it.

"Mike . . ."

It couldn't be true.

But if this world was real, then where was Annie in it? Could he believe in a world from which she'd been erased as though she'd never existed?

You don't have a wife.

I do.

This is the dream . . .

It had to be.

He turned from the window to look at Penny, anguish written in every plane of his features.

275

"How . . . can it be . . . possible . . . ?"

His voice was a ragged croak. He could feel the walls closing in on him. If he shut his eyes, the sounds and smells of the hospital flooded his senses. He lay helpless there.

"How . . . ?"

Penny shook her head slowly. "I don't know, Mike. I took those pills and I lay down on my bed, waiting for my mom to come home. And then I just drifted away. When I opened my eyes again, I was here."

"In . . . in this place?"

"Not this apartment—this world. It was like I was being given a second chance. I think this is a place where we go when we weren't ready to accept our deaths. A kind of echo of the real world. When you've died, when it wasn't your time to die, but you did anyway, it's like there's all this leftover stuff—all those months and years, all the pieces of your life that you didn't get to live—it all gets distilled into a kind of energy that you can use to make a place like this.

"There's probably hundreds of worlds like this—one for every person who died before his or her time."

"I . . . I'm dead . . . ?"

"Not yet. You're in a coma. And like the doctor said in your dream, when you come out of it—if you come out of it—you're going to be a vegetable. Or you're going to be a head attached to a body that doesn't work anymore."

A quadriplegic. Helpless.

"How . . . how can you know this?" he asked.

She shrugged. "I'm connected to you, Mike—I think of you all the time—so when the . . . accident happened, when I knew there was finally nothing left for you back there, I brought you here. I thought you'd be happy—that we could be happy here. I thought that when you finally let go of your body in that world, you'd be here with me and we could make a new life together. I didn't realize that you'd remember your old life so strongly."

Annie.

"There's nothing left for you back there, Mike."

Annie.

"Even if you don't die—what kind of life would it be?"

There'd be Annie.

"Everything will be changed. You'll be just a burden on . . . on your wife."

But we had a pact, Shiel thought. We swore an oath. We exchanged rings in the church and when the priest spoke—

(for better or for worse, in sickness and in health)

—we both said "I do."

He left the window and sat down on the couch again, cradling his head in his hands.

"Mike . . . ?"

He looked up at her.

"I know it wasn't right what I've done—manipulating you the way I have—but you can't go back. It doesn't have to be with me, but you've got to stay. How can you return, knowing the kind of half-life that's waiting for you there? At least here you can make a new life for yourself—be what you would be if you hadn't hit that tree."

"But it's a lie."

"Isn't a lie better than what reality's got to offer you now?" Penny asked.

"When I dreamt of you coming to me, dressed as a nurse . . . Did that really happen?"

Penny nodded.

Jesus.

"But that was me," Penny said. "Manipulating you. I'll leave you alone from now on, Mike. I promise. We can be friends, or not. You don't ever have to see me again if you don't want to. Just don't go back. There's nothing for you there."

"There's Annie."

"And if you're not a vegetable, then you'll probably be paralyzed from the neck down, so what good would you—"

"Do you *know* that?"

She shook her head. "But you heard what the doctor said.

277

And if that does happen, what will you have to offer her?"

Shiel slowly shook his head. "You don't understand. We love each other. If it was her—if it had happened to Annie—I'd be there for her. That's what it's all about. It doesn't matter how bad things get, so long as we're there for each other. If I stayed here, I'd be making a lie of everything we had between us."

"Can you even begin to imagine what your life will be like if you go back?"

"No. I won't pretend that I can. I know it'll be harder than anything I could imagine. But at least it'll be real."

Penny said nothing. Her eyes held her sadness. The lines of her body spoke her weariness. She looked away from him, off into unseen distances. Shiel closed his eyes and the smells and sounds of Intensive Care were back.

"If you go back," Penny said, "you'll think this was all just a dream. But it wasn't, Mike. It was real, too. It was how things could have been."

Shiel could sense Annie's presence in the hospital room, sitting beside his bed. Her love for him was so strong, it had physical weight.

It was like a lifeline, calling to him.

Calling him back to his ruined body.

Calling him home.

"I can't stop you from going back," she said.

"I don't know how to do it," Shiel said.

Penny's gaze returned to meet his. "Just let go," she said.

4

Shiel did as she said. He caught hold of the lifeline that was Annie's love, and let go of the world he was in. It was like falling into a pool of shadows, everything darkening, everything losing its definition, its connection to him.

He felt the hospital bed under his body. He heard the beep

of the monitoring machine, the sound of the IVAC pump. An antiseptic odor stung his nostrils.

His eyes were closed, but he could still see Penny. It was like looking at a television screen, the last scene of a made-for-TV movie before the final fade-out and the credits came rolling up. He wasn't *there* anymore.

"I really loved you," she said. "I never meant to cause you any hurt."

But he was gone now and she spoke to an empty room. He'd crossed back over, out of her life again.

No.

He'd never really been a part of her life.

Except in dreams.

Her dreams.

He saw her bow her head and finally set free the tears she'd been holding back until he was gone.

The screen in his head faded to black.